Praise for Sherrilyn Kenyon
and her novels

"[A] publishing phenomenon . . . [Sherrilyn Kenyon is] the reigning queen of the wildly successful paranormal scene . . . Just one example of arguably the most in-demand and prolific authors in America these days." —*Publishers Weekly*

"Kenyon's writing is brisk, ironic, and relentlessly imaginative. These are not your mother's vampire novels." —*The Boston Globe*

"Kenyon (*Born of Legend*) puts the lie to the old adage 'Dead men tell no tales' in the jam-packed, appealing first book of her Deadman's Cross historical fantasy series." —*Publishers Weekly* on *Deadmen Walking*

"[An] engaging read." —*Entertainment Weekly* on *Devil May Cry*

BY SHERRILYN KENYON

A
HERO
FOR THE
HOLIDAYS

SHERRILYN KENYON

St. Martin's Paperbacks

This is a work of fiction. All of the characters, organizations, and events portrayed in this book are either products of the author's imagination or are used fictitiously.

Published in the United States by St. Martin's Paperbacks, an imprint of St. Martin's Publishing Group.

A HERO FOR THE HOLIDAYS: A DARK-HUNTER CHRISTMAS copyright © 2003 by St. Martin's Paperbacks. UPON THE MIDNIGHT CLEAR copyright © 2007 by Sherrilyn Kenyon. HOLIDAY GATHERINGS copyright © 2007 by Sherrilyn Kenyon. SANTA WEARS SPURS © 2000 by St. Martin's Paperbacks.

For information, address St. Martin's Publishing Group, 120 Broadway, New York, NY 10271.

www.stmartins.com

ISBN: 978-1-250-88961-4

Our books may be purchased in bulk for promotional, educational, or business use. Please contact your local bookseller or the Macmillan Corporate and Premium Sales Department at 1-800-221-7945, ext. 5442, or by email at MacmillanSpecialMarkets@macmillan.com.

Printed in the United States of America

St. Martin's Paperbacks edition / October 2023

10 9 8 7 6 5 4 3 2 1

CONTENTS

A DARK-HUNTER CHRISTMAS

PROLOGUE

Born to impoverished Irish immigrant parents at the turn of the century, James Cameron Patrick Gallagher entered this world with a large chip on his shoulder.

It didn't help any that he was birthed in the backroom of a sweatshop that should have been condemned, to a timid, fretful woman who'd been forced to return to work just hours after she had delivered him into the hands of his nervous, alcoholic father. A father who was indifferent to the boy at best and violent at worst.

From the moment of that first wail forward, Jamie spent his life fighting for respect. Fighting his way out of the poverty that haunted him as he grew up in the Irish slums of New York.

At age fifteen, he found his way out.

The year was 1916 and two important events happened to him. His father died after he slipped and fell into the river on his way home from a three-day drinking binge. Two weeks later, Jamie went to work for the renowned gangster Ally Malone so that he could support his mother and eight younger siblings. A thug and a bully, Ally had shown him a way to make money that had made Jamie's poor mother's knees ache from the untold novenas she had prayed for her son.

But that was okay as far as Jamie was concerned. His new lifestyle afforded him the ability to buy his mother silk pillows to cushion her work-worn knees, and instead of praying with a cheap wooden rosary, she now had one made of gold and ivory.

It was a rosary she'd thrown in his face the day she had learned the real truth about her son: Jamie wasn't a poor innocent lad being led astray by those out to take advantage of him. By the time he was twenty, he was a fierce gangster to be reckoned with.

Disowned by his mother, he'd given his younger brother a reputable job so that Ryan could care for the family without their mother knowing it was Jamie's ill-gotten gains that kept them all fed.

Jamie had learned to harden his heart and to care for no one or nothing. He became Gallagher. A man who had no other name. One who let no one near him, let no one know him. He was ice-cold and rock-solid.

Until the day Rosalie had come into his life and chiseled away his granite casing. The daughter of

Portuguese immigrants, she had been walking home from an all-day Mass.

Jamie had stumbled over her in his haste to catch up with a "business" associate he needed to take care of.

It had been a cold winter evening with snow falling down on the city. February 11, 1924—a date that was branded into his heart and mind for all eternity. The minute Rosalie had turned her dark brown eyes on him, his entire body had been consumed by fire. For the first time in years, he felt something more than cold, blind hatred.

"I'm so sorry," she had whispered in her exotic accent, brushing at his expensive, handmade suit. "I didn't see you for the snow."

"It was my fault," he hastened to assure her. No doubt any other man in his position would have hit her or yelled at her. That thought sent a wave of unreasonable fury through him.

She was a complete stranger and yet he felt possessive toward her. Respectful. Two emotions he'd never accorded any woman not related to him.

"Rosalie!" her mother had snapped as she came back for her daughter. "You do not talk to such men. How many times must I say that to you." She took Rosalie by the arm and offered him a pleading, servile glance. "Forgive my daughter, *senhor*. She is young and foolish."

"It's fine, *senhora*," he said quickly. Then he met Rosalie's wide-eyed stare. She was truly beautiful. Her black hair was braided and coiled around her head, exposed to him when her church veil had fallen off after they collided. Her dark brown eyes were pure. Innocent. Completely unspoiled by the bloody violence that made up his life. Most of all, her eyes were kind.

He didn't want anything to sully that gaze. To make it hard and cold. Bitter.

Like his.

"May I have permission to court your daughter?" The question was out of his mouth before he could stop it. Her mother's expression was one of pure horror. White Irishmen didn't court Portuguese women. Society would never tolerate such a thing.

"No," she said sharply, hauling her daughter away from him.

Jamie might have taken no for an answer.

Gallagher didn't.

It had cost him well over one hundred dollars in bribes to locate Rosalie, but she had been worth every cent of it. Regardless of her parents, his associates, and society as a whole, he had made her his wife on June 17, 1925.

Rosalie alone had known Jamie. And he had died trying to get to her side while she struggled to bring his one and only child, his son, into the world.

It had been a cold snowy night then, too. Just days

before his thirty-third birthday. He'd known the authorities were after him, had known he had a mole in his company even though he had been trying to go straight.

None of that had mattered.

Rosalie had needed him, and he had refused to let her down.

It was a decision that had cost him his life and his soul.

1

Seventy years later
New Orleans

Gallagher frowned as he felt something tickling his lower back. It was a sensation that he'd learned years ago signaled a Daimon was nearby. He turned his one-of-a-kind 1932 Bugatti Atlantic Aerolithe down a side street and parked it.

Oh yeah, the feeling was there, even stronger than before. He left the car and paused as he got his bearings. In the last seventy years, he'd only been to New Orleans a handful of times, and though the city didn't change much, it still took him a couple of minutes to remember the lay of the French Quarter.

The moonlight filtered down past the wrought-iron railings and hanging plants to illuminate the old brick of the buildings. Faint laughter and music could be heard as well as cars passing by. He cocked his head to listen, hoping for a sign of where the Daimons were.

A scream rang out.

Rushing off after it, he tore through the back alleys until he found the young woman near a garbage

pile, surrounded by four male Daimons while a fifth
Daimon had already sunk his fangs into her neck.

Infuriated, Gallagher rushed them. They charged
him in unison, not that it did them any good. A couple of well-placed blows and one quick stab to their
chests, and they were history.

Gallagher ran to the woman and knelt down by
her side. Gently, he turned her over to find a girl no
older than twenty. He cursed at the fate that had
brought her into the path of the Daimons.

Luckily she was still alive, even though she was
struggling to breathe. He pulled his monogrammed
handkerchief out of his coat pocket and used it as a
makeshift tourniquet over her vicious neck wound.

Moving quickly, he carried her back to his car, then
rushed her to the nearest emergency room where he
learned that the hospital staff wasn't big into admit-
ting unknown women who were carried in by strangers in bloodstained clothes.

Once he had Nick Gautier on the hospital phone
with the clerk and he was sure the unknown girl
would be cared for, Gallagher took a deep breath.

He hung around the hospital, wanting to make
sure she would live. Anxious and unable to just sit
while the staff tended her, he found himself wandering around the corridors. The place was really decked
out for the holidays. The green and red garlands and
poinsettia cut-outs added a warmer feel to the anti-
septic white. A couple of nurses and young female

visitors smiled invitingly at him as he passed by. But then, women always had. At six-foot-four with black hair and eyes, he was well-muscled and hard-edged. The kind of guy that dames tended to notice.

He'd never been vain about it. It was just a fact of life that women liked to look at him and often propositioned him. And though he'd been tempted a time or two over the decades, he had never touched another woman.

Not so long as his wife had lived. Gallagher might have broken every law on the books, but he had never broken a single vow. Especially not one made to someone he loved. Even after Rosalie's death, he still hadn't felt the inclination to touch another woman. So Gallagher just nodded kindly to them and kept walking.

Before long, he found himself on the pediatric ward. His stomach knotted as he realized where he was. There had been a time once when he'd hoped to come to a hospital to see his son.

He'd never made it.

Hurried and not thinking, he'd left his office building at a dead run and had been trying to get into his car when he'd found himself surrounded by cops.

Gallagher, who had never backed down from a fight, had held his hands up. For Rosalie's sake, he'd been willing to surrender to them.

They had shot him dead in the street like a rabid animal.

Unable to deal with the memory, Gallagher was just about to turn around and leave when something odd caught his eye . . .

He saw a strange-looking elf dressed in a red Santa shirt with a very short red skirt, and red-and-white thigh-high stockings that vanished into a pair of scuffed-up black combat boots. She sang to a group of kids with a voice that would rival a heavenly choir for its melodic beauty. The woman was tall and in a freakish way extremely attractive, with eerie, reddish-brown eyes that must have been some kind of contact lenses, pointed ears, and hair that was jet black and streaked with red.

But what floored him most was the man with her.

Acheron Parthenopaeus. The glorified leader of the Dark-Hunters sat on the floor, surrounded by children while he played a black guitar and sang chorus to the woman's lead.

Gallagher was stunned by the sight. In all the years he'd known Ash, he had never seen the man relaxed. Normally, Acheron had a presence about him that was decidedly lethal and cool. One that warned people to keep their distance if they wanted to live.

But that wasn't the Ash he saw now. The man on the floor looked more like a kid himself. Approachable and kind. Ash's deep voice mingled with the elf's as they sang Jackie Deshan's "Put a Little Love in Your Heart."

"Now there's a sight you don't see every day, huh? Two punked-out Goths throwing a Christmas party for sick children."

Gallagher turned to find a middle-aged African-American doctor beside him. She looked tired, but amused, as she watched Ash and his elfin helper with the children.

"You've no idea," he said to her.

The doctor smiled. "I have to admit it took me some getting used to when I started working here a few years ago. I thought they were joking when they first told me about the Goth Guardian Angel and his children's fund."

Gallagher arched a brow at the nickname. "So he comes here a lot?"

"Every few months or so. He always brings gifts for the children and staff, and then plays with the kids for awhile."

Gallagher couldn't have been more stunned had she told him Ash routinely burned the hospital to the ground. "Really?"

"Oh, yeah. We figure he must be some rich kid with a need to do some good. The darnedest thing is, whenever he comes, the kids become perfectly calm and serene. Their blood pressure goes down and we never have to give them any painkillers while he's here. After he leaves, they sleep comfortably for hours. And best of all, the cancer patients go into remission for several weeks afterward. I don't know what it is about that young man, but he really makes a difference in their lives."

Gallagher could understand that. Even though Ash could be terrifying, there was something oddly comforting about the Atlantean.

The instant Ash realized he was there, he saw the veil come down over the man's face. The humor faded, and Ash stiffened noticeably. Ash became the grim, take-no-prisoners leader that Gallagher was well-versed with.

As soon as the song was finished, Ash handed his guitar off to one of the older children and excused himself. He stood up and left the room with a loose long-limbed, predatorial gait. Ash's face was impassable as he crossed his arms over his chest and approached Gallagher.

"St. Ash—who knew?"

Ash ignored his comment. "What are you doing here?"

Gallagher shrugged. "I was just passing through."

He cocked his head. "Passing through? Last time I checked, Chicago was north of Baton Rouge, not south."

"I know. But since I was so close, I just wanted to stop in at Sanctuary and wish everyone a Merry Christmas."

Ash listened to Gallagher's thoughts and let the man's emotions wash through him. Jamie's wife had died of old age this past summer, and her death had hit the Irishman hard.

As soon as he'd "heard" about her death, Ash had gone to Jamie immediately only to find out that Jamie had broken his Code of Conduct and visited her while she'd been in the hospital. Ash had chosen to overlook the breach. He might not have ever known the love of a human being, but he did understand those who were lucky enough to have it.

"Tell you what, since you're here, why don't you just stay on until after the New Year?"

Jamie scoffed at that. "I don't need your pity."

"It's not pity. It's an order. Since Kyrian is retired, Talon could use an extra hand. Things get rather rowdy this time of year. Lots of Daimons head down south where it's warmer and people are out for New Year's."

"Are you full of crap or what?"

Before Ash could answer, the elf woman came out of the room holding a young toddler to her hip.

"*Akri*?" she said to Ash in a strange sing-song kind of voice. "Can I keep him?" She patted the plump leg that was exposed from beneath the hospital gown. "See, he good eating. Lots of fat on this one."

The dark-headed toddler laughed.

"No, Simi," Ash said sternly. "You can't keep the baby. His mother would miss him."

She pouted. "But he want to go home with the Simi. He said so."

"No, Simi," Ash repeated.

She huffed at him. "No Simi, no food. Nag, nag, nag. Does your daddy nag you, too?" she asked the boy.

"Nope," he said as he pulled at one of the black and red horns on top of her head.

Ash sighed. "Simi, take the baby back inside."

She moved to stand before Ash. "Okay, gimme a kiss and I'll go."

Ash looked extremely uncomfortable as he glanced at Gallagher, then back at her. "Not in front of the Hunter, Simi."

She made a strange animal-like noise as she looked at Gallagher. "The Simi wants a kiss, *akri*. I'll wait all century. You know I will."

To say Ash looked peeved was an understatement. He leaned over and kissed her quickly on the brow.

She beamed proudly, then trotted off with the child.

"Who is that?" Gallagher asked. "Or should I say, *what* is that?"

"In short, she's not your concern." Ash rubbed his hand over his forehead as if he were in pain. "Where were we?"

"I asked why you were giving me temporary duty in New Orleans."

"Because Talon could use a hand."

"I wonder what Talon would say?"

"He would tell you not to piss me off."

Gallagher gave a half laugh at that. "All right then. I'll take it under advisement."

Ash watched the woman in the room with the kids. "You can camp with the Peltiers at Sanctuary. Right now I better go before one of those kids ends up on a milk carton."

Gallagher watched as Ash rushed into the room to take a little girl from the elf and then set the child aside. The elf danced away and moved on to another child.

Shaking his head at the oddity, Gallagher headed for the elevator to go back below and check on his patient. The nurse told him she would be fine. Gallagher let out a relieved breath.

The nurse stood up and patted his arm. "Come on," the woman said, inclining her head toward the back. "She wants to thank you."

"I don't need any thanks."

"Sug, we all need thanks. C'mon."

Before he could stop himself, he let the nurse lead him back to a small emergency room that had curtained walls. The petite brunette sat up on her stretcher with an oversized bandage on her neck. Her large green eyes were a bit dazed, but they brightened as soon as she looked up to see him. The nurse left them alone.

"Are you the man who saved me?" she asked.

Feeling awkward, he nodded.

The girl fidgeted with the blanket that covered her. "Thank you. Really."

"My pleasure. I'm just glad I found you when I did."

"Yeah, me too."

Gallagher turned to leave. "Well, I need . . ."

His voice trailed off as a lovely young woman came through the curtains. She was tall, probably around five-ten or so with jet-black hair and deep blue eyes. "Jenna!" she cried as she saw her friend on the stretcher. "Oh thank God, you're okay. The lady on the phone said you'd been attacked."

Jenna's eyes teared up. "I don't know what happened. I was just going out to my car, and I don't remember anything after that. If not for him, I'd probably be dead."

The girl turned around and froze. She looked at him as if she'd just seen a ghost.

Gallagher stared back defiantly. "Something wrong?" he asked.

She frowned. "No." She waved her hand around as if feeling silly. "I'm sorry, you just remind me of someone."

"Old boyfriend?"

"No, my great-grandfather."

"That's not particularly flattering. I thought I looked rather good for my age."

She laughed at that. "No, I mean . . . oh, never mind."

Jenna cocked her head as she looked at him. "He does look like him, Rose. You're right."

Rose. The name hit him like a blow.

Before he could move, the girl named Rose approached him. She pulled out an engraved gold locket from underneath her brown sweater. It was a locket he knew intimately. Right down to the garnet and diamonds that formed a circle on the front of it, to the inscription on the back.

For my Rose.

Happy Anniversary 1930.

She opened the locket to show him the two pictures inside. One was the photograph Rosalie had requested he have made just months before he died and the other was of his son at age two. "See," the girl said, showing him the photograph. "You look just like my Grandpa Jamie."

His heart aching, Gallagher swallowed. He wanted to reach out to touch it, but his hands shook so badly, he didn't dare. "Where did you get that?"

"My great-grandmother gave it to me last spring. Since I was named after her, she wanted me to have it." She smiled sadly and then closed the locket and returned it to rest under her sweater. "My father said Grandpa Jamie was a gangster, but I don't believe it. Gram Rose would never have married someone like that. She was a saint."

It was all he could do to breathe. To not crush her into his arms and weep. His great-granddaughter.

Rosalie.

This vibrant young woman was his living tie to his wife. When he spoke, his voice was thick and deep. "She must have loved you a great deal to give you that."

"I know. She wore it every day of her life until she gave it to me. It's just weird, you know? You looking so much like him and all."

Gallagher cleared his throat. "Yeah. Weird." He couldn't take his eyes off her. He didn't see much of himself or Rosalie in the girl, but he felt the bond of kinship deep in his heart.

She was his family. And he could never tell her. Just as he had never been able to tell her father or her grandfather.

Gallagher had bartered his soul for vengeance and then been forced to step back into the shadows and surrender the care of his family over to strangers. But at least the Squire Council had been there. After Gallagher had become a Dark-Hunter, they had sent in people to make sure his family survived.

The government had taken everything from Rosalie. Confiscated even his legitimate assets and left her destitute. The Squires had given her a job, and after a few years, they had sent in suitable beaux to date his wife and one of them had finally married her.

While Harris had lived, he had sent Gallagher updated photos and news about Gallagher's son and grandchildren. The Squire's Council had ensured the safety and well-being of his family while he had gone about his business of hunting and killing Daimons.

Ash had warned him how hard it would be.

"So long as you have direct descendants still living, it will haunt you. But it does get easier . . . in time."

Other Hunters had told him the same thing, but right now with his great-granddaughter standing before him, he didn't believe it. God, it was so unfair.

Or maybe this was his atonement for living the violent life he had chosen.

Always an outsider. A part of the world, but not in it. He winced at the truth.

Weary and hurt, he excused himself from the girls and made his way out of the hospital. The street outside was virtually empty. The late hour had sent everyone home seeking warmth. Comfort.

He doubted if he would ever feel either again.

When he pulled into the private garage that was across the street from Sanctuary, Elizar Peltier came out of the back door and stopped. The man's long, curly blond hair was pulled back from his face. He wore a pair of black chinos and a baggy black sweater.

"Jamie Gallagher," he said slowly. "I'll be damned." He turned and called into the open door, "Kyle, go tell *Maman* to put on a plate of corned beef and cabbage. We have a Dark-Hunter in need of food."

Gallagher nodded his thanks. "Hi, Zar. It's been awhile."

"About thirty or so years, I think, since we last had the pleasure of your company."

Time was truly fleeting to an immortal. "Yet you still remember my favorite food."

Zar shrugged. "I never forget a friend."

Neither did Gallagher. They were too few and far between.

Zar led him to the building next door to the Sanctuary bar. Built at the turn of the century, Peltier House was the home of the Katagaria family and their hodgepodge group of refugees. The house connected to the bar through a downstairs door that was guarded at all times by one of the eleven Peltier sons.

In the Hunter world, they were legendary because they greeted everyone as friends: Were-Hunters, Dream-Hunters, Dark-Hunters, or others. It mattered not. So long as you minded your manners and kept your weapons concealed, they let you enter and leave in peace. Those who broke the one house rule of "No Spill Blood" quickly found themselves leaving in pieces.

The elegant Victorian mansion was quiet now except for the muffled sound of the Howlers playing on the stage next door in the bar. It was furnished in expensive turn-of-the-century antiques that had been in the house since they were new. The bear clan didn't like change. Gallagher was glad for that. It felt strangely like coming home again.

"How long are you staying?" Zar asked as he led him up the hand-carved mahogany stairs.

"Until the New Year."

Zar nodded. "*Maman* will be glad to hear that." He showed Gallagher to a room at the end of the hallway.

Gallagher stepped inside and found a warm, cozy bedroom. The windows were well-shuttered and covered by heavy drapes that would keep the daylight from reaching him.

"Here's a cable modem for your laptop if you brought one."

The corner of Gallagher's mouth lifted. "All the comforts of home."

"We try. I remember well the days of running and hiding, and never having a single comfort. Take a few minutes to get settled in and join us when you're ready."

Gallagher watched Zar leave while feelings and memories went through him. He appreciated the bears' courtesy, but he would trade all his money and immortality for one single night spent with his wife and son.

One single Christmas with them, watching Rosalie's face light up as she opened a gift.

The pain of his loss racked him. He didn't want to hurt and wish for things he could no longer have. He sat on the bed and stared at the wall. He saw his great-granddaughter's face and wondered if she would go home at Christmas to be with her family.

For that matter, he wondered if he should go home himself. At least Chicago was familiar to him. Weary and heartsick, he lay down on the bed to just rest for a second. He only wanted to escape for an instant into memories of a time when he had been human.

Gallagher woke up to find that three days had passed while he slept. He didn't remember anything about his dreams.

"Why did you let me sleep so long?" he asked Mama Peltier as soon as he left his room and found her in the downstairs parlor on the right.

In human form, she was an elegant, tall blonde woman who most often wore a stylish suit. Though she looked no older than forty, she was in fact close to eight hundred years in age. "Acheron said you needed to rest and I agreed."

"But three days?"

She shrugged. "Do you feel better?"

Strangely, he did. At least physically.

It was just after dark on Christmas Eve. The bear clan was slowly filing down the stairs and gathering into the two main parlors where dual twelve-foot-tall pines were decorated.

Gallagher stood back, watching the whole crew of Katagaria and Arcadians who made Peltier House their home gather around for the coming celebration. The tiny bear cubs climbed over presents and tried to eat and climb up the trees while their fathers and mothers, in human form to make Gallagher feel more at home, pulled them back. Justin Portakalian came down in his panther form and picked up one of the smaller cubs by the scruff of his neck and rolled him playfully across the floor.

It was the most bizarre Christmas gathering Gallagher had ever seen in his one-hundred-plus years of living. He felt even more out of place than he had felt three days ago when he arrived. As members from The Howlers came in to join the party, Gallagher decided he needed a breath of fresh air and a moment of quiet to clear his head. He headed out into the cold dark night and drifted aimlessly through the French Quarter. Before he realized it, he was outside the St. Louis Cathedral.

It had been a long time since he'd last been in church. There were only a few people headed inside. No doubt most of the parishioners would wait until the Midnight Mass. He started to turn away, but instead found himself heading inside with the others.

The foyer was dark, but his Dark-Hunter sight saw the interior clearly and he moved toward the small font of holy water that rested on the wall to his left, just beside the church store. He blessed himself, then opened the dark wood doors that led into the cathedral. The beauty of the stained glass and statuary immediately took him back to the days of his youth.

Gallagher genuflected, then sat down on the last

row. Here, he felt his Rosalie. Devout, she had never missed a Holy Day of Obligation or Feast Day. He had dutifully gone with her even though he'd hemmed and hawed about it. Ever patient, she would sit by his side, patting his arm and smiling to herself over the fact that she had gotten him to do the impossible.

"I miss you, Rose," he breathed, his chest tight with the pain of her loss.

He wanted to stay here where he felt her, but he couldn't. No Dark-Hunter could remain in any old church for very long before the ghosts of the past came out to possess them.

And he was too weak at this moment to fight them.

Getting up, he made his way silently out back to the font, then out to the street.

It was cool out, but nowhere near the coldness he felt inside himself. Gallagher headed down Chartres Street. He didn't know where to go. He didn't feel like going back to Sanctuary and there was no real need to hunt on Christmas Eve. Since most humans were at home with their families, the Daimons tended to stay in as well.

"Hel-lo!"

He paused at the familiar sing-song voice. Turning around, he found "Simi" behind him.

"Hi," he said, half-expecting to see Ash with her.

But apparently she was out alone. Simi bounced up to him. "What'cha doing out here all alone?" she asked. "Did you forget how to find Sanctuary?"

"No. I want to be alone for a bit."

She cocked her head and frowned. "Why? Were the bears mean to you? Mama can get a bit cranky whenever I play with the cubs. She thinks I'm going to eat one, but bleh! They're way too hairy. Now if she'd let me skin one, I might be interested."

He laughed in spite of himself. "Are you joking?"

"Oh no. I never joke about hairy food. It's disgusting." She looked up at him. "If they weren't mean to you, then why did you leave?"

"I don't know. I guess I didn't feel right being there."

"Why?"

He shrugged. "What are you doing out here?"

"Not much. *Akri* is off with that red-headed demon so he said I could go play just so long as I don't eat nothing not cooked by a human. But all my favorite places are closed so I thought I'd go find the bears myself and see if Jose, since he's human, would make me up something good that wouldn't make *akri* mad if I ate it."

"*Akri* is Ash?"

"Yes."

"And the red-headed demon?"

"Artemis the bitch goddess. You know her. She's the one who stole your soul."

"She didn't steal it."

Simi blew him a raspberry. "Of course she did. She steals everything." She stood up on her tiptoes and stared into his eyes. "Hey," she said, taking his chin in her hand so that she could move his head back and forth while she examined him. "You're hurting in there. That would make *akri* very sad. He doesn't like for his Dark-Hunters to hurt and the Simi don't like it when *akri* is sad. Why are you hurt?"

"I miss my family."

Releasing him, she nodded sympathetically. "I miss mine, too. My mama was good people. 'Simi,' she would say, 'I love you.' *Akri* loves me, too."

She tilted her head down so that he could see her horns which were now covered by what appeared to be very small knitted hats. "See, *akri* even gave me hornay warmers so my horns wouldn't get cold. You want some hornay warmers, too?"

This had to be the oddest conversation of his life. He didn't know why he stayed here talking to her. Maybe it was her childlike manner. There was something very charming about her.

"I don't have horns."

"You want some?" she asked hopefully. "I could give you some real colorful ones. *Akri* has some black ones, but he doesn't let other people see them."

"Ash has horns?"

"Oh my, yes. They are quite lovely. Not as lovely as mine, but they are still very nice. The Simi would say she hopes you see them, but if you ever did, you'd be dead and I think the Simi would miss you. You seem very nice, too."

Gallagher frowned as she rummaged around in her

giant oversized, beaded purse. After a few seconds, she pulled out an oven mitt that looked like a fish. She handed it to him.

"That is quality. From QVC. My favorite place. Do you watch QVC?"

"No."

"Well, you should. *Akri* says I watch it too much, but he never complains when I shop there. They like me, too. Put me on television and call me Miss Simi. I like that."

He handed her the fish back.

"Oh no, that's for you. Presents make people happy. The Simi wants you to be happy."

Oh yeah, this was without a doubt the strangest moment of his life. Both mortal and immortal. "Thank you, Simi."

She waved his words aside with her hand. "No need to thank me. See, that's what families do. They take care of each other."

His stomach tightened at her words. "I no longer have a family. I had to give them up."

She looked at him curiously. "Of course you have a family. Everyone has family. I'm your family. *Akri* your family. Even that smelly old goddess is your family. She's that creepy old aunt who comes around but nobody likes her so they make fun of her when she's gone."

He laughed again. "Does she know you say that about her?"

"Of course. I say it to her face all the time. That's why *akri* told me to come play while he's with her. He don't like it when we fight."

She took his hand into hers. "Listen and I'll tell you what *akri* once told me. We have three kinds of family. Those we are born to, those who are born to us, and those we let into our hearts. I have let you into my heart so the Simi is your family and she won't give you up. If you are sad right now, then I'm thinking your family is still in your heart, too, and they are taking up so much room that you have no room for anyone else."

"I can't give them up."

"And you shouldn't. Ever. No one should ever forget those they love. But it's like with QVC— whenever I fill up my room with too much stuff, *akri* builds me another room. Somehow there's always space for more. Your heart can always expand to take in as many people as you need it to. The people who live there, they don't go away. You just make room for one more person and then another and another and another."

With her arm in his, Simi walked him down the street. "Don't you want Simi to be your family?"

He thought about her words and strange analogy.

She leaned forward and whispered. "This is the part where you say, 'Yes, Simi, I would like to be your family.' 'Cause if you don't, then I'll have to take my mitt back and barbecue you. *Akri* is still upset about the last Dark-Hunter I barbecued and that was . . . oh, a thousand or so years ago. He part elephant when it comes to remembering things. So tell me, do you want Simi to be your family?"

He smiled in spite of himself. "Yes, Simi, I would like to be your family."

She beamed. "Good. You're such a smart Dark-Hunter."

Before Gallagher realized it, Simi had led him back to Sanctuary. She opened the door and stood back, waiting for him to enter. The earlier loudness was nothing like what was happening now. There were four hawks lined up on one curtain rod, dancing in time to the rocking Christmas carols. The Howlers (all in human form) were singing while Dev Peltier played the piano. A white tiger was lying on its back on the sofa while Marvin the monkey jumped up and down on its belly.

A large black bear he assumed was Aimee Peltier was feeding two baby cubs peanut butter sandwiches. A red-headed human woman with a scar on her face came up to them and grabbed Simi into a hug. "Hey little demon, where's boss man?"

Simi shrugged. "He off attending to Lord Queen Pain-In-My-Butt. How are you, Tabitha? Is your sister and Kyrian coming?"

"No, they'll be here tomorrow. Morning sickness

hit Amanda as they were leaving, but Talon said he'd be here just as soon as he could." The two of them drifted off into the crowd.

Gallagher stood back, watching the revelry. There were Arcadians here, Katagaria, Dark-Hunters, demons, humans, and who knew what else. By all rights none of them should get along and yet they were together tonight.

Bound by something other than blood. They were bound together by their hearts.

Colt came up to him. An Arcadian Sentinel, his job was technically to hunt and slay the Katagaria. But years ago the Peltiers had rescued and protected Colt's mother and then raised him after her death. He was as loyal to the bear clan as any of their natural sons.

Smiling, he pulled a pineapple mitt out of his back pocket. "Man, Gallagher, you must really rate. You got one of the good fish. All I got was a lousy pineapple."

"What, does everyone she meet get one?"

"Nope. Only family."

Gallagher looked around at that and saw something he hadn't noticed earlier.

Everyone there had a mitt.

UPON THE MIDNIGHT CLEAR

The way to overcome the angry man is with gentleness, the evil man with goodness, the miser with generosity and the liar with truth.

—AN INDIAN PROVERB

It sounds good, doesn't it? If only people and life were that effing easy. Trust me, it takes more than a friendly biscuit to tame a hungry lion. And it's all fun and games until someone gets hurt. Then it's war.

—SAVITAR, CHTHONIAN GOD

PROLOGUE

Dolor smiled as he finally felt the call of his summoning ring. For countless centuries he'd been asleep—cursed to wait for another human to grow enough testicles to awaken him. How he hated the dream goddess, Leta, for her abilities to trap him to this fate. To make him the lapdog of a mere mortal.

Now the bitch would pay.

But first he'd have to deal with this pathetic mortal who had temporary power over him.

Leaning his head back, he allowed the conscious part of himself to travel through the darkness until he appeared as an apparition before his summoner.

"See! I told you it would work!"

Dolor frowned at the small, round male who had beady blue eyes, glasses, and a bald scalp that gleamed under the grueling fluorescent lights. He stood next to a taller human whose blond hair was cut close to his head. His green eyes were feral with madness and anger.

And those green eyes narrowed suspiciously on Dolor. "Who are you?"

Dolor snorted at the asinine question. "You summoned me. Don't you know?"

The human gaped as the smaller man pushed his glasses back onto his nose with his forefinger. His jowls flapped as he looked up at the taller man. "See, I told you, Donnie. The book of spells and ring worked just like Mark said it would. I told you Mark was a genius about all that weird occult stuff. He's never been wrong before. Now you tell the pain god who you want punished and he'll do it."

"For a price," Dolor added, reminding them that there was more to bringing him back from stasis than just reading the lines from his book and wearing his binding ring. Right now, most of his powers were still bound by Leta's curse.

The blond man crossed his arms over his chest and gave him a tough, smug grimace. "What price?"

Dolor shrugged nonchalantly as if the steep price was nothing at all. "The price of all vengeance—blood sacrifice. I will need you to kill someone in order to awaken me from my slumber."

The one called Donnie nodded as if he agreed to the terms. An instant later, he pulled a small shiv from his back pocket and cut the throat of the man beside him. The smaller man tried to scream, but the cut was too deep to allow it.

Dolor lifted an eyebrow as the shorter man fell to

the floor, clasping his neck and jerking until death finally claimed him. Donnie merely watched him die without a single sign of remorse or feeling for the person who'd been his cellmate for the last two years.

Good. Dolor needed someone this soulless to help him.

Smiling, he applauded the human. "Nice gesture, but not what I needed."

Donnie curled his lip. "What do you mean?"

"There is a ritual, you fool. I don't come back without . . ." Dolor hesitated at revealing too much lest he frighten the human away, "certain requirements."

"And they are?"

Again, Dolor hesitated, but there was no other way for the human to awaken Dolor's powers. Hopefully the human would continue to be heartless and cold. "The blood of a loved one. You must offer me someone important to you and you must utter my curse while you bleed them. When the words are spoken and they lie dead, my powers will be unbound and I'll be able to enter this world."

There was a little more to it than that, but the human didn't need to know the rest until the time came for it.

First things first. If Dolor could get this sacrifice, the rest would be easier . . . provided the human was serious about his vengeance.

Donnie scowled as if skeptical. "How do I know you're not lying to me?"

"Why would I lie?"

"Because everyone does."

And he would know. It was lies and deception that had landed this piece of trash in prison. Dolor gave him a soothing, if not insincere, smile. "True, but I want my freedom as much as you do."

Donnie scoffed. "And I've seen this movie a few times. You'll kill me once you're free, won't you?"

Dolor laughed. "My venom isn't for you, little human. I have my own person to bleed. Because of her, I have to do what you order me to first. Then and only then will I be free to exact my own revenge. Trust me, you'll live a long time once I'm gone."

Because living with the actions he'd have to take to free Dolor was the worst thing Dolor could do for this human and since he was the god of pain . . .

Dolor smiled and this time he meant it.

Donnie stepped over the body to approach his shimmering ghost form. "I've been waiting for this for far too long. Since the day I was first arrested, I've been trying any- and everything I could and nothing has worked. What I want more than anything else in this world is my kid brother dead and I want him to suffer unimaginable misery before he dies. We're talking pain of Biblical proportions. The kind that has him screaming out for mercy and begging me to kill him to end it while I laugh at his agony. Can you do that?"

"That is my specialty."

Donnie smiled as the insanity flared deep in his eyes. "Then tell me what I have to do to set you free. I will do anything to see my brother suffer and die, and I do mean *anything*."

Two days later

Dressed in a long, flowing, white Grecian gown, Leta came awake with a sharp gasp. It took her several seconds to acclimate to her surroundings. She was still in her cushioned pod, asleep in the hall of mirrors on the Vanishing Isle.

But something was wrong. She could sense it. The dark hand of evil slithered over her body with an unmistakable touch.

Dolor, the most vile of all gods, had been summoned back into the human realm which had triggered her own waking. The god of pain had been trapped centuries ago by Leta, who had fought him until they'd both been bloody and spent. Forbidden by Zeus to kill him outright, she'd been forced to trap him so that he would never do to another what he'd done to her.

And once he'd been trapped, she'd placed herself in stasis to heal and await the moment when he would stir.

Now someone had found Dolor's hidden ring and

uttered that which was never to be uttered again. Sucking her breath in sharply, she allowed her buried memories to assail her.

Morons! The stupid humans had no idea what they'd unleashed. Pain wasn't content to attack just the one person it was sent after. No, it was bloodthirsty and ruthless. Dolor respected nothing and no one was immune to Pain.

Sure, he'd stalk and kill the one he was sent after, but once that was accomplished, Pain would return to the one who'd summoned it.

May the gods help the summoner then. His torture would be without end.

Closing her eyes, she reawakened her dormant powers. She let her thoughts drift until she found Pain's target.

The target had his back to her, but even so she could tell he was tall and broad shouldered. His blond hair was tousled and wavy as it fell to the top of his black collar.

As a dream god, she could feel his bitter emotions calling out to her. They were so strong she could even feel them as her own.

"Yeah," he said, his deep voice filled with malice. "It never fails to amaze me how a single lie can undo an entire lifetime of good."

And it was then she realized something. This man didn't need Pain. It already lived inside him right alongside Bitterness and Rage. They had him nestled tight against their bosoms and from what she sensed they had no intention of letting him go.

Then she heard it . . .

That deep, blood-chilling laugh.

"Leta . . ."

She flashed herself from her sterile pod to stand on the cold marble floor. A bitter wind plastered her gown against her body, exposing her bare feet to the ankles. It made the gold bands on her upper arms bitingly cold. The walls around her were white; no pictures or curtains or anything else to break its sterile quality.

Still she felt the presence of the god of Pain.

"Where are you, you bastard?"

Dolor appeared behind her. Before she could move, he grabbed her by the hair and wrenched her head back against his shoulder. "You didn't really think you could keep me trapped forever, did you?"

She tried to fight, but he released her and vanished. "This isn't over, Dolor," she said, her voice filled with the weight of her promise.

His laughter filled the room. "No, it isn't. You bound me to this curse, and before this is over, you will pay for it. Now if you'll excuse me, I have a human to torture and kill."

She felt him receding all the way down her spine and there was nothing she could do to stop him. By the order of Zeus, her own emotions had been drained. Yet she felt something . . . some remnant emotions from the past perhaps?

She wasn't sure.

But one thing was certain, there were enough emotions inside her that she wasn't about to allow Pain to hurt another soul if she could help it. It was a solemn vow she'd made and it was one she would keep. So long as she had life in her veins, she would fight.

And as she started forward, Dolor's target turned in the mirror to face her.

Leta froze as she saw the man's features. He was as beautiful as an immortal. Through the mist that separated the Vanishing Isle from the human plane, she could see every curve and line of his perfect face. Sharp brows arched over eyes that were a pale green. Searing with intelligence, they showed her a soul that was tainted by betrayal. One completely devoid of trust.

And in that one single moment, she felt his sorrow inside her own heart. He wanted to trust someone. He wanted to reach out. But he'd forgotten how.

Alone and cold, he was pain personified.

Cocking her head, she realized something else. That pain that burned so fiercely within him was exactly what she needed to use in order to defeat Dolor. If she could channel it, it would meld with her powers and give her the advantage. There was no stronger emotion than rage . . .

He's been hurt enough . . .

It didn't matter. She couldn't see his pain for her own. Dolor must be defeated at any cost and if this human paid the price, so what? The life and soul of one would never be worth more than the lives and souls of many.

Aidan O'Conner would be her sacrifice and her past would finally be avenged. Pain would be defeated by her hand and laid to rest for all eternity.

1

Leta was completely baffled by the human world as she stared into the mirrors around her that showed the daily events taking place in the realm of man. Her gaze chased from mirror to mirror as she tried to make sense of the flickering images of people from all over the world. She was beginning to suspect that she'd made a horrible mistake by putting herself in stasis while waiting for Dolor to stir. Everything had changed.

Everything.

There were complicated contraptions—machines— that she couldn't even begin to fathom. And the languages had changed *so* much . . . She had to focus to understand the rapidly spoken words, which were riddled with colloquialisms and slang that flew past her understanding. Her head ached from the strain of it all.

"Give yourself time."

She turned to find her older brother M'Adoc behind her. For a creature whose emotions had been brutally taken from her, she felt her heart stirring at his approach. It was a muted joy that only reminded her of what real happiness had felt like. But phantom emotions were better than no emotions at all.

Tall and lithe like her, M'Adoc had black, wavy hair and eyes so pale a blue they were almost luminescent.

She held her hand out to him. "It's good to see you again, brother."

There was the subtlest of softening in his gaze as he took her hand and brought it to his lips.

Leta flinched as an unbidden and unexpected image of his being tortured went through her. Even after thousands of years, she could still hear his screams.

And her own.

As if he knew her thoughts, M'Adoc gathered her into his arms. He cupped her head in his hand and held her face against his shoulder. Leta gasped as he passed onto her the knowledge of the changed world and how it worked.

"You have set yourself a herculean task, little sister," he breathed against her hair. "You should have stayed with the rest of us and not isolated yourself."

"I couldn't." It had been too painful to see them all emotionless when she remembered the way they'd been before Zeus had punished them. The only emotion Zeus had left them with was pain, so that he could control and punish the gods of sleep, and that never-ending pain had eaten a hole inside her.

It was a cold world she'd been forced to live in and that as much as anything else was why she'd been just as content to sleep through eternity.

She stepped back from M'Adoc so that she could meet his gaze. "I have to stop him."

"He's not the only god of pain. Pain permeates everything in our world and that of man."

"I know. But he *is* ultimate suffering. It's not enough to make his victims cry. He destroys them, mind, body, and soul. You weren't there, brother . . . you didn't see."

Still, he flinched as if he could in fact see her memories. "Everyone does what they feel they have to do. I respect you for your choices. Doesn't mean I agree with them." His gaze sharpened before he spoke again. "Dolor will kill you if he gets the chance."

She let one side of her mouth curl up into the semblance of a bitter smile. "Good. I relish the fight just as I will relish the feel of his heart in my fist as I crush the life out of him."

M'Adoc inclined his head to her. "Then I leave you to your plans for revenge . . . except for one thing."

"That is?"

His eyes were haunting. "It's not the pain that's inflicted on us by others that destroys us. It's the pain we let inside our hearts that does that. Don't let the human's anger become yours. It can drive you mad if you do." And with those sage words spoken, he vanished.

Leta drew a deep breath as she considered what he'd said. She knew he was right. But knowing something and doing it were often two entirely different things. She needed Aidan's anger. She wanted it.

Closing her eyes, she focused on the target.

Aidan.

He was asleep in his bed, dreaming that he was lost in a thundering storm. The rain slashed painfully against his skin as he trudged along. His breathing was ragged, his handsome face contorted by rage.

Leta was baffled by his actions. By his will to carry on even as lightning struck the ground, barely missing him. The static from the blasts caused his hair to rise and fan out around his steely features. It was a feral determination that carried him onward. And before she even realized what she'd done, she'd stepped through the portal and entered the dream beside him.

He froze in place as he became aware of her. The cold rain pelted her flesh, plastering her hair against her body as she watched him curiously. In this state, all of his emotions were laid bare to her. She could feel every ounce of his rage, his betrayal.

His unsated need for revenge.

It was so close to her own feelings that it fed her powers and brought her emotions back with a clarity so crisp, it stung.

He uncoiled his arms from around his chest as he

stared at her with those icy, probing eyes. "Who are you?"

"A friend," she whispered, catching a chill from the wind that started blowing against them.

He laughed bitterly. "I have no friends. I don't want any."

"Then I'm here to help you."

He snorted in derision. "Help me do what? Freeze? Or is your plan to hold me still in this storm to make sure the lightning kills me?"

Leta snapped her fingers and the rain instantly stopped. The clouds roiled above as they parted to show the sun. The rays illuminated the bleak landscape and painted it in bright greens and yellows.

Aidan wasn't fazed. "Neat trick."

He was a hard man to impress and his jaded causticity made her wonder what had happened to him to cause it. She dried their clothes and hair. "Why did you summon the rain?"

"I didn't summon shit," he growled. "I was minding my own business when it came down on me. All I was trying to do was get through it."

"And now that it's gone?"

He looked up at the clear blue sky above them. "It'll be back. It always comes back and it hits you when you least expect it."

She knew he wasn't just talking about the weather. "You should find shelter."

He scoffed at her. "There isn't any. The storm tears

it down and leaves you naked in the hurricane, so why bother?"

And she'd stupidly thought *she* was bitter. Then again, outside the dream world, she could only feel a twinge of what she felt now. Even so hers was nothing in comparison to his. His bitterness ran so deep, it scalded her tongue with the taste of it.

But beneath that hostility she sensed a raw vulnerability in him. Something about him that had been crushed and yet was still struggling to survive even though he didn't want it to. It reached out to her own grieving heart and made her want to touch him.

Without a second thought, she took a step forward to lay her hand to his cheek.

He hissed at her like a cat before he moved away. "Don't touch me."

"Why not?"

"I don't want your lying kindness. Sure, you'll smile and be so sweet to me that I'll trust you, but the minute I don't give you *everything* you want the instant you demand it, you'll turn on me and try to crush me. You're just like everyone else in the world. No one matters but you."

And with that, he turned and walked away.

Leta crossed her arms over her chest as she watched him put distance between them.

Oh yeah, she had enough bitter emotions here to more than defeat Dolor. Little did the god know that his current victim was going to be his downfall. Aidan might seem insignificant to the god, but his determination and spirit would be the fuel she needed to avenge them both.

And just like Dolor, she wouldn't show any clemency or weakness. Nothing was going to stop her from destroying him. For once Dolor was going to know exactly what it was like to have someone come for him and leave him quivering on the ground, begging for a mercy that would never come.

She couldn't wait . . .

2

It was just another frigid day in hell as far as Aidan O'Conner was concerned. Nothing ever changed and he liked it that way.

At least that was what he was hoping for until his cell phone started ringing. Picking it up from his breakfast counter, he looked at the ID. He started not to answer it, but it was his agent, Mori, and if he didn't answer Mori would worry him like a neurotic puppy with a urinary tract infection needing to go piss in the snow.

Definitely not what he needed in his life or, more importantly, in his current mood.

Aidan flipped the phone open with his chin as he simultaneously turned down his stereo, which was playing his Bauhaus CD. "Hi, Mori."

"Oh, Aidan, there you are. I've been worried about you."

Yeah, right. The only thing Mori ever worried about was where his next check was coming from.

The bastard was just like everyone else Aidan had ever known. Greedy, self-serving, narcissistic, and wanting a piece of Aidan's flesh.

Just the sound of his whiny voice telling Aidan what to do made him all warm and toasty inside.

"I have another offer for you, A. They're up to thirty-five million dollars plus a significant share of the profits, and believe me, with the costars in this movie there will be enough profits to make even a Scrooge like you smile."

Aidan remembered a time when he would have choked and died at such an offer. A time when that kind of money had seemed like an unimaginable dream.

And like all his dreams, that one too had been brutally shattered.

"I told you I'm not interested."

Mori scoffed. "Of course you're interested."

"No, Mori, I'm not."

"Oh, come on, you can't keep hiding out on top of your little mountain. Sooner or later you have to come back to the real world. And this will be the perfect comeback. Think of how much money you'd be throwing away if you say no."

Aidan flipped the CD to the song "Crowds" and let it remind him of why he had no interest in going back to Hollywood . . . or anywhere outside of Knob Creek, Tennessee, for that matter. He didn't like people and he hated the thought of ever doing another movie. "Thanks, but no thanks. With a hundred million dollars in my bank accounts, I don't ever have to come back to reality again."

Mori made a deep sound of disgust in the back of his throat. "Damn it to hell, Aidan. You've been gone from the scene so long you're lucky anyone is wanting you at any price. Even the tabloids have forgotten you at this point."

"Really?" he said, glancing down at the stack on his coffee table that he'd picked up a week ago when he'd been in the supermarket. His face was plastered all over them. "Funny, but I seem to be the talk of the tabloids. They're speculating on everything from whether I had a disfiguring car wreck to being kidnapped by aliens or an insane fan, to my favorite of all—which claims I'm having a sex change operation at a Swedish clinic. I particularly like the Photoshopped picture of me in a dress. At least I look better than Klinger, huh? But in all honesty, I'd like to think I'd look more like Alexis Mead from *Ugly Betty* than this hairy yeti they have me pictured as."

Mori cursed again. "You're really not playing with me, are you? This isn't a stunt to get more money from the studio. You really are serious about retiring."

"Yeah, Mori. I'm through. I just want to go back to being a plain, normal guy that no one knows."

Mori snorted. "It's too late for that. There's not a person in the world over the age of two days who doesn't know the name and face of Aidan O'Conner. Christ, you were on more magazine covers than the president."

And that was why he had no intention of leaving his mountain top except for food, beer, and maybe once a year to get laid . . . then again, given all he'd been through, he might consider using blow-up dolls instead—some of the ones he'd found online were getting seriously high tech. "You're not helping your case. Besides, I thought they'd all forgotten me."

Even over the phone, he could hear Mori blustering in his office. "You know better. I don't get you, man, I really don't. You could own the world if you wanted to. It's yours for the taking."

As if Aidan cared about that . . . What good was owning the world when he'd have no choice except to defend himself against every person in it? Personally, he'd rather be a beggar with one true friend than a prince surrounded by two-faced assassins.

"I'm hanging up now, Mor. Talk to you later." Aidan clicked the phone off and tossed it back to the counter where it landed on another photo of him in a bad wig and a dress. God, he remembered when a lie like that would have sent him off on a rage that would have lasted for days.

But that was before the betrayal that had cut so deep it had destroyed every sensitive nerve in his body. Unlike the firestorm he'd been through, these attacks weren't personal and they weren't directed at him by people he'd once called family. These attacks were all highly laughable.

He flicked the lid off his beer and held it up to the photos of his "family" that he kept on his mantel next to his five Oscars. "Fuck you all very much," he said snidely.

But in the end, he knew the truth. He was the only one who'd been royally screwed. He'd put his trust in all the wrong people and now he was left alone to deal with the devastation they'd foisted on him— because he'd dared to love them more than he'd loved himself.

Life was nothing if not pain and he was the king of it.

Two years ago, he'd lived and died for those assholes on the mantel. Had given freely to them, hand over fist, wanting them to have a better life than the hell he'd known growing up.

And even though he'd given all but his life to them, it hadn't been enough. They'd been deceitful and selfish. Unsatisfied with his extravagant gifts, they'd begun taking, and when he'd dared to question them about their theft, they'd gone after the only thing he'd had left.

His reputation and livelihood.

Yeah, people were sick and he was tired of the Judases around him. His days of being used by others for what they could suck out of him were over.

He wanted nothing more of this world or those who were in it.

His gaze slid to the shotgun that he kept in the corner of his cabin for snakes and bears. Sixteen months ago, he'd loaded that gun, intending to kill himself and end his pain for real. The only thing that had kept him here was the fact that he wouldn't give them the satisfaction of knowing they'd weakened him to that point.

No, he was stronger than that. He'd come into this world alone and alone he would stand and defend himself until the day God above saw fit to take him from it. He'd be damned if some two-bit backwoods trash would get the better of him. He hadn't clawed his way out of poverty and built up his life to where it was, to give it all up because of some backstabbing bastards.

He hadn't started this fight, but he was the one who'd ended it.

"The trust of the innocent is the liar's most useful tool." Aidan flinched as he remembered the quote from his favorite Stephen King novel. They'd certainly proven that to be true. And no one had been more innocent than he in all this. Because of them, his gullibility had been slaughtered on the altar of treachery.

But no more. Now there was nothing left except a man so strong he would never again allow anyone that close to him. He'd banished all trust. Banished all tenderness. He now gave to the world what it had given to him.

Anger, hatred, and venom. And that was why he kept their smiling faces on the mantel. It was to remind him how two-faced everyone was.

Aidan paused as he heard a slight banging. It sounded like someone at his door . . .

No. It wasn't possible. He was too far out and away from everything. No one ever came up the isolated dirt road that led to his log cabin. Cocking his head, he listened again, but the sound seemed to vanish.

He snorted. "Yeah, great, now I'm hearing things."

Aidan took a step, then heard the banging again.

Maybe something had come loose. He reversed course and headed back toward his great room.

"Hello?"

He cursed at the muffled feminine voice. Damn it. The last thing he wanted on his mountain was a woman. Growling, he snatched open the door to find a white, bundled form on his porch step. "Get off my property."

"P-p-please. I'm freezing and my car broke down. I need to call for help."

"Then use your cell phone." He slammed the door in her face.

"I can't get a signal up here." Her voice was faint and the softness of it cut through him.

Don't you dare feel sorry for her, putz. No one takes

pity on you. Give only what you're given. Hatred. Contempt. He glanced to the pictures on his mantel.

"Please. I'm freezing. Please help."

If you don't do something she's going to freeze out there. Her death will be on your hands.

So what! Let her die for being stupid. Sometimes Darwinism was the best way to go . . .

But no matter how much his anger gnawed at him and his inner voice called him an ass, he couldn't leave her out there to die.

You're a freakin' idiot.

"Ten minutes," he snarled as he snatched open the door. "That's it. Then I want you out of my house."

"Thank you," she said, stepping inside.

Aidan kept his lip curled as he watched her drift toward his fire. She left a trail of snow on his hardwood floors. "Don't mess up the place."

"I'm sorry," she said, her voice still distorted by her pink woolen scarf that she had pulled up over her mouth and nose. All he could see of her face was a pair of eyes so pale a shade of blue they practically glowed. "It's really cold outside."

"Like I care," he said under his breath before he moved to get his cell phone from the countertop. He went back to her and held it out. "Make it quick."

She pulled off her white leather gloves to expose dainty hands that were bright pink from the cold. Shivering, she pulled the scarf down.

Aidan couldn't breathe as he saw her face, and a

wave of lust bombed his system. Fine boned and patrician, she was beautiful. But more than that, it was the same woman he'd seen in his dream last night who had stopped the rain.

How freakin' weird . . .

Without a word, she took the phone from his hand and dialed it.

He couldn't move as he watched her. What were the odds of some unknown person coming out of his dreams and showing up at his door needing a phone? Especially the woman whose face had been haunting him all day.

You should play the lottery . . .

She shut his phone, then held it out to him. "Yours isn't working either."

"Bullshit." He flipped it open, then realized she was right. There was no signal at all. Baffled, he scowled at it. "I was just on it a minute ago."

She shrugged before she returned to his fire. "Looks like we're both out of luck then."

"I'm not out of luck. I live here. You're the one who's screwed, 'cause you're not staying."

She gaped in disbelief. "You would really throw me out of your house in the middle of a blizzard?"

He scoffed. "There's no . . ." His voice drifted off as he looked outside and realized she was right. It was a total whiteout.

When had that happened?

"Un-friggin'-believable," he snarled. Then again, it was just his luck. His uncle had always told him he was born under an unlucky star. The man had been more right than either of them had ever guessed.

She turned her haunting eyes toward his. "Should I leave?"

Yes. Something in his soul screamed for him to shove her out the door and then lock it tight. It was that part of him that had been battered to the brink of suicide.

But even after all he'd been through, he couldn't bring himself to cause her death. Unlike him, she most likely had someone out there who would actually mourn for her if she were to die. Bully for her.

She gave him a look that rivaled the freezing temperature outside before she pulled her muffler back over her face and started for the door.

"Don't be stupid," he snarled. "You can't go out there."

She raked him with a stern look, then lowered the muffler. "I don't like staying where I'm not wanted."

"So you want me to lie?" He fell into the acting that had won him his Academy Awards. "Oh, baby, please stay with me and don't leave. I need you here. I can't live without you."

Leta arched a brow at his words, which lacked the sarcastic tone she was certain lay beneath them. Little did he know how true they were. He did need her here because she was the only thing standing between him and death.

"How nice. You practice those lines much?"

"Not really. Usually I just tell people to fuck off and die."

"Ooo," she said in a seductive tone. "That just gives me goose bumps all over. I love it when a man sweet-talks me."

"I'll bet you do." Scratching his jaw, he indicated the wooden tree by the door. "You can hang your coat there until the storm or the phone clears."

She shrugged the coat off and unwound the scarf from around her before she pulled away her hat and tucked it in the pocket of her coat. "What's the gun for?"

"I would lie and say it's for bears or snakes, but mostly I use it for trespassers."

"Wow, Dexter," she said, using the name of the serial killer from the Showtime series M'Adoc had shown her. "I'm impressed. Since we're not in Miami and you haven't a boat to hide the hacked-up bodies at sea, where are you keeping them?"

"Under the woodshed out back."

"Nice." She smiled. "At least that explains the odor I smelled coming up the driveway."

His gaze lightened as if he found her entertaining. "You're right. That's the septic line. I'm not stupid enough to put corpses that close to my house—it'd bring the wildlife too close to my back door. I leave the bodies in the woods for the bears to eat."

"What about when they're hibernating?"

He shrugged. "The coyotes get them."

He was quick, she'd give him that. "Well, then, I guess you need to go ahead and shoot me and get it over with. The coyotes are probably starving in this weather."

Aidan was completely baffled by her lack of fear. "You're not afraid of me, are you?"

"Should I be?"

"You're trapped in the woods during a snowstorm with a man you've never laid eyes on before. My nearest neighbor lives six miles away. I could do anything I wanted to you and no one would ever know."

She looked to the corner behind her. "True, but I'm the one closest to the gun."

"You think you could beat me to it?"

Leta wrinkled her nose at him. She didn't know why but she was enjoying this banter and she shouldn't be capable of enjoying anything at all. "I think I can handle you, Dex. After all, you don't know anything more about me than I know about you. For all you know, I could be a crazed serial killer on the run from the authorities. Might even be a body in the trunk of my car waiting for me to bury it."

Aidan was intrigued by the fact she was playing the same game that he'd started. He admired courage and she seemed to have more than her share of it. "Are you a serial killer?"

She lifted her chin. "You first, Dexter. Who are you and why are you up here alone?"

He stepped around the counter to approach her. Pausing before her, he held out his hand. "Aidan O'Conner. Former actor, but I'm sure you know that."

She shrugged. "It means nothing to me. I'm Leta."

"Leta what?"

"Just Leta." She hesitated a moment longer before she took his hand and shook it. "Nice to meet you, Dexter."

He studied her carefully. Her winter-white clothes, while nice, weren't extravagant. They didn't say much about her except that she was caught in a snowstorm unprepared. She didn't have any jewelry or anything else that marked even the most basic thing about her. She was like a blank slate. "And what do you do for a living, just Leta?"

"I'm a professional bodyguard."

He laughed at her unexpected answer. "Yeah, right."

She shook her head slowly. "Nope. All true. I know seventy-two ways to kill a man and sixty-nine of them look like an accident."

That should probably scare him, but instead he was intrigued. "And what brings a bodyguard to this neck of the woods? Did Mori hire you to protect me from my brother?"

"I don't know any Moris. I'm currently between assignments and was looking for a change. I heard there was work in Nashville and it seemed like a good place to start over. So here I am stuck in the freezing cold with a . . . serial killer. Has the making for a great horror movie, huh?"

He still wasn't satisfied with her answer. "How are you in the profession of protecting people without knowing who I am? I've been told I have one of the most recognizable faces in the world."

"Wow . . . Just out of curiosity, when you go to bed at night, do you find yourself ousted off the mattress by that ego?"

"It's not ego. It's the truth."

She folded her arms over her chest as if she didn't believe it for a minute. "Well, then, if I admit I know who you are and really couldn't care less will that assuage your damaged manhood enough that we can get past this and move on to something that ends with your giving me a sandwich?"

He ignored her question. "So you do know me?"

"Yes, Dexter," she said, her voice laden with sarcasm. "I know who you are. You feel better now?"

Not really. Her sarcasm rather sucked all the joy out of being right. It also made him see red. "Then why the lie?"

Leta realized she'd just made a big mistake with him. This was a man who'd been lied to enough, and it was obvious if she were to stay, she'd have to be as honest as possible. "Well, since you're hidden away in the middle of nowhere, I figured you didn't want to advertise the fact you're a world-famous actor, though to be honest the Oscars on the mantel aren't exactly subtle."

A tic worked in his jaw. "Are you a reporter?"

She rolled her eyes. "No. I told you what I am. I protect bodies."

"How do I know I can believe you?"

"You don't. But why would I lie?"

If anything, that made his anger increase. "You lied about knowing me. You could lie about anything. People lie all the time, usually for no reason whatsoever."

"But I'm not lying about being hungry." She gestured toward the loaf of bread on the counter. One of the problems with entering the mortal realm was that it tended to make Dream-Hunters extremely hungry, and right now her stomach was cramping and aching. "Could you toss me a piece of bread before the interrogation continues? Or do I have to beat your butt for a spoonful of peanut butter?"

Aidan grabbed the bread from the counter and chucked it at her. She caught it with one hand. Stepping back, he swept his hand toward the door next to the fridge. "Peanut butter is in the pantry."

She narrowed her eyes on him suspiciously before she moved to open the door and search through his staples. She emerged a few minutes later with the peanut butter. Her gaze unamused, she set it on the counter. "Knife?"

"Drawer in front of you."

After opening it, she twirled the knife in her hand with an expertise that said she wasn't lying about her occupation.

"Who was your last job?" he asked, tucking his hands under his arms.

"Terrence Morrison."

He frowned. "Who?"

"A billionaire playboy who made the mistake of putting his balls on the wrong billiard table."

Aidan could just imagine the trouble something like that could get a man into, especially depending on who thought they had rights to that billiard table. "Why did you leave?"

She spread the peanut butter over a slice of bread. "I took care of the person harassing him. Threat gone. Job eliminated." Her look smug, she took a bite of her sandwich. "Anything else you want to know? Dental records, fingerprints? Retinal scan?"

"Urine sample would work."

She rolled her eyes. "What cup you want me to use?"

He was intrigued by her comebacks and the fact that she didn't appear angry over his questioning and word choice. "Does anything faze you?"

"I fight people for a living. Do you honestly think peeing in a cup is going to frighten me?"

She had a point . . . providing she wasn't lying about her occupation.

Without a word, Aidan pulled a glass out of his cabinet and handed it to her.

Her jaw dropped. "You've got to be kidding me? You really want a urine sample?"

He actually smiled at her question. "Not hardly, but I thought you might be thirsty. The drinks are in the fridge."

For once he saw relief in her gaze before she went and poured herself a glass of milk. "Thanks for showing some mercy."

"Yeah," he said bitterly. "Just remember to return the favor."

"Is that supposed to mean something?"

He shrugged. "Just in my experience, all people do is take. None of them give a damn about helping someone else."

"And sometimes people can surprise you."

"Yeah. You're right. I'm constantly amazed by the unprovoked treachery they're capable of."

She shook her head. "Wow, you *are* jaded."

If she only knew. Besides, he had every right and then some to it. He'd had enough knives planted in his spine to make a stegosaurus envious. "Look at you." He indicated her body with his hand. "Do you protect people because they need it or do you protect them because they pay you?"

Leta hesitated. She most certainly didn't get paid

for what she did, but he'd never believe a human would be so altruistic. So she opted for a semitruth. "Girl's got to eat."

"And I rest my case. People will knife you in the back for a stinking crumb and then go on with their lives as if you're nothing but a worthless roach."

She let out a slow breath as she saw in his anger exactly what M'Adoc had seen in hers. His was an unreasonable master that wouldn't release him. The worst part was the degree to which he'd embraced his rage. It controlled and distorted everything around him to the point he was unable to see past it. "There are sorry people out there. But I promise you not everyone is like that. For every act of cruelty mankind is capable of, they're just as capable of kindness."

He sneered at her. "You'll forgive me if I ruthlessly disagree." He shook his head as if the mere sight of her disgusted him. "I marvel at the fact you've lived to your age and no one's taken those rose-colored glasses and shoved them up your—"

She held her hands up in surrender to silence his tirade. "You're entitled to your opinion just as I'm entitled not to listen to it."

That set him off even more. He pushed himself away from the counter and headed toward the front door. "You're irritating. If I had to have someone barge into my home, couldn't they at least have been mute?" He picked up the gun and started for the small hallway that led to his den. "Don't make yourself too comfortable. I want you out of here the instant the weather clears."

Her gaze sharpened on the gun in his hands. "Trust me so little?"

"I don't trust you at all." And with that, he went off to his den and left her standing in his kitchen.

Leta took a deep breath as she felt his hostility reaching out to her. Good.

So far Dolor hadn't managed to break into the mortal plane. But it wouldn't be long.

Dolor had been summoned to kill Aidan and he would do everything within his power, which was great, to succeed. There would be no stopping him.

Which meant she wouldn't have long to build up her own powers by feeding from Aidan. She frowned as she felt a twinge of guilt. As a Dream-Hunter, she shouldn't feel anything like that at all and yet she couldn't squelch the part of her that didn't want to hurt Aidan when it was so obvious he'd been cut enough by those around him.

It's for his own good.

Odd how the gods and humanity used that so often to justify brutality.

Zeus had even said that when he'd ordered all the emotions stripped from the Dream-Hunters. When he'd had all of them punished for a crime only one god had committed. And even that hadn't been a crime. It'd been intended as a joke on old Thunderbutt to make him not take everything so seriously. Instead of laughing, Zeus had abused his powers to lash out against everyone who didn't agree with him.

The rest of the dream gods had merely been innocents caught in the crossfire. But Zeus's fear of being overthrown and mocked had caused him to punish them all. How pathetic to live his existence in such paranoia.

However, Zeus's god complex didn't concern her. What she needed to focus on was saving Aidan's life if she could and killing Dolor at any cost.

Dolor's laughter from the past filled her head. *"I am Pain. I am eternal. And you are insignificant, Leta. You will never defeat me."*

So far he was right. She hadn't defeated him, but she had wounded him.

His arrogance would be the tool she would use to break his strength and Aidan was the hammer she needed to drive her spike right between Dolor's eyes.

Her resolve set, she went to find Aidan and anger him some more.

3

Aidan sat in his chair, strumming the Indigo Girls' "Strange Fire" on his electric guitar, as he realized tomorrow would be Christmas Eve, and for the third year in a row, he'd be all alone for it. It was why he hadn't bothered decorating anything. All that would do was remind him of just how lonely his life had become.

He sighed wearily as he thought about all he'd been through. How could one man be adored by millions and loved by no one? Yet that was his fate. The only people who claimed to care for him didn't know him at all, and the people he'd once loved with everything he had spent every moment of their lives trying to end his.

"Merry fucking Christmas," he muttered.

Trying to forget the past, he focused on the song in his head. Since the guitar wasn't plugged in, the notes were only a whisper around him but it was enough to soothe his ragged state. Music had always been his sanctuary. No matter how hard life was, it was music and movies that he ran to for comfort and inspiration. They gave him solace when nothing else could.

He was so intent on the song that it took him several minutes to realize he was no longer alone. Opening his eyes, he looked up at Leta and paused mid-strum. The light formed a soft halo around her, making her black hair appear luminescent. For a solid minute he couldn't even breathe. Every hormone in his body was on fire.

It'd been way too long since he'd last touched a woman, other than to hand over his credit card to her in a checkout line. And to think he'd almost convinced himself that he didn't need a woman's softness.

Yeah . . .

With her looking at him while a beguiling half-smile touched her lips and her bright eyes shone, his resolve shattered. All he wanted to do was set the guitar aside and pull her into his arms for a long, wicked kiss until both of their lips were numb. It was way too easy to imagine her in his lap, naked. That one image seared him from the inside out.

His cock hardened to the point of pain.

"You need something?" He hated that his voice had a hollow note in it and not the venom he wanted to give her.

"I was just curious what you were doing in here by yourself. You're very talented, by the way."

He sneered at the compliment. "Don't flatter me."

"No, you really are."

"Yeah, and don't flatter me," he repeated, finally finding the venom he wanted in his tone. "I don't like or want compliments."

A sharp frown wrinkled her brow. "Are you serious?"

"Deadly." He strummed an idle chord. "See, I know this game. You flatter me, make me laugh and feel good about myself. Then the next thing I know you're walking out the door with your pockets stuffed with my money, telling the world what an asshole I am. Let's just skip straight to the end where you get out of my house and tell everyone I'm a dick." Cradling his guitar, he nodded. "Yeah, that works for me."

Leta couldn't believe what she heard. His anger sharpened her powers even as his words flabbergasted her. She sucked her breath in sharply. "What did they do to you?"

He set the guitar aside before he stood up. "Don't worry about it."

She reached out to touch his arm as he started past her. "Aidan—"

"Don't touch me." His voice was a feral snarl.

But that only made her want to touch him more, even though she knew she should anger him as much as possible in order to strengthen herself. "I'm not here to hurt you."

Aidan wished he could believe that. But he knew

better. How many times had he heard that lie? And in the end, they always hurt him and laughed while they did so.

He was tired of falling for it.

"You know, if I had a nickel . . ." His gaze sharpened on her face. He wanted to reach out and touch her too. But he couldn't bring himself to do it. Not after what had happened with Heather.

"I would never hurt you, baby. You can always trust in me. I'm here for the long haul. You and me, forever. Us against the world. No matter what. You can always be yourself and know that I will love you regardless. I don't care about your career or fame. If it all ended tomorrow, I would still be here for you, with you."

Those words had made his heart soar—they had been a symphony to his ears, which were tired of the liars around him. Most of all, he'd trusted them just as he'd trusted Heather. As an orphan, all he'd ever wanted in his life was a family of his own. Someone who wouldn't hurt him. Betray him.

Someone who would accept him for the man he was, regardless of fame and wealth or even poverty.

Unfortunately, he'd never once found that. The moment he'd started making real money and people had begun to recognize him, Heather had felt threatened by it and by the women who threw themselves at him. She'd become catty and biting. Criticizing everything he did and resenting him for wanting more.

Even now, he could hear her caustic words. *"There are two kinds of people in Hollywood. Actors who want to act and those who want fame. The ones who go after fame deserve everything they get, so don't cry to me about the tabloid liars. It's what you wanted, Aidan. Everyone knows who you are. You should have been satisfied with the acting alone. But no, you had to have more. So now you got all you wanted and everything that goes with it."*

Ultimately, because she couldn't cope with it all, she'd carved his heart out and handed it to him on a silver platter. Not in private like a decent human being. She had done it publicly by seeking out the same tabloids that had already eviscerated him. Even worse, she'd helped his enemies come after him and had done everything in her power to embarrass him before the world.

And this woman before him now was no exception. He had no doubt. If he let her in, she'd hurt him too. The only person in this world who cared about him was himself.

He indicated the door with a jerk of his chin. "Can't you just stay here for a couple of hours and not speak to me? Is that really too much to ask?"

"I don't like silence."

"Well, I do."

"And it's my house," she said in a deep voice, imitating him with the voice of an irate parent. "While you're under my roof, young lady, you'll do as you're told!"

Aidan wanted to be offended by her mockery. But a smile tormented the edges of his lips. "You're not funny."

"Of course I am." She winked playfully at him. "You wouldn't be smiling inside if I wasn't."

His stomach tightened as he realized that she was charming him with her actions and that only made him angry again. "Look, I really don't want to talk to you. I just want to be left alone. Get out."

She released a tired breath and shook her head. "When was the last time you talked to a friend?"

"Nineteen months ago."

Leta felt her jaw drop at his disclosure. She couldn't believe that. Even with her emotions muted and basically gone, she still confided in others. The only exception being the time she was in stasis. "What?"

"You heard me."

Yes, but hearing and believing were two entirely different things. "You're not serious."

"Oh, I'm serious all right. I called up my best friend to confide in him because I needed someone to talk to and the next thing I knew our conversation was not only in the paparazzi rags, but on blogs and in every industry magazine the bastard could find. 'Aidan O'Conner: The Truth Behind The Legend. Read how his girlfriend betrayed him and left him a drunken sot on the street, begging for change while assaulting his fans.' What killed me most, there was so little truth in what he told them. Instead, he distorted my words and embellished them until I couldn't even recognize what I'd said. Let's just say I learn from my mistakes. So no, I don't talk to friends. Ever."

Well, she could understand that. Back when she'd still had her emotions, she'd once shoved M'Adoc from behind when he'd told their brother M'Ordant that she thought he was a prig at times. She'd been humiliated and mortified that M'Adoc had repeated a private conversation and then used it to hurt someone she loved dearly. It'd made her cautious for weeks about saying anything to anyone, but eventually she'd gotten over it and moved on.

That experience was certainly minor in comparison to what Aidan had been through. Honestly, she couldn't imagine having to cope with something so intrusive or a person so slimy. M'Adoc had only told one person, not the entire world, and he had quoted her verbatim without embellishment.

That being said, it didn't mean Aidan should give up on people and trust no one at all. People needed friends in this world. "Well, one person's betrayal doesn't—"

"We'd been best friends since junior high school," he said between clenched teeth. "We're talking twenty years of friendship flushed away in three seconds because someone was willing to give him five thousand dollars." He curled his lip bitterly. "Five grand. That's all my friendship over the years was worth to him. Funny thing is, I'd have given it to him if he'd just asked."

Leta cringed in sympathy. No wonder he was so bitter. She knew such things went on, but as a rule the gods of dreams didn't betray each other like that—especially now that their emotions were gone. There had been a few over the centuries, but not many, and they had been an exception who had been hunted down and killed.

Aidan narrowed his eyes on her. "Now tell me again how you can be trusted when you just walked through my door."

She held her hands up in surrender. "You're right. You can't trust me or anyone else. Never in my life have I understood why people betray others. I don't guess I ever will."

He scoffed at her words. "Like you've never betrayed anyone."

Leta quickly countered with a simple question. "Have you?"

"Hell, no," he roared as if the very thought sickened him. "My mama taught me better."

"And so did mine." She paused before she added, "Actually, that's not true. My brother taught me better. And when we were under fire, he did his best to protect me no matter the cost to himself."

"Then you're lucky. My brother sits in jail for his attempt to take my life."

That unexpected bit hit her hard. "What?"

"You heard me." His voice broke even though she saw no emotion except anger in his expression. "Didn't you read about it in the papers? For six months, I couldn't watch TV without seeing his face staring at me from his mug shot."

Since she couldn't explain why she hadn't heard it, she simply shook her head "I don't understand. Why did he try to kill you?"

He gave a dark laugh. "Oh, killing me would have been far kinder than what he did. He wanted to take everything in this world that I'd built. He was trying to blackmail me."

"Over what?"

"Nothing more than his own willingness to lie and people's gullibility to believe it. He said he'd make up everything from I was a pedophile to acts of animal sacrifice to brutality against women and children. He even went so far as to accuse me of mocking my fans and attacking the reputations of other actors, producers, and agents. No part of my life was spared from his lies and he didn't hesitate to forge documents or to lie to the courts or the police. Thank God, McCarthyism is dead or I'm sure I'd have been blacklisted and imprisoned."

That didn't make sense to her. "But that's just stupid. Who would believe such ridiculous lies?"

"Everyone who's ever been jealous because it's my face in the magazines and not theirs. Every person who can't believe or accept that someone can reach my level of success without being a total prick. Trust me, it's not the lies that hurt people. It's the willingness of everyone else to believe them. And then there are those who come out of the woodwork to back your accuser because it gives them the spotlight for three seconds. They can't stand the fact that you've risen above your past and that they have no excuse for never rising above theirs. In their minds, you need to be taken down a notch and they need to be raised a few, off the lies they tell about you. Because in the end, *they* know you, *they've* seen the real you, and by backing your accusers, they make other people think that maybe they were close to you—at least that's what they claim. It's a sick world and I'm disgusted with it."

She flinched at the fury and hurt that bled from every part of him.

He was right; there was no way she could argue with him. Life could be cruel and people were even more so. There was so much agony inside him that she should be grateful for the strength it gave her.

But honestly, she wasn't. His emotions were so potent that they were feeding her even in this realm.

And those emotions made her want to weep for him and the hard layer of ice that encased his heart. No one deserved such isolation. No one.

Wanting to comfort him, she reached out and took his hand in hers.

Aidan closed his eyes at the softness of her skin on his. It burned him to his core. It'd been so long since someone had reached out to him in kindness that he wanted to savor the sensation of her gentle touch.

But he knew better.

Kindness today . . . a kick in the teeth tomorrow. *Don't you* ever *forget that again.*

No one would protect him. Everyone had shown him that when the fires came blazing down around him. He'd been left alone, bereft of friendship, family, and kindness.

And he was too scarred by it to simply move past it and trust again. The wounds were too deep and damaging.

Reminding himself of Heather, he moved away from Leta to look out the window. Damn the snow. It was still coming down, even faster than before. "You should try the phone again."

"I just did. It's still not getting a signal."

He'd once considered that a drawback. How many times had he wanted to talk to his brother when the signals went down? He was so far away from everything that the phone company had refused to run a line to his cabin. So he'd relied on his cell phone, which was haphazard in this area at best.

Now he wished he lived in the middle of city so he could toss her out on the very ass that was making him crazy with lust. God, how long had it been since he last smelled a woman this close to him? Heard the sound of a feminine voice inside his house, saying his name?

It was heaven.

And the lowest level of hell.

"Look, I admit you seem like a decent person. For all I know you stop and move turtles out of the road whenever you see one to keep someone from running it over. But this turtle is tired of having his guts spattered on the pavement while other people drive right over him. I just want to scrape myself up and hide in the woods, okay?"

She nodded. "I'll leave you alone." Clearing her throat, she stepped back from him, and it took all his strength not to pull her closer.

"Just remember, sometimes people will put you ahead of themselves. It does happen."

He snorted. "Yeah, the whole world is just rainbows and puppies. Boy Scouts really do help old ladies cross the street without mugging them and no one ever ignores a trauma victim's screams."

"Aidan—"

"Don't. It's impossible to believe in the world you describe when your own family sold you out for nothing more than cruelty and money."

He saw the acknowledgment in her gaze before she withdrew from the room.

Yeah, he knew he was a bastard. Just like he knew

there were decent people out there. They just didn't exist in his world. When he'd been poor no one had ever helped him. People had gone on with their lives as if he were invisible and that had been fine with him. He didn't mind invisibility.

Actually, that wasn't true. He'd wished repeatedly in his life that he really had been as invisible as other people had made him feel.

Closing his eyes, he could still see Heather's beautiful face. Hear her laughter. When it had all begun, he'd thought losing her would be unbearable. That it would destroy him.

By the end of it, he hadn't missed her at all. Not even a little, which made him realize why they'd been able to turn on him without remorse. There was no such thing as real love. The heart was just another organ, pumping blood through his body. There was no magic to it. No spiritual bonding between friends and family.

People were users, plain and simple. Hoping for anything better only led to bitter disappointment.

No, this was his life. He'd be alone until the day he died. But deep inside him was still that stupid, insipid dream of one day having a family. Ever since his parents had been killed by a drunk driver, he'd missed that sense of bonding. Of family belonging. His parents had loved each other dearly and had had mutual respect—at least it had looked that way to his seven-year-old mind.

Who knew what the truth really was. Maybe they'd hated each other as much as his brother hated him, and like Donnie they'd kept it a secret.

As for Heather, that bitch was the one who should have an Oscar on her mantel instead of him. Her acting had been exceptional right up until the end.

And right outside his door was the first woman to set foot in his house since Heather had walked out of it . . .

"So what?" he asked himself under his breath. One woman was as good as another and most likely she was twice as treacherous.

Disgusted with it all, he lay down on the couch and turned on his TV to let his *Star Wars* DVD distract him from the madness of letting a stranger into his home.

Leta paused as she felt the slight unconscious tugging in the back of her mind. There were really no words to describe the sensation, but anytime a human target went to sleep, a dream god could feel it.

As quietly as she could, she made her way back to Aidan's den where she found him dozing on the couch.

He was leaning back with one foot still on the floor and one arm draped over his face. Cocking her head, she stared at how strangely attractive his pose was. His faded T-shirt was stretched tight over a chest that was absolutely ripped.

The stubble on his cheeks only emphasized the rugged handsomeness of his features. He looked vulnerable and yet at the same time she had no doubt that if she made the slightest sound, he'd jerk awake, ready for battle.

As she closed her eyes to spy on his dreams, she saw the snowstorm outside that she'd started was permeating his subconscious. Kneeling on the floor by his side, she let her thoughts drift until they connected more fully with his.

Here in the dream world she was an observer who followed his lead.

He stood outside a basic Cape Cod house where lights twinkled against a dark snowy storm. She heard the sounds of laughter and music coming from inside the home. Curious, she moved to stand beside Aidan as he spied on the party's attendants through a frosted window.

"Look at them," he said as if accepting her presence in his dreams without question. His lips were curled disdainfully.

Leta scowled at the revelers who were toasting each other during a Christmas party. "They seem very happy."

"Yeah, like a nest of scorpions waiting to strike each other down." He jerked his chin toward a thin, pretty woman in the rear of the group. "The blonde in the corner is my ex-fiancée, Heather. The balding guy she's draped over is my brother, Donnie."

The two were making cooing noises at each other before they drank out of the same wine glass. Boy, Freud would have had a field day with Aidan's dreams.

"Why are they together?" she asked him.

"That's an interesting question. After I gave Donnie a job, Heather threw a fit over it. Next thing I knew he'd started snaking on the bitch. The most amazing thing is she always told me she absolutely hated him. She thought he was brainless redneck trash who needed help to tie his own shoes."

He shook his head as he pointed to a brown-haired man at the table across from Heather and Donnie. "That's Bruce. He was the president of my fan club and a longtime personal friend. My nephew Ronald befriended him and the next thing I knew the two of them were off spreading more lies than even my publicist could counter. What kills me is that I know exactly what my nephew really thinks about Bruce. Man, if he only knew what Ronald said about him the minute he was out of earshot. For that matter, all of them. They never hesitated to insult each other to me because they knew I wouldn't betray their trust. A more treacherous bunch of snakes never existed. And what really baffles me about them is that after having seen the way they all turned on me for no other reason than simple jealousy, they're dumb enough to believe that the same people who screwed me over would never do it to them. Unbelievable idiots."

Leta tilted her head as she heard his memories in her mind. As he said, each of the people in the room had said horrible things about one another to him. They'd played against each other and done anything they could to keep their hands in Aidan's fame while trying their best to alienate him from the others in hopes of hanging on to him tighter. It was frightening to think they would be capable of getting along with each other given the things they'd said behind each other's backs to Aidan. "I don't understand. Why would they do this?"

Aidan led her away from the house, through the storm, until they were again inside his cabin. He went to the desk she'd seen just inside his living room. It was a tall, Colonial-style writing desk, complete with leaves and Chippendale trim.

Without a word, he opened a drawer and pulled out a folded sheet of paper. His gaze was dark as he handed to her.

Unfolding it, Leta glanced over the list of names. Some had marks through them while others were marked with stars. "What's this?"

"Donnie's list. He'd gone through all my contacts and friends, systematically trying to befriend them. He kept telling me that I had to pay him whatever he wanted because if I didn't, he'd ruin me since all of my friends were now his. 'They'll believe me over you anytime,'" Aidan mocked in what must have been his brother's voice.

Leta was aghast. "You've got to be kidding me."

"Trust me, I'm not that creative. Everyone from my agent to my banker is on that list. The names with marks through them are the friends he couldn't convert with his lies."

"What happened to them?"

"Donnie and Heather ran them out of my life without my even knowing it. I was off on a trip making my last movie when he ousted my booking manager. Richard had been with me since the very beginning. Apparently something had happened between them and Donnie fired him and threw him out of my house and office. I didn't even find out about it until I'd gotten back weeks after the fact."

"Did you call Richard?"

"I started to when word got back to me of the lies he was then spouting about me to my so-called friends. It wasn't until later that I realized it was Ronald's girlfriend who, at Ronald's behest, was playing as everyone's friend, and she'd goaded Richard into it. She was moving between everyone, spreading crap just to watch all of us fight."

"Why would she do that?"

He sighed wearily. "I've asked myself that a thousand times over and I'm no closer to an answer now than I was when it began. I think that's why I always loved movies so much. In a movie, everything has to make sense. The characters always have to have motivation. Good, *solid* motivation for everything they do. They can't be a dickhead without reason. If someone turns on a character, they have to have a hardcore, believable reason for it. Unfortunately, in real life you don't. People turn on each other for anything from catching a constipated look on your face when you had gas and thinking it was directed at them, to not liking the brand of shoes you're wearing. People are sick."

Leta glanced down at the list of names in her hand. She couldn't believe anyone would be so cold. So conniving. Surely there was more to it than what Aidan was telling her.

Wasn't there?

Surely he'd done something to deserve it. Yet as she used her powers to look over the situation, she realized that he hadn't. Unlike his brother and nephew, he'd been giving to a fault. Loving to a fault. Unfortunately, he'd given his love and trust to the wrong people.

"The simplest reason," Aidan continued, "is my brother was jealous. He wanted to have my life and he did everything he could to take it. He got Heather on his side and into his bed. Then for a time he'd wooed my fans, even though he kept stirring them up and had them turning on each other more times than he didn't. For whatever reason, he thought he could use them to blackmail or steal my money from me. What he forgot was that I didn't get to where I am by being afraid to stand up for myself. More than that, he wasn't the first person to try and ruin me and I doubt he'll be the last. But I am still standing and it's going to take a lot more than his crap-ass lies to knock me down."

Leta wanted to weep at the conviction she felt inside him. At the raw pain. She didn't know where it came from, but admiration for him swelled deep inside her. He was strength personified.

Everything about him was integrity and honesty, even in the face of such unrelenting hatred and hostility.

His eyes burning, he cupped her cheek in his warm hand. "Why are you here with me?"

Several lies came to her mind, but she didn't want to lie to a man who'd been dealt more than his share of them. And since they were in a dream state, there really was no reason to. "Your brother has summoned a demon out to kill you."

He laughed.

"I'm serious, Aidan. As crazy as it sounds, your brother found a way to summon a god of pain from his slumber and he has commanded him to torture and kill you."

"And *you're* going to save me." He laughed again, then sobered. "Why would you do that?"

"It's my job."

The expression on his handsome features looked

less than convinced. "So you just randomly follow the god of pain around trying to protect his targets. What are you, the antipain fairy?"

"Something like that."

He snorted. "Note to self on waking. Lay off the beer on an empty stomach. This dream is even more screwed up than the time I had a donkey and a corkscrew."

Leta frowned. "Donkey and a corkscrew?"

"I don't know you well enough to fill you in on those details."

Before Leta could ask more, she felt that deep sense of foreboding in the pit of her stomach. She looked around, but the cabin was the same in this realm as it had been in the mortal one.

"Aidan—"

Before she could say anything more, Dolor grabbed him from behind and knocked him to the ground.

4

Before Leta could move to protect him, Aidan rolled to his feet to confront the god. The rage that roiled through him was so potent that it actually made her gasp as it struck her like a hostile jolt of electricity. She threw her head back as it ripped through her like acid. Never in all eternity had she felt anything like this. It was hot and blazing.

Dolor swung at Aidan who blocked the punch with his arm, then head-butted the god back. Before Dolor could regain his balance, Aidan scissor-kicked him in the ribs. Twisting around, the god fell to the ground.

She knew it was only Dolor's arrogance that had allowed him to be taken by surprise. He hadn't expected Aidan to fight him.

But that was over.

Dolor shot a god-blast at Aidan's head. Aidan ducked it, then flipped to pull Dolor off the ground to hit him again. But this time Dolor saw it coming.

He slung Aidan up into a steel wall that appeared out of nowhere.

Leta manifested her two whips—one for each hand. She snapped them briskly to capture Dolor's arms. He hissed in pain before he wrapped his forearms around them and yanked.

She didn't budge even though it felt as if he'd wrenched her arms from their sockets. "Leave him alone."

Dolor laughed at her. "You're a fool to protect him."

"Then I'm a fool." She tried to uncoil her whips from his arms, but he held them firmly in place.

Aidan shook his head to clear it. He could actually taste blood in his mouth. There was a real quality to this fight even though he knew it was a dream. He wiped the blood from his face and frowned as he studied it.

Wasn't it?

He watched as Leta hurled the larger man into a wall an instant before the man turned and kicked her to the ground. He ran for the man and caught him about the waist with his shoulder before the man could attack her again. "Don't you touch her."

The man laughed as he sank his hands into Aidan's hair and wrenched it.

Aidan growled at the agony but it wasn't the yank on his hair that hurt as much as the images that appeared in his head. Images of Heather in bed with

Donnie. The lost feeling he'd had the morning they'd all attacked him at once and tried to destroy him.

He cried out as his heart splintered from that one moment in time when all of his delusions of love and family had been shattered.

Suddenly Leta was there, shoving the man back from him. "Stop it, Dolor. Now!"

Dolor turned on her with a smile. He pulled her into his arms. "Hear the baby crying?"

She screamed in horror.

Aidan tried to shove the god back, but he refused to let go of Leta. "Go to hell, you asshole!" He manifested a sword in his hand and stabbed Dolor straight through the heart.

Releasing Leta from his hold, Dolor staggered back. His black eyes were large with disbelief as he disintegrated into a thousand sparkling pieces. They fell slowly to the ground before a feral wind carried them away.

Still Leta continued to scream as if she were caught in the middle of a nightmare she couldn't wake up from. She pulled at her hair as if she couldn't bear whatever images were in her head.

Aidan scooped her up in his arms to hold her close. "Shh," he breathed as she trembled in his arms.

Tears streamed from her eyes. "Make it stop! Please, God, make it all go away. I can't breathe. Can't think. I can't . . . I can't . . ."

He winced as he heard the same agonized pleas

from her lips that he'd uttered on countless days of bitterness. It made him hold her closer and touched him on a level unimaginable. Whatever her past, it was obvious it was as bad as his own.

"I've got you, Leta," he whispered, rubbing his chin gently against her wet cheek. "I won't let him hurt you." He didn't know why he made that promise, but even more surprising than the words was the fact that he meant them.

Something about the sharing of this moment broke through his own pain. For the first time in over two years, he felt human again and he didn't even know why.

She drew a ragged breath. "He'll be back."

"No he won't. I killed him."

"No," she said, her eyes sparkling from her tears, "you didn't. You can't stop Pain. He's coming back and now he knows . . ." Her voice faded out as if she were too afraid even to finish her sentence.

"Shh," he repeated as he held her close and let the warmth of her body seep into the coldness that had gripped him for all this time. He hadn't comforted anyone in years. Literally. The last person he'd sat up with all night had been his nephew. Ronald had just broken up with his first fiancée, so the two of them had gone out drinking. Even though Aidan was supposed to be studying a script he'd been prepping for, he'd taken the entire night off to soothe Ronald's grief.

And what had it gotten him?

Ronald had eventually sided with Donnie and turned on Aidan even after all Aidan had done for him over the years—paid for his private school and college, paid for his high school graduation trip to Florida for him and his best friend, given him a job, bought him a car, a house . . . Nothing had been enough. And this after Ronald had told him how badly his father had treated him growing up.

Now he didn't know if Ronald had ever spoken the truth or if it'd been nothing but lies designed to gain Aidan's sympathy so that he could take more money from him.

And in the end, none of what Aidan had done to help the kid had mattered. Like his father, Ronald had demanded that Aidan give him everything he wanted whether he deserved it or not.

His heart pounding, he looked down at Leta and wondered if she was just as cold inside as they had been.

That was when Aidan made the most grisly discovery about himself.

He still cared.

In spite of everything the scum had put him through. In spite of how carefully he'd sealed himself off from the world, he cared about Leta. He didn't want her hurt and he damn sure didn't want her hurt because she'd tried to help him.

In that moment, he hated himself for the weakness of caring.

How much could one human take?

But it was there. That internal ache that only wanted to tend to her injuries and make sure she was okay. Grinding his teeth, he pressed his lips to her soft, sweet hair and carried her out of the snow to a sandy beach where the sun was shining brightly above them.

With her still cradled against his chest, he fell to his knees in the sand and set her down before him. He cupped her face in his hands and wiped the wet tears that still rolled down her cheeks. "It's okay, Leta. I've got you."

Leta sniffed back her tears as she stared into those eyes that were as green and stormy as a deep sea. For once they weren't filled with hostility. They were open and caring, and that literally stole her breath.

She lifted her hand to lay it to his cheek where the stubble of his whiskers teased her palm. His masculine scent filled her senses . . . it'd been so long since she last tasted passion. Since she'd been held by a man who wasn't related to her. And in that moment, the pain of her own past overwhelmed her with misery.

Choking on the raw agony inside her, she leaned against him and tucked her head under his chin, against his chest. She didn't like being in this dream. She didn't want these feelings anymore. Not having them was so much better than what she felt now. If only she could banish them forever.

"How do you cope with it all?" she breathed against Aidan's chest.

"Don't think about it."

"Does that work?"

"Sometimes."

"And when it doesn't?"

He shrugged. "There's beer and cheap whiskey but not even that does anything more than add a headache to what already plagues you. Sooner or later you sober up and it starts all over again."

That wasn't the answer she'd wanted from him. "I hate crying."

His eyes scalded her with their intense heat. "Then do what I do. Turn your tears into rage. Crying will only make you sick. But anger . . . anger infuses you. It strengthens you. It crawls through your body until you're forced to act. There's no dwindling of strength, no mewling blurry vision. It clears your head and focuses your actions. Most of all, it empowers you."

"Is that why you stay angry?"

"Absolutely."

And his rage was strong enough to feed them both. But even so, she didn't understand it. Her anger had always spiked quickly and then faded. More than that, her tears had always negated her anger. The second her tears started, any rage she had evaporated underneath them. "How did you learn to stop crying?"

His expression was harsh. "I nailed my heart shut and learned to stop caring about anyone except me. They can't make you cry when you don't give a shit about them or their opinions. You can only be hurt by the ones you love."

"And by the god of pain," she whispered. "He knows what weakens us. Look at what he's done to me."

"It's because he knows you and where to strike." Aidan shook his head. "He doesn't know anything about me. There's nothing he can use to hurt me anymore. I let it all go except my anger."

Which was why Aidan had been able to fight Dolor even though Aidan was only a mortal man.

But she didn't know how to hold on to anger. Every time she thought of her daughter or her husband, it brought her to her knees. They had been innocent of any crime except belonging to her and they had been coldly executed by Dolor and his ilk. It was why she was here.

No more innocents would die.

Ever.

No one deserved the pain she felt. No one. And she would die before she allowed Dolor to destroy another person this way. To take from them what they loved, and for what? Over one god's vindictiveness because someone else played a prank on him and he lacked any sense of humor? It was cruel and it was wrong.

"Teach me your anger, Aidan. Show me how to hold on to it no matter what."

He nodded grimly before he dropped his hands from her face. "Let go of your pain. If there's any kindness inside you, kill it. Now, remember the only person in this life that matters to you is you. No one else will ever care about you. No one. The only person who can protect you is you. Let everyone else go to hell. In fact, rush them to it."

She couldn't believe what he was telling her. It seemed easy, if she were mad enough, but how did he sustain it? "How do you manage to stay there?"

"Remember that whenever you were being kicked, there was no one standing beside you to soften the blow. No one there to help you lick those wounds or protect you."

But in her case, that hadn't been true. M'Adoc had stayed by her side, trying to protect her family. That was how he'd been captured and then tortured. He would have been able to escape and save himself. Instead, he'd chosen to come warn her and to stand with her when Dolor and his minions had attacked.

They'd almost killed him too.

"And if I wasn't alone?" she asked, her voice only a whisper.

"Then imagine them taking the one who stood with you. Imagine your defender's blood on your hands as they stab him through his heart."

It was enough to make her want to scream and it gave her the rage he spoke of.

Aidan was right. If he could, Dolor would kill M'Adoc in an instant.

"I don't know how to defeat Dolor," she confessed. "The best I could do last time we fought was
to freeze him and make him the slave to a human's
summons. I thought by doing so no one would be so
stupid as to release him. Now that they have . . . I
don't know how to return him to stasis until after he
completes his task."

"And that is?"

"To kill you—and I won't let that happen."

Aidan was glad this was a dream. Otherwise he
might think himself insane. But as the purple surf
crashed against a crystal beach he knew he was safe.
There was no reality here. There was just Leta and
him.

Still, he was curious about why his subconscious
would create all of this. "You said my brother conjured him to kill me."

She nodded.

"He did this from prison?" It made as much sense
as anything else.

"He must have. Can you think of anyone else
who'd want you dead to the point they'd give up their
soul for it?"

Aidan gave a bitter laugh. "The list of those who
hate me is lengthy, but those who want it to that extreme is much shorter. You're right. Donnie stands out
among the really big haters."

She nodded.

Aidan sat quietly thinking about the tragedy of his

past. After the death of their parents, he and Donnie had ended up being raised by their alcoholic uncle. As a single parent, the man had left much to be desired and basically Aidan and Donnie had always joked that they'd been raised by wolves.

All they'd had was each other. He still couldn't believe what something as petty as jealousy had done to his brother. How it could take a guy who'd once taken punches for him and turned him into a cold-blooded user who was willing to do anything to hurt him. It didn't make sense.

And now this . . .

No wonder his dreams were so whacked out. He was still reeling from the betrayal and obviously his subconscious continued to try and reconcile all of it.

Those thoughts reminded him of his early years in Hollywood. "One of the first movies I appeared in was a zombie flick. I remember that in the film, if you killed whoever was controlling the zombie, you took out the zombie too. Would this work the same way?"

Leta scowled at him. "Are you willing to kill your own brother?"

He didn't even hesitate with his answer. "Blood stopped binding us the instant he came at my throat. If this thing is stalking me because of him, then I'm more than ready to slash his throat and laugh while he bleeds to death at my feet. Give me the knife and stand back."

Leta let out a slow breath at the hostility in his

tone. She should be appalled by his brutality, and yet she understood the sentiment. "Unfortunately, that doesn't work in this case. Dolor isn't a zombie. He's an ancient god who is only held in check by a curse I put on him."

"Can't you put him back in stasis?"

She shook her head. "Not so long as you're standing. The strongest curse I could find would only work so long as the summons wasn't in place."

He narrowed his gaze on her. "Who the hell came up with this brilliant curse?"

"It was the best I could manage in a hurry," she said defensively.

He rolled his eyes. "With those kinds of critical assessment skills you should consider running for political office."

Before she could respond, a loud growl rent the air. Leta ground her teeth in disgust as she recognized the sound.

"What the hell is that?" Aidan asked.

"Timor."

"I hope old Tim's an ex-boyfriend."

How she wished. "No. He's the personification of human fear."

"Oh, goody," he said in a jovial tone. "Just what I wanted to add to my dream. Should we invite him over for tea?"

While she found his sarcasm entertaining, it still failed to make her laugh or smile given their worsening situation. "Aidan, this isn't a dream. I mean, yes, we're in a dream state, but when you wake up, it doesn't mean that Dolor won't be real. He is real and he's out to kill you."

He moved away from her. "Fine. Bring him on. I *will* be the last one standing."

"Bravado doesn't defeat a god."

"Then what does?"

She really wished he hadn't asked that particular question. "I don't know. Each one of us has something that will render us weak and allow someone to kill us. But we're not real big on letting other people know what those weaknesses are."

"And neither am I. I have no intention of letting anyone or anything knock me down."

She admired that about him, especially since he was human. "I want you to hold tight to that courage, Aidan. It might be the only thing that saves your life."

And with that she pulled him toward her and kissed him.

Aidan's breath caught at the forgotten sensation of a woman in his arms. She tasted of bliss and woman. Of wicked delights. And God help him, he wanted more of her.

His heart thrumming, he deepened the kiss as he pulled her even tighter against him.

Leta couldn't think straight as her tongue danced with his. It'd been centuries since she'd last kissed a man. Centuries since she felt this compelled to touch a man unless she was throwing a punch at him.

Aidan's desire set fire to her own bound emotions. But more than that, they unleashed the long-buried part of herself that missed her family. Closing her eyes, she remembered her husband and that miraculous feeling of belonging. Of loving someone and being loved by them.

She missed it so much. Craved it even more. No one should have to spend eternity alone, isolated from everyone, devoid of all emotions. What Zeus had done to her kind was deplorable.

Again, she heard the cry of Timor from across the sea that splashed against the crystal sands. Dolor was trying to use him to break through the barrier of the dream world so that he could fight them on the mortal plane where they were weakest. She needed to wake up Aidan and make him understand the threat they posed to him.

"I'll see you on the other side," she breathed before she pushed him away and forced him to wake up.

Aidan jerked awake. His heart pounding, he lifted his arm from his face to try and get his bearings. His movie was still playing in the background as the logs popped and settled around him.

It was then he saw Leta at his feet.

She blinked her eyes open as if she too were just waking up.

"What the hell are you doing here?" he demanded.

Leta started to answer, only to realize that if she told him, he'd toss her out. He would never believe her in this realm.

Dear Zeus, how was she ever going to convince him of the truth?

"Aidan . . ." She hesitated as she tried to think of something reasonable to say to him.

"Leta . . ." he mocked. "I told you to stay out of here."

"I know you did. It's just that I wanted to see you for a few minutes and you were asleep. I didn't want to disturb you."

"So you slept at my feet like a puppy? No offense, but that's creepy as hell. Next thing I know, you'll be trying on my clothes and sleeping in my bed."

She scoffed as she pushed herself to her feet. "Brad Pitt you're not."

"You're right. I'm the man who kicked him out of the number-one slot for best-looking actor three years in a row."

Leta rolled her eyes. "That's some ego you've got there."

"Yes it is and it's constantly being reinforced by women willing to do anything to get my attention."

He raked her with a cold look. "How far are you willing to go?"

She screwed her face up at him. "Don't let that kiss go to your head. I was just curious."

"Yeah, babe, that's what they all—" Aidan froze as her words permeated his ire. "What kiss?"

Her face went pale. "There was a kiss?"

"In my dreams. How did you know that?"

She became suddenly fidgety. "Lucky guess."

"Yeah, right. The only person who's a worse actor than you is my old roommate whenever he was drunk. How did you know about my dream kiss?"

Leta swallowed as she grappled with what to tell him. But she kept coming back to one truth . . . "You're not going to believe me."

"Try me."

What the heck? The worst he could do was throw her out and he'd been trying to do that since the moment she arrived. It wasn't like she could die in the storm. For that matter, the storm only existed because she'd created it to give him a reason to invite her in.

"All right. I'm an Oneroi."

His features didn't change as he appeared to accept it. "An honor what?"

"Not honor. *Own-nuh-roy.* It's a god of sleep and I'm here to protect you."

He didn't even blink at her words. He merely stared at her with a blank expression as he continued to lie on the couch without moving.

Finally, he inhaled deeply. "Why am I having this bad Terminator flashback . . . My name is Kyle Rhys. Come with me if you want to live."

She crossed her arms over her chest. "This isn't a joke, Aidan."

He shot off the couch and moved to tower over her. Now there was no missing the disdain and disbelief bleeding out of every part of him. "No, it isn't and I don't find you amusing in the least."

"Then how did I know about the kiss you and I shared in your dreams?"

"Wishful thinking on your part."

She shook her head. "I told you in your dream and I'm telling you again . . . bravado won't defeat a god. If you really want to be the last man standing, you're going to have to trust me at your back."

Aidan reeled at her words.

No. It wasn't possible. Yet he recalled that moment from his dreams when he'd told her that. Clearly. Normally his dreams dissipated whenever he woke up. But he remembered every part of the last few minutes in his mind.

It wasn't possible. She couldn't have been there. She couldn't.

"How much beer did I drink?" he whispered, raking his hand through his hair. "Am I in a coma?"

She shook her head. "You're alive and awake. Fully conscious."

Yeah, right. "No," he said, still shaking his head at

her. "I can't be. This is all wrong. *You're* all wrong. Things like this don't happen in real life." He felt as if he'd been trapped inside one of his movies.

In a script, he'd accept this.

In real life . . .

Bullshit!

She reached for him, but he quickly moved away from her. "Aidan, listen to me. Everything I told you is the truth. You have to trust in me."

"Uh-huh. If you're a god prove it. Make it stop snowing."

She gave him a peeved glare. "Parlor tricks to entertain humans are beneath us. But since you insist." She snapped her fingers and instantly the snow stopped.

Aidan felt his jaw drop again as he saw the clouds literally part to reveal a bright, sunny day—just like in his dreams. The rolling landscape was completely white as if fully cleansed.

Still his mind wouldn't accept it. This just couldn't happen. "Nice coincidence. Now get the hell out of my house."

"I can't," she said from between clenched teeth. "I need your anger to fight Dolor. If I leave you, he'll cut through you like a hot knife on butter."

"I already kicked his ass."

"In a dream, Aidan. Ever tried to manifest a sword with your thoughts in the real world? It doesn't happen, does it?"

Aidan hated to admit that she had a valid point. But it still didn't change the fact that this was lunacy.

"How do I know you're not lying to me?" he asked. "Show me something I can't argue against."

She spread her arms out, and as soon as she did, a sword appeared in her right hand. She turned the blade around and offered him the hilt. "Test it for yourself."

He did and it felt real enough. Sharp, heavy. There was no way she could have had something like this concealed on her body without his knowing it.

As much as he hated to admit it, it was beginning to look like she was telling the truth and that somehow the impossible was possible.

He lowered the sword. "How can this be?"

"We've always been here. Sometimes living among all of you, sometimes just as innocuous viewers of your lives. I'm one of those who volunteered to protect humanity."

"And why would you do that?"

He saw pain flash across her light eyes before she answered. "Because I have nothing else to live for. You told me of your brother's betrayal. Imagine your own father calling out his hounds to kill your infant daughter and your husband. Imagine what it was like to watch them die and then be taken and punished for something you didn't do. To be stripped of your dignity and emotions because your father was embarrassed by a stupid, insignificant dream he'd had and he blamed everyone who walks in the dreams for it. You feel your pain, Aidan. I feel mine."

He winced at the unimaginable horror she described. "Why would he do such a thing?"

"Because he was a god and he could. He didn't want another dream god in his sleep ever again, playing a prank on him. He thought if he took away all our emotions, we would no longer be creative or derive pleasure from teasing him or anyone else. All that mattered was *his* life and dignity. Ours was nothing in comparison to his."

Aidan felt a tic begin in his jaw as her words seeped in. "So the Greek gods are just as petty and selfish as humanity. Nice."

"And just like humans, we're not all like that. Some of us are quite aware of our powers and we know better than to abuse them."

Maybe. But it sounded pretty bad to him. Aidan couldn't fathom what she must have gone through—if this wasn't a delusion brought on by a brain tumor and if she wasn't lying. It made his own betrayal seem as insignificant as her father's dream that had caused him to kill her family. "Why would you come to help me?"

"Because you don't deserve to die after all you've been through. Your brother has taken enough from you. And you have so much anger that I'm hoping we'll find some way to kill Dolor and stop him from ever harming another person. Someone has to take a stand against him. All I can hear when I think of him is the way he laughed with pleasure when I begged him to spare my daughter's life. The bastard actually smiled as he suffocated her while his henchmen held me back."

Aidan winced as his heart seized under the weight of what she described.

Her eyes burned him with their own misery. "You want to hurt the people who hurt you, Aidan . . . Now imagine my need to taste his blood."

He stood there as he tried to sort through this. Could he still be dreaming?

"No. You're not," she said out loud. "This isn't a dream. I swear it."

Aidan frowned at her. "How did you know what I was thinking?"

"I can hear your thoughts when I focus on them."

"Good. Then you know I think you're insane."

She smiled at that. "The truth is, I am. I lost all sanity the night my daughter died and I couldn't prevent it. All I have left in this world is a thirst for vengeance. And the mere fact I can still feel it—when I shouldn't have any emotions, tells you just how badly I need it."

He held his hand out to her. "Then we have a lot in common."

She nodded before she took his hand into hers. That one action sent a chill down his spine and he wasn't sure why.

Her hand tightened on his before she spoke. "We have to find some way to stop him."

"Don't worry. We will. As I said, I will be the last man standing."

Leta closed her eyes as his words ran through her mind. Last man standing. She remembered a time when she'd felt that way too. Now all she wanted was to strike back at Dolor, and if she had to fall to do it, then she was more than willing. She didn't care about surviving so long as he died with her. For that, she would crawl naked over broken glass.

All of a sudden, Aidan started laughing and let go of her.

Leta scowled at him. "What's wrong?"

"Mori said that being up here alone would make me crazy one day. Damned if he wasn't right. I have totally lost my mind."

His misplaced humor wasn't quite enough to ease the pain inside her. "No you haven't. I told you I was a bodyguard and so I am. We're going to get through this together. You and me."

His laughter died instantly as he glared at her. "The last time a woman said that to me, she handed me my heart cut into pieces on a platter. What organ are you going to carve out of me?"

"None, Aidan. I'm going to leave you as I found you. You will be here in your cabin, standing stronger than ever."

"Why don't I believe you?"

"Because people are ever willing to believe the negative over the positive. It's easier for you to think me corrupt and evil than it is for you to see me for what I really am. No one wants to believe that some people are willing to help others out of the goodness of their hearts because they can't stand to see someone suffer. So few people are altruistic that they can't understand or conceive that anyone else in the world could ever put someone else's good above their own."

Aidan froze as those words permeated his mistrust. He was doing to her exactly what everyone had done to him.

Assuming the worst even when she hadn't done anything to warrant it.

The world had wanted to believe he was cold to his family, that he'd done something to warrant their cruelty, because that was a lot less frightening than the truth. No one wanted to think that they could give everything of themselves to someone, only to have the recipient turn on them like a rabid dog for no logical reason.

If they accepted the truth—that Aidan was innocent in all of this, that his only crime had been the fact that he was too giving, open, and kind to someone who didn't deserve his trust—then it left them vulnerable and questioning everyone around them. But in their hearts, they all knew the truth. At some point in their life everyone had been betrayed like this. No rhyme. No reason. Just human deficiency in some people who were users and abusers.

As his mother used to say, it's people who have no home training.

But as Leta had pointed out not everyone was a user. Aidan had never once betrayed anyone. Never once had he set out to destroy or hurt another human being. It wasn't in him to bring more misery to anyone.

He alone in his world had been loyal and trustworthy. Maybe, just maybe, he wasn't alone after all.

His throat tight, he glared at Leta. "I'm still not sure this isn't a hallucination brought on by carbon monoxide poisoning from my stove or heater, but in case it's not I'm going to trust you, Leta. Don't you dare let me down."

"Don't worry. If I let you down, we both die and our pain ends."

"And if we win?"

The teasing light in her eyes went dead. "I guess we live on to ache some more."

He laughed bitterly. "Not much of an incentive to fight, is it?"

"Not really," she said, her gaze softening. "But it's not in me to lie down and die."

"Me either." He glanced out the window at the world that looked so bright compared to the earlier storm. If only it would stay that way. "So tell me . . . what do we do now?"

"We are going to see an old friend of mine about some serious pain repellent."

"Do they make such a thing?"

She shrugged. "We're going to find out. And while we're at it, we're going to see exactly what Dolor needs to cross into this plane."

That made sense. "If he crosses over, how strong will he be?"

"You remember the plagues of Egypt?"

"Yeah. I was in that movie too."

She ignored his acidic comment. "That was him just practicing and having fun. If we don't stop him, he'll release all his playmates and they will spread utter misery and torment throughout the world."

"Cool. Can't wait for it." He let out a tired breath before he spoke again. "And what about the other gods? Will they help us?"

She patted his cheek in an almost playful manner. "That, my friend, is what we're about to go and find out. Buckle up, Buttercup. This ride could be bumpy."

The only problem was, he was used to that. It was when things went smoothly that he became scared.

But even as that thought went through his mind, it was followed by the realization that things weren't going to be bumpy.

They were going to be deadly.

5

"I can't believe you cheated!"

"I can't believe you didn't know it. Man, what kind of god are you? I never knew stupidity had a divine representative. Guess I was wrong, huh?"

"You're such an asshole."

Aidan frowned as Leta took him into a white marble room where two men were playing a game of chess. Everything in the room was sterile white, except for the two men dressed in black and the odd chess pieces who had been dancing and fighting around the board on their arrival—chess pieces that were living, breathing creatures who now watched the arguing gods with great interest.

At a quick glance, the two gods appeared to be twins except that the one cheating had short brown hair with black streaks laced through it. He also had what appeared to be black tattoos running down his face at sharp lightning-bolt-style angles from his tear ducts to his chin. The man across from him had black hair with tribal tattoos covering his arms from wrists to shoulders. They were both dressed in jeans and sleeveless T-shirts. An odd style for two gods.

Then again, what did he know of such creatures?

"Deimos?" Leta called as she led Aidan toward the players.

The one with the facial tats looked up. "Leta, my lovely. What brings you here?" he asked in a jovial tone—as if he hadn't been in the middle of a verbal smackdown with his brother three seconds ago.

The other man stood up as if to leave.

"Sit down, Phobos," Deimos snapped. "We're not through."

"Yeah, we are. I don't play with cheaters and I don't care if you are three seconds older than me, you don't tell me what to do. I'm not your bitch, boy."

Deimos grimaced. "Then stop acting like one. Whoever heard of Fear being a crybaby?"

Phobos crossed his arms over his chest. "The same people who made Dread a cheater."

Deimos scoffed at him. "Oh, go cry to mama, you nancy-boy." Then Deimos looked at Aidan. "You play chess?"

"Extremely not well."

He indicated the chair across from him. "Take a seat while we talk."

"Don't," Phobos warned. "It's like playing against a two-year-old who can blast your soul right out of your body. Last time Demon played a human who beat him, he sliced him open from asshole to appetite."

Aidan arched a brow at the vivid description. "Interesting turn of phrase."

"Consider it a warning."

Leta leaned against Aidan and smiled. "Pay Phobos no attention. His job is stir fear in others. He's good at it, too."

Aidan shrugged her warning away. "Not really. I have no fear of anything."

Phobos grinned as if he enjoyed the thought of a challenge. "I assure you, I can rectify that."

"I'd rather you didn't," Leta said quickly before she waved the god away. "Now go scare an old woman or two."

Phobos saluted her with two fingers before he vanished into a circle of flames.

She turned to Deimos who was in the process of directing the chess pieces back into their starting places. "You got a minute, Demon?"

Deimos laughed. "An eternity of them. Why?"

"I need to know how to stop Dolor."

That got him to finally look up at her with a quizzical expression. "Dolor? When did he wake up?"

"A couple of days ago. Now he's after Aidan here to kill him."

Deimos tsked. "Poor you. It really sucks to be human."

Leta narrowed her gaze at him. "Demon . . ."

He was unfazed by her chiding tone. "Don't nag me, little cousin. I don't want to hear it."

"You're a Dolophonos, a god of justice. Are you really going to sit there while an innocent man is put to death because someone has PMS?"

Deimos gave her a droll stare. "I'm an executioner, Leta, hence my Demon nickname. They send me in to take the heads off people and gods who've stepped over the line, usually only because someone has PMS. You want justice, Themis's office is down the hall on the left." He flashed an evil grin at her. "You want death and dismemberment, I'm your man . . . or rather god."

She let out a long-suffering sigh. "So you're not going to answer my question?"

"I don't have the answer for you. Just because I've been drinking buddies with Dolor in the past doesn't mean I know how to stop him, especially since no one has ever sent me in to kill him. I only know he prefers double-shot lime-flavored tequilas with bourbon chasers. Sick, I know, but far be it from me to mock his tastebuds. I'm just glad they're not mine."

Aidan stepped forward with a question of his own. "What about you? Could you stop him?"

Deimos gave him a smug look. "No one stands before me for very long. Dread always trumps pain. Besides, I fight dirty. Chess isn't the only thing I cheat at." He leaned back in his chair and folded his hands behind his head before he returned his gaze to Leta.

"If you really want the inside weakness on Dolor, I'd suggest you try his sister, Lyssa."

Aidan could tell by the look on Leta's face that she'd rather not. "Who's Lyssa?"

"Personification of Insanity," they answered simultaneously.

Leta gave Deimos a chiding stare before she elaborated. "She often works as a demon in conjunction with other gods, to incite madness in their victims so that the Erinyes or Furies can do their work. Because of that, she's a little hard to handle and the madness she used to give to others has nicely taken root inside her own mind."

It figured. "Ooo, perfect. I do believe that in the last twenty-four hours she and I have become really good friends."

Deimos laughed. "I can tell you haven't met her."

"Maybe not personally, but I've definitely been skating around her block a lot today."

"Around the block's okay. Just don't stop and knock on her door."

"Why?"

Deimos gave him a sinister smirk. "She's special. We used to unleash her on ancient battlefields just to see soldiers chop their best friends into pieces before falling on their own swords."

Leta screwed her face up at his brutal imagery. "You're so sick, Demon."

He shrugged nonchalantly. "Trust me, they deserved it or I wouldn't have been so mean. Besides, my mother is a Fury and my father War. What more would expect of me?"

"Compassion," she said softly. "The Erinyes aren't always cruel."

"True, but not for the wicked. Our job is to punish and that, my cousin, I'm more than capable of doing. Grisly though you may think it." He indicated the door with a jerk of his chin. "See Lyssa. If Pain has a weakness, she alone would know it."

"But will she share?"

He shrugged. "You know her as well as I do. Depends on her mood and degree of clarity when you speak to her."

Aidan frowned. "Degree of what?"

Instead of answering, Leta took his arm before she flashed them into an Escheresque garden. It was so complicatedly intricate, with twisting staircases that defied logic, misaligned arches, and backward-growing shrubs, that Aidan couldn't even grasp it. He literally felt as if he'd just stepped into Escher's *Other World* engraving. It made him dizzy to try and make sense of the nonsense around him.

No wonder Lyssa was nuts. Trying to walk through her garden would drive anyone crazy.

Leta led him up a small set of stairs that twisted into a dragon's scales before dissolving into a river of blood that lapped against the small rock they both stood on.

"What is this place?" he asked.

"Lyssa's home. Like Deimos warned, she's not exactly right in the head and hers is a very unique view of reality. The garden reflects her quirky nature."

Quirky? Yeah, she'd blown right past quirky to dive headfirst into all-out strange. He was beginning to understand that as the rail under his hand licked his palm. Curling his lip in disgust, he jerked his hand away to find eyes watching him instead of the tongue he'd felt an instant before.

Yeah . . . if this was true insanity, he suddenly felt normal.

"Lyssa, Lyssa," Leta called. "Light and fair, 'tis Leta come to you with words to share."

Well, this was a new side to Leta. That being said, she did have a beautiful voice when she sang out the words. "What are you doing?"

Her smile dazzled him. "Lyssa likes rhymes. She will only speak in them."

"You've got to be kidding me?"

Before she could answer, a swirling blue ball appeared in front of them. The ball moved in a jagged path until it touched the top of the stairs behind him. There it grew until it formed a young, beautiful woman. Her long, curly blond hair shone as if it were made of pure spun gold and she stood with the regal demeanor of a queen. More than that, each feature of her face was so carefully sculpted that she didn't appear real.

Until one looked at her eyes. They were jet black and cold. Soulless. There was no white, or color of any kind. And when she turned them on him, he could feel the chill of madness all the way to his soul.

When she spoke, Lyssa's voice was as light and delicate as the goddess herself. *"Leta, Leta, born of dreams,*

"Through the centuries you have screamed.

"Now you come to my fair land,

"Only to ask for my helping hand."

Aidan leaned forward to whisper in Leta's ear. "Nice stanza."

She elbowed him hard in the ribs. "Can you help me, dear cousin?"

A whimsical smile curved Lyssa's red lips. *"Help is all they ever say,*

"Even though it seldom stays.

"It'll leave you too you'll see

"And then alone you will bleed."

Infuriated with her cryptic words, Aidan stepped around Leta. "Look, we don't have time for this. We need—" His words stopped instantly as his lips were sealed shut.

Lyssa shook her head in reproach. *"Men will ever speak their way,*

"Regardless of those who hold sway.

"'Tis time you pause to listen instead of hear,

"Only that will save what you hold dear."

Leta placed a tender hand on his arm, before she

looked back at Lyssa. "Are you telling me that we can defeat Dolor?"

"*Pain is here,*

"*Sharp and clear.*

"*Even so, it must fade,*

"*And a new way should be made.*"

He saw the relief on Leta's face even though he was having a hard time following the nonsense. And not being able to open his mouth was seriously starting to piss him off.

"How do I defeat him?" Leta asked.

Lyssa lifted her hand so that a bird that was flying backward could rest on her extended finger. Picasso would have been proud of the bizarre image the two of them made. "*True pain is born,*

"*When the heart is worn,*

"*On the sleeve*

"*For all to see.*"

By the aggravated look on her face, he could tell Leta wasn't any more satisfied with that answer than he was. "But how does it end?"

"*An ending is a beginning in disguise.*

"*But it is seen only by those who are wise.*

"*For pain to be returned to its place,*

"*You must confront it to its face.*

Leta shook her head. "I don't understand, Lyssa."

She gave Leta the same look a kindergarten teacher would give an aggravating child. "*In time there is clarity to be found.*

"But not now on this most hallowed ground.

"You have the answers you have sought.

"Now it is time for battles to be fought." And with those words, the bird let out the croak of a frog, then dissolved into dust. Lyssa raised her arms skyward before she sank into the ground.

Yeah . . .

Aidan sucked his breath in sharply as he was finally able to open his mouth again. He gave Leta a deadly stare. "Interesting woman. Must get tiring though trying to always rhyme everything you want to say."

"Not after as much experience as she's had."

He didn't want to argue that point. He was just glad Lyssa was gone. "Did you learn anything from this?"

"Yes. I learned that we can defeat him before he kills you. That's at least a start."

She was definitely an optimist. He on the other hand . . . "Call me crazy, then again compared to Lyssa, Sybil was normal, but all I got out of this meeting was a headache. Actual directions on how to kill him would have been nice."

"True, but in this case, I think we got the best we could hope for."

"Then why did we waste our time?"

She patted him indulgently on his cheek. "Who said we wasted time?"

"I do, for the record."

"And for the record, you're wrong. Trust me."

Yeah, sure. He wasn't about to make that mistake. "No offense, but the last person I trusted tried to barbecue me—personally and professionally."

Instead of angering her, his words turned her expression soft and gentle. "I'm not a jerk, Aidan. I wouldn't have come to you if I wanted you hurt."

It made sense when she said it, but he couldn't shake the bitterness inside him that didn't want to get burned again. He was so tired of people playing him, using him to get what they wanted, then casting him aside the minute he displeased them.

He wasn't disposable waste. He was a human being with feelings just like everyone else.

Afraid of what Leta might do to him and afraid of his past, he reached out to touch her cheek. Her skin was so soft, her lips inviting. There had been a time in his life when he wouldn't have hesitated to make a move on a woman like this. A time when he'd have had her laughing and naked in his bed.

Now that part of himself was dead. He would never again be so carefree and full of life. His soul had been kicked to the ground where it was still mired by memories and pain so profound that he wondered if he would ever be able to resuscitate any part of the man he'd once been.

Did he even want to?

There was something to be said for being numb.

There was no liability. No harm to himself or anyone else. It was a nice place to live once you got past the loneliness.

But as he stared into those eyes so blue and sincere, all the isolation of his life hit him square in the chest.

If I have gone insane would it be so bad to kiss her? Would it?

And before he could second-guess himself, he dipped his head to taste the sweetest lips he'd ever known.

Leta buried her hands in Aidan's soft hair as her breath mingled with his. For a mortal man, he knew how to kiss. She could feel the steel of his body pressing against hers, feel the heat of his embrace all the way to her immortal soul.

She shouldn't be doing this. Yet she couldn't make herself stop. It'd been way too long since she last touched any man. Since she'd allowed any passion to touch her life. She was supposed to be devoid of emotions, but here she stood, feeling his presence with every part of herself.

Was she siphoning from him? That was the most logical explanation for these emotions and yet that didn't seem right. Her feelings were too vivid. They felt like hers. This wasn't his anger. It wasn't his lust. It was a longing that she, herself, had and it came from deep inside her battered heart. A need to be close to him.

Afraid of losing her feelings, she wrapped her arms around him and transported them back to his cabin. She deepened her kiss as her heartbeat quickened and her blood fired. This was what she needed most.

Aidan.

She pulled back to stare up at him. "I want to be with you, Aidan," she whispered as her hands paused at the hem of his shirt.

Honestly, she expected him to push her away again. She certainly wouldn't blame him if he did after everything he'd been through. No one would blame him for it.

But he didn't. His green eyes blazing with heat, he jerked his shirt off over his head, and pulled her back into his arms to continue their kiss.

Closing her eyes, she savored the taste of him, the feel of his hands skimming over her body as she held him against her. His muscles bunched and tightened under her palms, reminding her of a time long ago when she'd been afraid of touching a man like this. But that had been eons ago and she'd changed so much since then.

For centuries, she'd fought Dolor alone, trying to save as many humans from him as she could. She'd felt it was her duty even though she was numb to everything but pain.

After a while that absence of feeling had worn on her and weakened her resolve. She'd learned to siphon emotions from humans in their dreams. For a time, she'd started relying on those emotions and had been afraid of turning Skoti—one of the dread dream gods who preyed on humans so that they would have feelings. It wasn't necessarily a bad thing, except when they took too much and drove the human hosts insane and shattered their lives. It was something she couldn't allow herself to do to an innocent person. The moment she'd truly seen herself slipping into the Skoti mindset, she'd locked Dolor and herself away.

Now she wasn't afraid of her emotions or of Aidan's. She wanted them. Needing to feel more, she flashed them into the bedroom and onto the bed.

Aidan pulled away from her lips as he realized where he was. "Nifty trick."

"I can do one better."

Their clothes vanished.

Aidan laughed deep in his throat. "Yeah, that could definitely come in handy."

She rolled him over, onto his back. He looked up at her, drinking in the sight of her bare body against his. Her breasts were the most beautiful he'd ever seen, and he'd seen some of the best in the world. His mouth watering, he pulled her closer so that he could draw her puckered nipple into his mouth.

Leta shivered at the sensation of his hot tongue teasing her. She cupped his head to her as her mind reeled with forgotten sensations. It'd been too long since she'd been intimate with someone. Too long since any man had touched her . . .

He growled deep in his throat before he pulled back and rubbed his whiskered cheek against her sensitive breast. She sucked her breath in sharply as chills erupted all over her.

She was drunk with her lust as she skimmed his body with her gaze. Every part of him was sculpted with muscles. There was so much strength to him, inside and out. And all she wanted to do was to touch that strength and hold him close.

More than that, she wanted to taste him.

Aidan watched her as she kissed her way down his body. Her long black hair teased against his skin, giving him chills and setting him on fire. It'd been so long since he'd last had a woman that he was actually afraid of coming before he even really touched her.

That was all his bruised ego needed. He'd rather die than embarrass himself like some jacked-up high school kid seeing his first naked woman.

Closing his eyes, he tried to think of anything else besides those dainty lips that brushed against his flesh. Of her tongue flicking over his body. His heart hammering, he wanted this moment to last.

And when he felt her nibble the tip of his cock, it was all he could do not to scream out in pleasure. He opened his eyes to watch as she took him even deeper into her mouth. It was the most incredible sight he'd ever beheld. Her tongue teased and tormented him to the highest level.

Leta smiled at the salty taste of Aidan and at the joy she could feel coming from inside him. It was unbelievable. And most special of all was the feeling she had from him that he was afraid of disappointing her. The fact that he even cared made her heart light.

His kindness reminded her of a time when she'd been like him. When her feelings had been her own and when she'd owned her life. When she'd been free to make her own decisions. She missed that so much . . .

Most of all, she'd missed feeling connected to someone else. Being a vital part of them—aching when they were on a trip, knowing that someone was out there missing her and counting the heartbeats until they were back together again. There was nothing else like living and breathing for the smile of someone she loved.

Aidan drew a ragged breath as he cupped her head in his hands. He wanted this to be plain, animal sex. No commitment, no promises. Nothing but the two of them scratching a biological itch.

And yet, as he watched her pleasing him, that disgusting, tender part of himself that he hated stirred. It was the part that wanted a woman who didn't cheat on him. One he could trust not to hurt or betray him. One person who would stand by his side no matter what was thrown his way.

Other people had it. Why couldn't he?

Because you don't deserve it . . .

He didn't want to believe that. Surely to God, given all he'd been through in his life, he was worthy of someone's loyalty. Someone's love.

"Did you ever cheat on your husband, Leta?" He cringed as the words left his lips. Mentioning her husband would probably be a sex-kill for her.

But even so, he needed to know if she'd been trustworthy or like Heather, a liar who sold herself to the highest bidder.

Her eyes were pain-filled as she pulled away from him. "No. Never. I loved him completely, and so long as he lived, I didn't even look at other men. There was never anyone else in my world except him."

"Was he a god?"

She shook her head as she made slow circles with her hand over his abs. "He'd been a warrior. A kind man whose dreams I'd once visited. For a soldier, he'd been amazingly artistic and his dreams had been vivid with colors and sounds." She swallowed as if it were almost too much for her to think about. "And when I saw him tremble from holding our daughter for the very first time . . . every part of me loved him more."

Aidan's stomach tightened. That was what he

wanted. Someone to love him like that. "Did he ever cheat on you?"

Her gaze fired. "I would have killed him."

Aidan cupped her cheek in his hand as he stared into those luminescent eyes. "Do you think he ever knew what a lucky bastard he was?"

"I wouldn't call him lucky. Because of me, and for trying to protect my back, he was gutted on the floor like a pig."

Aidan felt sorry for her loss, but it didn't change the fact that he'd kill to have what she'd shared with her husband. "I don't know. I think to have one day of what you described would be worth being gutted."

Leta was amazed as she felt tears for him sting her eyes. "You didn't deserve what happened to you, Aidan."

"Deserving's got nothing to do with anything. You didn't deserve to lose your family. And they definitely didn't deserve to die because Zeus was an idiot."

A single tear fell down her cheek where it was stopped by his finger. Inside, she felt something she hadn't felt in centuries. An emotional bond with someone else. He understood her tragedy. Most of all, he felt for it.

Wanting to take him away from his sadness, to give him even a moment's worth of peace, she crawled up his body so that she could kiss him deeply.

Aidan's head swam at the fierce passion of her kiss.

He couldn't remember anyone ever kissing him like this. It was demanding and hot, and it fired every nerve ending in his body. All he wanted was to touch her. To feel her.

To be inside her.

She clutched his body close before she dipped her head to tease his throat. Aidan growled as her tongue danced across his flesh. All thoughts fled his mind. She was the only thing he could focus on, the only thing he could feel. Her touch branded itself into his flesh as he let her take him away from a past he didn't want to dwell on.

Leta rolled him over, onto his back. She was molten inside and all she wanted was to feel him deep inside her body. Unable to wait, she straddled his hips and impaled herself on him.

He threw his head back as if he'd just been electrocuted. "Oh, God, Leta," he breathed. "Don't . . . stop."

She hesitated at his words. "You want me to stop?"

"No," he all but roared. "You stop now and I swear I'll die."

She laughed at his desperate words before she resumed her strokes.

Aidan couldn't breathe as she thrust against him. He honestly wanted to die in this one perfect moment. Nothing had ever felt better than the woman on top of him. She was like an angel sent to save him from his isolation.

And he never wanted to let her go. He wanted this time to freeze and stay right where it was as he gripped her soft thighs with his hands. He lifted his hips, driving himself even deeper inside her. This was where he wanted to stay. He wanted to pretend there was no world outside this cabin, no one waiting there to rip him to pieces. No one out to do him harm.

There was only Leta and the pleasure she gave him. This, this was heaven.

And when she came, he bit his lip so hard, he tasted blood. An instant later, he joined her release.

Her breathing ragged, she collapsed on top of him. Her sweet breath tickled his chest as he watched shadows moving on the ceiling. He couldn't remember the last time he'd been this relaxed. That he'd been so at peace.

Yeah, he was definitely insane. This entire day, including her presence, had to be some kind of hallucination. He must have fallen and struck his head. Hard.

But honestly, if this was a dream, he didn't want to wake up from it.

Leta pushed herself up on her elbows to stare down at him as he watched her through half-hooded eyes. She cocked her head in curiosity. "What are you thinking?"

He smiled at her very human question as he wound his hand in her silken hair. "I'm thinking about how wonderful you feel in my arms."

Her smile made his heart soar and his groin jerk. "I've only been with you and my husband. I'd forgotten how incredible this could be." Her eyes turned stormy. "Unlike you, I don't like being alone."

His grief and pain gathered in his throat to choke him, and he confided in her something he hadn't confided in anyone—not even himself. "Neither do I. Alone sucks."

She closed her eyes before she covered his hand with hers and turned her face into his palm to kiss it.

That single act shattered him. "If you betray me, Leta . . . Kill me. Be kind and don't let me live in the shadow of your cruelty. I can't take another blow like that. I'm not that strong."

A tic started in her jaw as she released his hand and gave him a hard stare. "I didn't come this far to betray you, Aidan. I came here to fight *for* you, not against you."

His vision blurred and he despised the tears he felt welling. He hadn't cried in so long . . .

He wanted his anger back. Anger didn't hurt. It didn't make him feel worthless or powerless.

Not so with these confusing feelings that he couldn't even sift through enough to identify. They left him vulnerable and weakness was something he'd learned to despise early in his bitter life.

I will be the last one standing. It was the one motto he'd always lived his life by. It was what had gotten him through countless attacks from other actors. Countless brutal reviews that had assaulted everything from his wardrobe, to his looks, to his past, to his abilities as an actor. Reporters and studio execs who'd laughed at him and his ambitions.

He wouldn't let them win.

He would be the last one standing.

Leta frowned as she felt his turmoil inside her own body. He was standing on a precipice. Scared. Furious. Strong and at the same time weak.

"Together we will see this through, Aidan. I promise."

He blinked as if her words had jogged something loose in his memory. *"Alabaster."*

She scowled at the unexpected response. "Alabaster?" What on earth? "There's no alabaster here."

"No," he said quickly. "It was a movie I was in a couple of years ago. One of the ones I won an Oscar for." A slow smile spread across his face. "It was a movie about a man's wife who was being targeted by an unstoppable serial killer."

That was not a pleasant thought after the sex they'd just had. "Okay . . ."

He looked at her. "Don't you see? That's what Dolor is—he's a sociopathic serial killer. And in the movie we didn't wait for the killer to come up on us unawares. We took the matter into our own hands. We chose the battleground and *we* chose the time and place to fight. The killer didn't come to us. *We* went to him."

It was a brave move. "I've never drawn Dolor into a fight before."

He nodded. "Exactly. It'll surprise him."

Leta froze as she remembered something Lyssa had said to them. *"For pain to be returned to its place,*

"You must confront it to its face." Maybe this was what Lyssa had meant. "You're brilliant!"

"Not me. Allister Davis is the one who wrote it. I'm just taking a page from his script. You said Dolor needed to come to this realm, but what if instead we fought him in yours?"

"What do you mean?"

"In the mortal realm, he's immortal, right?"

She nodded. "He's immortal in dreams too."

"Yeah, but like you said earlier, in dreams, we can create weapons to fight him with, right? We'd have an ax if we needed it or better yet the fabled Hollywood gun that never needs reloading."

"True. But he's stronger in dreams than he is here. He's had a lot more experience manipulating that realm than you have. If you kill him without knowing his weakness, he will regenerate. If he kills you there, you're dead."

He brushed her hair back from her face before he smiled, then kissed her. "I didn't say it was a perfect plan, but it's the best shot we have. Besides, I have a really good idea . . ."

"And that is?"

He answered her with another scorching kiss. "Just hang on, dream lady. We're about to take the home team advantage."

6

Leta stood on the top precipice of the tallest mountain on the Vanishing Isle. She held a vial of sleeping serum that she'd borrowed from her uncle Wink—the Sandman. With it, she and Aidan would be locked into the realm of sleep and Dolor wouldn't be able to throw them out of it.

What Aidan planned was so risky . . .

She shouldn't care. She shouldn't even be able to care, but as she stood there watching the ocean waves crash down on the rocks below she realized that she did. Aidan's pain did more than fire her emotions and powers, it touched her heart.

It had been so long since she last experienced real tenderness. She didn't want to lose it again. She didn't want to lose Aidan. He wasn't just an assignment to her.

He was so much more.

How that could be she couldn't even begin to understand. They'd only known each other in his dreams and for one human day. Yet she knew him on a level that defied logic. Her soul *felt* him.

And she didn't want to let him go, or worse, watch him die the way she had her family. She couldn't stand to go through that again.

Leaning her head back, she let the salt-scented breeze soothe the restlessness inside her. The weight of the vial lay in her palm like a heavy piece of iron. She didn't want to make a mistake. Trapping Aidan in the dream world might kill him.

He was certain it was their best chance to defeat Dolor. But she wasn't so sure. Dolor could be crafty and, most of all, he was deadly. Aidan had courage, there was no doubt. Unfortunately courage didn't always win the fight.

"Give me strength," she whispered to the gentle breeze that danced around her. In the back of her mind, she saw the slaughtering of her family. Nothing could dull that pain. Nothing.

But at least that pain showed her that she was alive. She wasn't completely empty and devoid of feelings.

Closing her eyes, she tried to channel it to anger. Aidan was right. It was the only way to cope with it. And yet at the mere thought of Aidan, her anger faded and a strange sense of peace overcame it.

"Leta?"

She turned at the sound of M'Adoc's voice behind her. He was dressed in a loose white shirt and white pants. His black hair curled becomingly around his face as he slowly approached her.

"What are you doing here?" she asked him.

"I heard you asked Wink for serum."

She nodded.

There was a deep understanding in his blue eyes as his gaze held hers captive. "It's a brave move to call Dolor out. Highly risky."

She didn't want him to know of her uncertainty. As one of the dream god leaders, he'd be honor bound to tell Zeus of any Dream-Hunter who might be getting their emotions back. That was something she couldn't allow. "Victory never goes to the coward."

He inclined his head respectfully to her as if he agreed with that. "By the way, I should warn you that you're not feeling Aidan's emotions."

A chill of strange apprehension went down her spine. "What do you mean?"

He leaned down to whisper softly in her ear. "Zeus's curse is weakening. Every year more and more of our emotions are coming back."

Leta paled at his disclosure and the ramifications of it. "Does he know?"

M'Adoc shook his head. "And we can't afford to let him learn it either. He will rain down on us with every thunderbolt he has."

Agony poured through her as she remembered the last time Zeus had come for them. Her vision was still tainted by the blood spilled that day and by those that followed as Zeus demanded they each be beaten and stripped of their emotions.

It'd been a harsh time for everyone.

"I thought it was part of your job to report that."

His look was harsh. Cold and determined. "I don't betray my family."

Her heart lightened at his words. Better than anyone, she knew he meant it. He'd already proven those words to her. "Can I trust what I feel?"

He gave the subtlest of nods. "But remember, don't show it. More lives than just your own are on the line with this. I'm one of the three chosen to report anyone who begins to feel and if Zeus ever finds out that I've failed in that he will have no mercy for me."

As if she would be so cold—too bad others weren't so trustworthy. "Have no fear, brother. I would *never* betray you."

"I know. It's why I came to talk to you. I wanted you to know that everything you feel is your own. I don't want you to get into trouble for it."

"Thank you."

He inclined his head to her before he stepped back and vanished.

Leta stood there, rolling the small vial of purple serum between her palms. So what she'd shared with Aidan hadn't been a farce. These weren't his emotions siphoned.

It was *her* determination. *Her* compassion. *Her heart*.

Grateful for that fact, she smiled. Kissing the bottle in her hand, she flashed herself back to the cabin where Aidan sat before the fire he must have started in his hearth after she left.

There was an odd look about him. He was somber, but there was something underneath that that hadn't been there before.

"Are you okay?"

He nodded without looking at her. "Tomorrow is Christmas Eve."

"I know." She glanced about the room that had nothing in it to mark the coming human celebration that she'd witnessed in the Hall of Mirrors. "Should we get a tree for you?"

He snorted as if the mere thought offended him. "When I was a kid, my mother used to make us watch that 1950s movie, *A Christmas Carol*, and then after she died, my uncle would put in Bill Murray's *Scrooged* every year while we decorated the tree. Do you know the story?"

She shook her head as she sat down beside him.

He turned away from her so that he could stare into the crackling fire. "The basic story is about a miser named Scrooge. In the beginning, he's harsh and unyielding. He hates Christmas and refuses to celebrate it.

"Scrooge gets taken to task for being so selfish and in response he says 'Bah Humbug'! Then during the course of the night, Scrooge is visited by three ghosts—Christmas past, present, and future and they show him the error of his ways. In the morning, he wakes up refreshed and confident in his new, reaffirmed life of giving. He tosses coins to the orphans in the street and he gives gifts and food to his employee, Bob Cratchit's, family." He gave her a hard, steely stare. "But you know, even as a kid there was something about those movies that always bugged me."

"And that was?"

"Why Scrooge was Scrooge. They never really explained to my satisfaction what had made him so miserly. But the toasty little Christmas story stayed with me, and all my life, I wanted to be the man Scrooge had become—always giving to those in need. Do you know, in the course of one year, I donated over a million dollars anonymously to charity? My mother taught me that no one should advertise their good deeds. You do them because you care and you should never accept any kind of benefit from those acts. It belittles them."

Leta smiled at that. There was a lot of truth to his mother's statement. "I can understand her sentiment."

He nodded. "I agreed with it too. But one thing I realized with my brother is that you can't toss your pearls before the swine. I think that's why my mother insisted you give anonymously. The instant anyone sees that you're kind and giving, they immediately take advantage of it. They seem to mistake kindness for weakness and giving for stupidity."

"How do you figure?"

He sighed. "My brother sent my nephew to me for a job when Ronald was still in high school. Donnie told me that he couldn't afford the tuition for Ronald's private school and asked if Ronald could work for me part-time while he went to school. Like a fool, I agreed, and even though I didn't have that much money back then, I started paying his tuition for him. Six years later, Donnie came to me telling me that he was getting divorced and that his wife was taking everything from him. He was about to lose his house, his car, everything. He told me he didn't want a handout, but wanted to know if I had some work he could do."

"So you hired him."

Every emotion left his face except for the harsh twist of his lips. Even so, she could feel his bitterness burning inside his heart. "Yeah. I seriously overpaid him to be my manager. God knows, I didn't want my own brother out on the street. And for a about a year, everything was great."

"Until?"

"I started noticing that money was missing. Mysterious charges were being made with no explanation. Worse, neither one of them would do their job. They always had some excuse for why they were about to get to what I needed them to do or why it wasn't done yet. Time after time, I'd walk into the office and find Ronald asleep in my chair—at least on the days he actually showed up to work. It was unbelievable. I told them that if they didn't straighten up, I was going to fire them."

"And what did they say?"

He curled his lip before he mocked in a gruff tone, "'You can't fire me. If you do, I'll ruin you. I know all your fans, all your friends, and all your business associates. I'm untouchable, hah, hah.'"

Aidan cursed before he spoke in a normal tone again. "At first I thought it was a joke at best and an idle threat at worst—until I looked around and realized that they really had ingratiated themselves with everyone in my life. Methodically. One by one. They went after them all. Those who wouldn't befriend them and fall in line with their vicious insanity, they cut out and kicked to the curb. Then in a show of power right before Christmas, they turned six of them solidly against me, cut one of them completely out of my life, and it was then they turned really brazen."

"How so?"

"'Give us five million dollars or we'll take everything you have. By the time we're through with you, every fan and friend you have will hate your guts and never pay a dime to see another movie of yours again. You'll be ruined.'"

He drew a ragged, angry breath. "*That* was my

Christmas gift from my brother. After I'd bought him and his son a car each and a house each, paid them far more than their skill levels warranted. It still wasn't enough for them. They had to take more because I had it and they didn't. Of course I was the one working twenty hours a day for months on end at shoots, attending publicity functions and interviews, and busting my ass reading and learning scripts while I was at home while they stayed up all night partying, playing games online, and then slept until noon or later. Blowing money on women, beer, and expensive toys. Gee, I can't imagine why they had so little, huh? As my mother used to say about Donnie, a hard day's work would have killed him."

She leaned against his arm, wanting to comfort him. "I'm so sorry, Aidan."

"Don't be. I should have known. Scrooge was right. You can't let people know anything about you. You can't give freely to them, because it's never enough. They always want more of you than any human being can give. If you let them, they'll suck your soul right out of your body. The golden rule really is if you give an inch, they take a mile." He shook his head bitterly. "There was a movie last year that I was in called *300*. It was about the ancient battle of Thermopylae—"

She frowned as he finally mentioned a reference she completely understood. "Where King Leonidas and his band of three hundred warriors held off the Persian army?"

He looked shocked by her question. "You know the story?"

She gave him a chiding smile. "I'm a Greek god, Aidan. Of course I know the story."

There was a light in his eyes that said he still had a hard time accepting who and what she was. "Yeah . . . anyway, I was curious about the history of the battle, and unlike you, I wasn't fortunate enough to be an eyewitness to it. When I looked it up, I learned that they were betrayed by a fellow Spartan soldier."

"Ephialtes."

Aidan nodded. "He wanted money, so for that, he sold out his own countrymen and fellow soldiers and told the Persians about the small goat path that allowed them to slaughter all of Leonidas's men. Men who had protected his back in battle. Men with families to feed. Men who fought to protect his own homeland and his own family and son that he'd left behind with theirs. A family that would suffer under Persian occupation. But none of that mattered to the greedy, selfish bastard. All he wanted was more and the rest of the world be damned. It appalled me when I found out about that. I didn't understand then and I still don't understand how someone could do such a thing."

Unfortunately, she understood. She'd seen people do it time and again over the course of history. "Simple. There's always some sorry human being who wants what other people have and they don't want to have to work to earn it."

"Exactly, and the part that kills me is the lengths to which they're willing to go and how they feel so justified in their theft. If they'd apply half the effort to earning the money that they spent trying to steal it, they'd be far richer than me."

Leta couldn't agree more. Such people had always angered her too. "Familiarity breeds contempt. By bringing them in close, they realize that you're just as human as they are. That's when the madness sets in. They can't understand why you have more than they do when you're just a regular human being the same as them. Then they hate you for it."

"Yeah, but why?"

Leta sighed. "I truly don't know. Humans are capable of so much creativity and goodness and at the same time they are destructive and cruel. It's as if your kind needs adversity in order to achieve."

"No, we don't. That's just a lie people tell themselves to feel better about all the people who kick them in their teeth when it's just as easy to help a man up as it is to knock him to the ground. That's why I've withdrawn from this world. I don't want to have to watch my back all the time and I'm tired of trying to figure out if the loyalty someone professes is real and true, or just another lie that will crumble the instant they taste jealousy."

"I'm incapable of being jealous."

"Are you?"

She cupped his chin and forced him to meet her gaze. "Seriously, Aidan. In my world, jealousy is a man, Phthonos. He walks in the court of Aphrodite and he has never taken root in my heart. He never will. Even when I had all my emotions, I never let him in."

He pulled her to his lips for a kiss so wickedly sweet it literally made her toes curl. That kiss was the most incredible one she'd ever known and the knowledge that this couldn't last made her ache.

As if he sensed her fear, Aidan stiffened an instant before he pulled back from her. "I just thought of something. What happens to you when this is over?"

Leta looked away, unable to answer that question. The pain of it was unbearable.

Aidan cursed before he answered for her. "You'll have to leave, won't you? I mean, you're really a goddess. I can't exactly keep you, can I?"

"Would you want to?"

He shot up off the couch so that he could pace the floor in front of her. His entire body was tense as he moved, and it showed off every corded muscle in that lean, hard body. She could feel his turmoil. "I don't know, Leta. I really don't. But you're the only person I haven't wanted to throw out of here in a really long time."

She smiled at him. "Well, that wasn't from lack of trying on your part."

"Yeah, but I brought you back."

"True . . ." She sobered as she considered what lay before them. "I don't know either. I personally think we should focus on surviving the next few days and then we'll see where we stand . . . if we're still intact."

He paused before he raked his hand through his tousled blond hair. "What aren't you telling me about what we're up against?"

She pulled the small square pillow under her arm into her lap. "Our only option with Dolor might be putting him back to sleep again."

"And?"

"The last time I did that, my injuries were so extensive that I had to go into stasis with him in order to heal. That was almost two thousand years ago."

No part of him moved except for his gaze, which fell to the floor in front of her. "I see."

Her heart shredded at all the meaning in those two simple words. "Don't, Aidan. Don't look like that." His hurt made her ache too. "I need you angry. Your anger feeds my powers and makes me stronger. The stronger I am, the less he's capable of hurting me or you."

He laughed at the irony. "I've never had a woman ask for my anger before."

She tossed the pillow aside before she rose and crossed the short distance between them. "I'm not your typical woman."

"In more ways than one." He lifted her hand that still held the vial. "So what do we need to do?"

"We need a bed."

He arched a brow at that. "Really?"

She laughed. "Stop that. You know why. We need to be comfy because one shot of this will put us out for a full night . . . or longer."

He gave her a becoming pout. "You take all the fun out of this."

His words confused her. "Fighting is fun?"

"Oh, yeah. The adrenaline rush ranks up there right below sex."

Uh-huh . . . "It's a man thing, isn't it?"

"I would say yes, but I've known enough women to say that it's not unique to my gender. I've met plenty of marathon sluggers in high heels."

She rolled her eyes at him. Stepping back, she held her hand out. "C'mon, soldier. Let's go feed your need."

He slid his gaze hungrily over her body. "Which one?"

"Let's save your life, then we'll worry about your body."

He let out a sound of disgust. "There are some pleasures worth dying for."

"Yes. But I don't want to be one of them."

He was still pouting as she tugged him toward the bedroom. Leta made him lie down first so that she could place three drops of the serum on his tongue.

Aidan made a terrible face. "Ack, that's bitter."

"I know."

She watched as he started blinking, trying to stay awake.

"Don't fight it. I'll see you on the other side."

His green gaze met hers. "You better. I'm trusting you to be there, Leta. I *need* you there." And with that, he was out.

Leta took a moment to run her gaze over him. He really was beautiful. Wanting nothing more than to save him, she lay down by his side and rested her head on his shoulder before she drank the serum.

She didn't know what awaited them in the dream realm, but it would be harsh and it would be cold.

Even so, they would face it together.

"I won't betray you, Aidan." Yet even as she said the words, she wasn't sure she would be able to keep that promise. The one thing she'd learned in her long life was that the best intentions were often the most lethal.

All she hoped was that Aidan wouldn't be her next regret.

7

Aidan stood in the center of a blinding gale. Harsh winds cut against him, howling in his ears. All around him was darkness so bitter that it permeated every part of him. He didn't know where to turn. Every move was buffeted by winds so brutal that they all but suffocated him. He didn't dare take a step for fear of it getting worse.

Panic set in as he struggled for his footing and bearings. He hadn't felt like this since the day his brother had turned on him and taken from him every person he'd ever trusted and left him standing alone. Rage clouded his sight, but it didn't do him any good. His anger was nothing now against the lost feeling that overwhelmed his entire being.

And still the winds tore at him.

Save me . . . please . . . The call inside his weary heart was weak, like that of a small child, and he hated that part of himself that felt so lost and abandoned.

Save yourself.

The anger was trying to surface again. That was what he knew. That was who and what he was. Yet he was so tired of being alone. Tired of fighting on his own.

How could he keep going alone?

"Aidan?"

His heart clenched at the soft call of Leta's voice that somehow drove back the madness seeping into him. Then he felt it . . . that tender touch that cut him soul-deep. It steadied him and jerked him back from the edge of panic.

Acting on instinct, he pulled her against him and held her tight. He let the scent of her settle him even more. This was what he needed—someone to balance the insanity. Someone he could believe in even during the most brutal of attacks. Someone who wouldn't flee in fear, anger, or jealousy.

And she was here, standing by his side without flinching or adding to the pain of it. That knowledge seared him.

Leta closed her eyes, amazed by the way Aidan held on to her—as if she were sacred to him. More than that, he actually trembled in her arms. It was a vulnerability she was sure he would have shielded from anyone else. She was the only one he still trusted to show this part of himself to and it filled her with an unbelievable joy.

"You didn't doubt me, did you?" she teased.

His grip on her tightened. "Everyone else has deserted me, why wouldn't you?"

She heard the ragged, raw emotion in his voice and it brought tears to her eyes. "I will always be here."

"Yeah, right."

She pulled back to cup his face in her hands. "Look at me, Aidan. Don't you ever doubt my sincerity. I don't make promises I can't keep."

And there in the meager light she saw the most incredible thing of all, the glimmer of trust in his green eyes an instant before he gave her a kiss so powerful, it stole her breath.

Elated over it, she snapped her fingers and pulled them away from the storm into a quiet meadow. Still, she felt his uncertainty as he looked about as if expecting the storm to return. He needed distraction. An enemy he could focus on to take his mind off the fact that he'd exposed himself to her and let her see a part of him that he preferred to keep secret.

"Shall we summon Dolor?"

He shook his head. "Not here. It's too open. In a fair fight, he might take us."

She hated to admit it, but she was grateful he understood the danger they were facing. "Then what do you suggest?"

The world shifted until they were again in Lyssa's garden. Leta scowled as she looked around—everything was completely different than it'd been earlier. Now the colors were muted and the shrubbery looked to be made out of water. It still twisted and turned in sharp angles that made no logical sense. "What are you doing?"

His smile dazzled her as he stepped away and released her hand. "Unnerving my opponent."

She cast a suspicious glance to a shrub that turned from a whale into shark shape—one that tried to bite her as she walked past it. "What about us? Won't it do the same?"

Aidan shrugged. "I don't know about you, but I've been living in madness for years now. I find this place kind of comforting."

"That's not what you said earlier."

"I wasn't planning on fighting here earlier. If we're going to do something as insane as calling out the god of pain to fight him to the death, what better place than this?"

He did have a strange point with that logic. "Are you sure you want to do this?" she asked.

"It's a little late to doubt ourselves, isn't it?"

Perhaps, but she still had the bad feeling this was a mistake. If it was, then she intended to make sure that Aidan was shielded. And in the back of her mind, she knew this was the best shot they had. This environment, they had some control over.

"All right then." She took a deep breath before she bellowed. "Dolor!"

The god flashed in before them and this time he wasn't alone.

Aidan felt a tic begin in his jaw as he glared at the two gods.

Dolor stood a good foot taller than him with a bald head and intricate tattoos that covered his entire face and body. While he was tall and lean, the man to his left was short and beefy with hands that would easily make two of Aidan's fists.

Aidan looked over at Leta for confirmation of the other god's identity. "Timor?"

She nodded glumly.

Nice to know his usual luck was holding. He now wished he'd stayed home. Then again, he wasn't about to lie down in this fight and let them roll over him. He'd been born two months prematurely and his mother had always said that even as an infant he'd had more fight in him than a ring of boxers. He'd come into this world as a scrapper, and if he was going to leave it, then he'd go down swinging.

Dolor arched a brow as a cruel smile twisted his lips. "I'm impressed, Leta. You said you'd be quick bringing him to me, but this is fast even for you. Nice work."

A chill went down Aidan's spine as his old mistrust burned through him. "What?"

Timor smirked. "Didn't you know she was working with us to lead you straight into our hands?"

"Liar!" Leta snapped. She turned toward Aidan with large, fear-filled eyes. "Don't listen to them. They're just trying to hurt you."

But it was hard not to believe it as old scars and fears were ripped open with a brutality that left him feeling naked in front of them. Everyone else had betrayed him . . . his own flesh and blood had thrown him to the dogs and laughed while they did so. It wasn't a big leap of faith for him to think she'd toss him to the dogs too.

"Aidan," she said, reaching out for him. "Trust me. Please."

He wanted to, and when her hand touched his face, he felt himself coming undone at the emotions that tangled deep inside him. Fear. Anger. Agony. And yet beneath all that was a glimmer of something he hadn't felt in years. Hope. He wanted desperately to believe in her.

Was she lying?

Closing his eyes, he covered her hand with his and savored the softness of that touch. But did he dare believe in it?

Did he?

Taking a deep breath for courage, he braced himself for a brutal moment of truth.

"You know what?" he asked, opening his eyes to glare at Timor and Dolor. "When I spoke the truth no one wanted to believe me even though I gave them no reason to doubt me. Even though they had seen the truth about me time and again. They wanted to believe the trash and the lies about my character. It's so much easier to believe the lies over honesty. So much easier and safer to blame than to love."

He took her hand from his face and looked into her eyes that were filled with apprehension. "Until *you* give me a reason not to, Leta, I trust you." He kissed her hand before he reluctantly let it go.

Leta's emotions choked her as she realized what he'd just given her. But she didn't have time to dwell on it before Dolor bellowed in rage and launched himself at Aidan. The two of them tangled and fell to the ground.

She barely had time to duck the punch Timor swung at her. Stepping back, she elbowed him hard in the ribs. The sky above them darkened dangerously, as if it were responding to their fight. Leta rained blows on Timor as he blocked and returned punch for punch. When he landed one solid blow to her chin, she tasted blood. Her face stung from the solid hit, but she couldn't let it faze her.

Growling at him, she pulled out a short staff and blocked his backhand. He came back with a sword that he manifested out of thin air. She rolled to the grass that began slithering like snakes as he lunged and lunged again. One swing came so close to her that she felt the blade graze her skin. She kicked up, catching him in the ribs again and knocking him back.

Timor staggered sideways.

Aidan took a second to check on Leta. It literally

pained him that he couldn't help her, yet she seemed to be holding her own against the larger god.

Because of Aidan's distraction, Dolor landed a solid blow to his jaw. Before he could recover, the ground under his feet shifted. He cursed as the blades of grass wrapped around his feet like long, skeletal fingers, clutching him and holding him in place. Aidan tried to shake them off, but they were persistent.

Dolor laughed. "Thank you, Sister Lyssa."

Aidan narrowed his eyes before he flung his hands out. Using his imagination, he conjured a sticky solution to blast from his palms. It wrapped around Dolor like a rope. He jerked the god forward to head-butt him. "Yeah," he said with a sinister laugh. "Thanks, Lyssa, for reminding me I'm in a dream."

Dolor let out a bellow of rage. Aidan laughed again before he flipped away from the grass. He ran up the side of the nearest wall and manifested a long staff.

When Dolor tried to follow, Aidan used the staff to knock the god off his feet. Dolor shot a blast at him. Aidan held his arm up and used his mind to block it with an invisible shield.

"Damned if it doesn't work," Aidan laughed.

Oh, yeah, this was making him feel better. He was beginning to think they might stand a chance after all. If only he could find some way to kill the beast.

"Aidan!"

He turned at Leta's call to see eight more Dolors coming at him.

And all of them looked pissed off.

The first one caught him about his waist and knocked him to the ground, flat on his back. Before he could move another one brought a sledgehammer down on his head. He managed to block it with his arm, but he swore he felt the bone shatter.

Cursing, Aidan tried to clone himself, but he couldn't focus on his goal enough to accomplish it as they hit him over and over again and his entire being ached from the attacks. So much for not being able to feel pain in a dream, huh? His body throbbing, he tried to manifest a shield, a weapon, anything.

But he couldn't.

He heard more laughter.

Suddenly, Leta was there, trying to pull him away from the others. He felt her cover him with her body as Dolor's clones continued to beat him with the sledgehammers.

The ground below them was trying to swallow them. "We're losing," she breathed in his ear.

"No shit," was all he could manage.

The skies above them opened up with rain so strong it slashed against his body like needles lacerating him. Yeah, this wasn't looking good for the home team.

He rolled with Leta, trying to keep her from taking any more damage from Dolor. The blows continued down his back until he feared they'd broken it.

His only thought to protect her, he cradled her under him even as she fought to shield him. "Stay safe, Leta," he breathed in her ear. "Don't fight me."

"Dolor's going to kill you."

Strangely, that didn't matter to him. It wasn't like he had anything to live for anyway.

Tired from the fight and weary from the loneliness, he laid his head down against her shoulder and waited for death. But as he did so and caught a teasing scent of her feminine skin, he realized that there was something left in this world that mattered to him. Something that was worth fighting for.

Leta.

His blood fueled by his fight, he let out a feral growl and closed his eyes. He would not be defeated.

Last man standing.

With his mind, he splintered the sledgehammers and sent the gods flying. He shoved himself to his feet and spun around to face a single Dolor whose eyes were widened.

"Shove it up your ass." Aidan delivered a blow to his jaw that lifted the god up two feet from the ground. In slow motion, the god arced over before he landed on his back with a solid thump.

Timor ran at him. Aidan clotheslined him and followed him to the ground so that he could punch Timor in the chest. Dolor came at his back, but before he could reach him, Leta kicked the god back.

Still the rain poured down on them while lightning flashed. The shrubs around them began to bleed.

Timor splashed in the mud that covered them before he sprang to his feet and flew at Aidan and caught him in the shoulder. Aidan heard the fabric of his shirt tearing. He tasted blood from his nose an instant before both gods blasted him.

"Side with us, Leta," Dolor growled. "We'll get your emotions back for you."

She answered by blasting him with a bolt that took some of the pain away from Aidan.

Aidan manifested another sword. Twisting around, he lifted it to strike down at Timor who caught the blade with his left hand. He moved to kick Aidan. Releasing the sword, Aidan flipped around and manifested another sword to cut deep into Timor's side.

The god went down with a bright flash of lightning. Dolor threw Leta into Aidan's arms an instant before the god drove his own sword through her.

Aidan bellowed in pain as he saw the blood pouring out of her body. "You bastard!"

Dolor laughed as he launched himself at Aidan.

But he never made it.

Just as he would have reached him, Dolor vanished. Aidan scowled as he looked around, expecting the god to attack from another area. "Dolor?"

There was no answer, except for the torrential rain that spattered the grass around them.

Forgetting about the god for a moment and focusing on the woman who was bleeding in his arms, Aidan lowered Leta to the ground. He felt sick at the sight of her blood mixing with the mud.

How could this be?

"Leta?" he asked, not bothering to cover the note of fear in his voice.

"Sh," she said, touching his lips. "I'm immortal. I won't die from this."

"Then why are you bleeding?"

She smiled wanly. "Because this is your fear. Let it go, Aidan."

That was easier said than done. "I don't know how."

"Yes you do. Think back to the time before your brother turned on you. What was your fear then?"

That he'd lose his career and the studios would stop calling him. That the fans who paid to see his movies would turn on him and no longer show up at the box office. That he'd be alone in the world with no one to rely on.

"I was afraid of bad publicity. Of people hating me."

"Now?"

He hadn't been hurt by it. Even though the world had heard the lies, had seen his family come for his throat, the fans had stayed and seen the truth of him. He'd even won the Academy Award that year and had starred in one of the highest-grossing movies. A movie that had set him free to retire if he wanted to. Professionally, no one had cared what lies his brother had spewed.

As for being alone, he'd learned that it wasn't so bad. It'd taught him self-reliance. He'd come away from Donnie's machinations even stronger than he'd been before.

He'd become fearless, with an inner strength and clarity that was unrivaled.

But that wasn't the same as Leta bleeding and hurt. "I don't want to lose you, Leta."

"Then don't fear it. Believe that I'll be here with you, always."

Again, that was easier said than done. But he had to put faith in her. Believe in her even though the hurt part of himself didn't want to have faith in anyone but himself.

He pulled her against him and laid his head against the hollow of her throat. "I believe in you, Leta."

She lifted her hand to bury it deep in his hair as she kissed him. And with every heartbeat inside him, he felt her growing stronger.

He broke off the kiss to find her smiling at him.

"Your fears have power. It's what feeds Dolor and Timor. Don't give them a power they don't deserve."

Nodding, he glanced around. "Speaking of Timor, what happened to him?"

She shook her head. "I'm not sure."

"Did we defeat them?"

"I wish I could say yes, but I don't think so."

Damn . . .

"You didn't beat them . . . yet."

They looked up to find Deimos standing over them with a cold, gloomy expression.

"What are you doing here?" Leta asked.

He let out a tired breath even though there was a hint of amusement in his eyes. "Getting involved in something I should leave alone but thought I ought to stick my neck out for it anyway. What the hell? Pissing off gods is what I do best."

Leta frowned at him. "And what exactly are you talking about?"

"In short, Dolor found a human sacrifice to the other side. He's now in human form. His highly non-entertaining birth is why he vanished from here so abruptly. He's on his way to kill Aidan's body while his consciousness is trapped here."

Leta cursed to learn that Dolor had found a body donor. Most people tended to pull back from being killed so that a god could use their body to murder their enemies. Apparently they weren't so lucky this time. "Who was the sacrifice?"

He jerked his chin toward Aidan. "His nephew. Donnie gave the kid up to the ghost to provide a body for Dolor's use."

Aidan went cold at the news. "No way!"

He shook his head grimly. "You want the god of

pain to do your bidding, you have to pay a steep price for it. Blood and bone, my friend. Blood and bone."

That sent Aidan's senses reeling. He knew his brother hated him, but not this much . . . Surely to God, Donnie wouldn't have killed his own son just to get back at him.

Would he?

No, it wasn't possible. "He couldn't have done something like that."

But by the light in Deimos's eyes, he knew the truth he wanted only to deny. "You're talking about a man who set out to ruin the doting brother who gave his lazy ass a free ride. Why do you think this is beyond him?"

Because Aidan remembered when they were kids together. He remembered the laughter they'd shared. The hard times when they had been a united front against a world that was out to beat them down. Without Donnie, he wouldn't have made it through the death of their parents. He wouldn't have had the confidence to go out and make it on his own.

How could that boy who used to laugh with him have turned into the kind of monster who could kill his own son? "I can't believe this. I just can't. How could jealousy do this? How? It can't sour someone to this extreme, can it? I mean really . . ."

Deimos gave him a sympathetic look, but there was no relief or comfort in that stare. No peaceful understanding to such a brutal reality. "It can and it does. Believe me. I've seen a lot worse than this in my billion or so years of existence—the first murder man committed was one brother against the other for no other reason than that one petty emotion. Jealousy turns to hatred which then turns to poison. It infects and it destroys until it eats someone alive. Your brother was so angry that you made something out of your life, that you had fans who would do anything for you. He couldn't take it; he couldn't understand why you would have something like that while he didn't. His only goal has been to take you down a notch and put you back where you belong . . . underneath him. If he can't have it, then damned if you will."

It still didn't make sense to him why Donnie felt like that about him. "But I never let the fame get to me. I never changed. I've always remembered who I am and where I come from."

"Yeah," Deimos said. "And do you remember the old Joe Walsh song 'Life's Been Good'?"

"What of it?"

"Everybody's so different, *I* haven't changed."

Aidan stood there in silence as the words echoed in his head. He hadn't thought about that song in years, but Deimos was right. He was still the same boy who'd run barefoot in the summer because they needed to save their shoes for school. He still said "please" and "thank you" to everyone around him, regardless of who they were.

But Donnie . . . he wasn't the man he'd once been. The minute Aidan had given him a taste of wealth, he'd begun to treat people like they were beneath him. Like he was somehow better even though he wasn't the one who'd earned it.

And Donnie wasn't the only one who'd changed. So many people had come and gone through Aidan's life. Those who'd had no use for him when he'd been a starving actor trying to get a break had become his bosom buddy the moment he'd begun getting choice roles. Suddenly he was important and people wanted to meet him. But Aidan still felt like the young actor who'd been left outside of hot nightclubs because he didn't rate. The same actor others had brushed off as insignificant.

And then there had been Heather . . .

Damn, old Joe had been a prophet with that song. It made him wonder who had screwed over the song-writer so that he'd been able to express it so elo-quently.

Deimos stepped forward. "We have to get the two of you awake. Dolor is on his way to your place to hit the two of you while you're unconscious."

Leta cursed. "We're sleeping ducks."

Deimos nodded. "It's a good plan on his end."

Yes, it was. Aidan glanced to Leta before he asked Deimos, "Can you wake us?"

"I don't know. But here's to trying." The god van-ished.

Aidan turned toward Leta who watched him carefully. She had a red spot on her face from a backhand one of the other gods had given her. Her hair was tousled and her pale eyes were filled with admiration. That look tore through him and it made him ache.

He held his hand out to her.

Her gentle touch set him on fire as she wrapped her fingers around his. His cock hardened instantly, making him wish they had a moment alone. He couldn't believe she'd infiltrated his life so easily, but he was so glad she had.

"If I end up dead tonight, I just want to say thank you."

She gave him an arch stare. "For what?"

"Knocking on my door and forcing your way into my life."

She smiled at him. "No problem. I'm just sorry I didn't do a better job of saving you."

Those words were a symphony to his ears. "You know, in a weird way, I think you did."

"What do you mean?"

He tugged her closer to him so that he could feel her body heat against his skin. It set his nerves on edge and reminded him exactly what she had brought into his life. "I've been asleep for a long time. Living in an empty place. I don't feel so empty now. There's something else there."

"Something else?"

He nodded, wrapping his arms around her. "It's

you." He touched his heart. "You woke me up and I feel again. It's actually kind of nice, and if this is the last chance I have to say it, I just thought you should know."

Leta's heart pounded at the words she knew were so hard for him to utter. They meant everything to her. And she felt the same way. "After my husband died, I never thought I would be able to care for another person. And then I found you. I won't let them have you, Aidan. I won't."

He kissed her hand before he cupped her face in his hands and placed the tenderest of kisses on her lips. Her senses spun. If she could, she would stay right here with him. There was nothing she wanted more than to be human and to stay by his side.

If only she could . . .

"Leta?" She heard Deimos's voice as a faint whisper in her head.

One more minute.

But it wasn't meant to be. She felt something pulling her back, away from Aidan.

No!

And still she felt herself slipping, falling down a dark tunnel until she was again waking up in the human plane. So groggy she could barely move, she blinked open her eyes to find Deimos staring at her.

"Aidan?"

He indicated the area beside her with a lift of his chin. "I can't get him to wake up."

"Where's Dolor?"

As if in answer to her question, she heard someone coming up the stairs outside.

Her heart hammering, she rolled over to shake Aidan. "Aidan!" she snapped.

He didn't move.

Deimos grimaced. "How much did you give him?"

"Apparently more than I should have. I wanted to make sure that neither of us pulled out of the dream early." Leta shook her head as she stared at Aidan lying there in perfect repose. In spite of the turmoil and battle in his dream, his handsome features were so peaceful, his body still and relaxed. However, the time for dreaming was behind them. They now had an enemy to face in this realm.

"Please wake up," she breathed, but she knew better. He was too far under. There wouldn't be any more waking for him. At least not for a long time.

Someone was kicking against the cabin door, trying to break it down.

She brushed her hand against Aidan's whiskered cheek before she rose from the bed. "We have to defeat them."

"I'm right here by your side."

She impulsively kissed Deimos' cheek. "Thank you."

He inclined his head before he flashed himself to the living room. Leta followed after him, knowing they were the only thing standing between Aidan and death.

She glanced back to the bedroom where he slept before she whispered a solemn vow. "I won't let you down, Aidan. I swear it."

Aidan jerked back in surprise as he heard Leta's voice in his dream state. He hovered in the room, unable to wake up. It was as if he were caught between the dream and reality. That strange nether realm where lucid dreams were made. He could see her and Deimos, see Dolor and Donnie as they broke through his door and spilled into his living room.

"I have to wake up." But no matter what he tried, he couldn't. It was the most frustrating thing he could imagine.

He looked at his brother, whose blond hair was shaved close to his head. Donnie had beefed up in prison and his green eyes were insane as he looked about. Aidan wasn't sure how Dolor had gotten his brother out of jail, but then it probably wasn't hard for a god to do whatever he wanted to.

"Where is he?" Donnie snarled. "Aidan!"

Leta braced herself in the middle of the room. "You're not getting him."

Donnie turned on her with a look of steel. "Like hell, bitch. He's mine, and if you don't move, I'm going through you to get him."

She closed her eyes an instant before a staff appeared in her hands. "Then let's dance because the only way to get to him is through me."

Dolor, who was in Ronald's body, stared at Deimos.

"You don't belong in this fight, Demon. You sure you want to stand there?"

"No place I'd rather be."

Ronald/Dolor blasted him off his feet. Deimos rolled with it before he returned the blast with one of his own.

Leta scissor-kicked Donnie and drove him back from Aidan's room.

Aidan watched the fighting with bated breath. It was inconceivable to him that the two of them were willing to be battered to protect him. No one had ever done that for him before.

Donnie swept Leta off her feet. As he went to kick her, she rolled away and twisted her body to knock him down. Damn, the woman was a better fighter than Jackie Chan. But Donnie was no slacker and obviously jail had taught him a few things.

Deimos and Dolor were locked in a massive battle as they slammed from wall to floor to wall again. They were equally matched, and there wouldn't be an easy victor in that fight.

And just when he was certain Leta would take Donnie, Donnie caught her from behind with a garroting chord.

Aidan's heart stilled as he watched her struggle.

"I can't flash out," she called to Deimos.

Dolor laughed. "It's one of Artemis's toys. You're snared."

"No," Donnie laughed in a sinister tone. "You're dead."

Aidan felt his rage building to an unbelievable level. There was no way in hell he was going to let her die because of him. He threw his head back and roared with the ferocity of everything he felt.

His adrenaline pumping, he ordered himself awake.

Still Donnie tightened the chord.

"Leta!" Aidan shouted.

Her face was turning blue as she fought for breath. He reached out to touch her, but it was too late.

Leta slumped in Donnie's arms.

8

Aidan came awake with the taste of rage bitter on his tongue. As he heard the fighting outside his bedroom, his anger built to a stellar level.

"Leta," he snarled, throwing himself toward the door. He snatched it open to see her on the floor at Donnie's feet.

Without stopping, he dove at his brother, catching him about the shoulders before they fell to the ground. His gaze turning red, Aidan slugged him with everything he was worth, over and over again. Donnie tried to throw him off, but he was having none of it. He was through with his brother's crap.

"I hate you," Donnie shouted.

"Feeling's mutual," Aidan said an instant before he slammed Donnie's head against the slate floor as hard as he could. Blood exploded over the hardwood floor. His brother's blood should have appeased him. It didn't.

And as he looked into his brother's dilated eyes

that were an exact match to the shade of his own, Aidan wanted to weep.

How had they come to this? How?

That moment of weakness cost him as Donnie kicked him back. His brother grabbed him by the shoulders and rolled until Aidan was pinned to the floor. There was no mercy in Donnie's eyes as he rained blows on Aidan.

"How could you?" Aidan demanded furiously as he blocked most of the hits.

"Because I hate you, you piece of shit. You got everything that should have been mine. Everything! The looks, the money, the hot girlfriend. It's not fair for you to have so much and for me to have so little."

That was so not true. Donnie had been even better looking than Aidan when he'd been younger. Where Aidan had been lean and had to work for muscle tone, Donnie had always been naturally muscled. Donnie had been the one to get married and have a family. Tracy had only left him because he'd cheated on her. As for the money, Donnie could have had that too, but rather than start a business for himself, he'd been content to make the steady salary of a cable installer. Good money that he'd spent on drugs, alcohol, and strippers—which had also caused the break-up of his marriage. "You're insane."

"Yeah and you're a dick. Do you have any idea what it's like to watch your wife lust after your kid brother? To listen to her sing your brother's praises and tell you how you don't measure up?"

What was he talking about? Tracy had never seen him as anything more than a little brother. Donnie's wife had barely even spoken to him the handful of times he'd been around her.

"*You* stole Heather from me."

"No," Donnie said bitterly. "The bitch still loved you even after we hooked up. All she could talk about was you and how good-looking you were. How much money you made and all the great places you'd taken her when you dated. How you couldn't go out without being mobbed by people who loved you. She was as obsessed with you as Tracy was. It's why I offered her soul to Dolor first."

Aidan was so stunned by the words that he allowed Donnie to land a solid punch on his jaw. He tasted blood before he kicked him back. "What?"

Donnie caught himself. He stood before Aidan with twisted lips, clenching and unclenching his fists. "Whiny fucking bitch. The only reason she even went with me was to hurt you. She didn't care about me. She just wanted you to think there was someone out there who didn't find you irresistible. She thought you'd come crawling back to her, begging for her to take you back. So I broke out of jail, cut her throat, and used her blood to wake Dolor."

Aidan cursed. His heart bleak, he rushed at Donnie and caught him in a headlock. He glanced to Leta on the floor who appeared to be breathing easier than she had before. He wanted to check on her, but knew better than to try. Donnie wouldn't let him near her until he was down for the count.

Aidan tightened his hold on Donnie's neck. "How could you kill Ronald? He was your son!"

"He may have been my blood," he said in a raspy tone, "but he wasn't my son. He loved you more than me. He always did. My house wasn't as fancy as Uncle Aidan's. My money wasn't as good. He wanted to apologize to you. Tell you how sorry he was for everything we'd done. He said we had no right to hurt you, so I told Dolor to take him out and use his body to get to you."

Aidan felt sick at the words. How could his brother be reduced to this? "I loved you, Donnie. I would have done anything in the world for you." His grip loosened as he tried to reach through the hatred to find the brother he'd once known and loved.

"Then die." Donnie spun on him with a kick that landed hard on Aidan's ribs.

Aidan grunted as he caught his balance.

Donnie pulled a knife out of his pocket and flipped it open. Aidan caught his wrist before Donnie could plunge it into him. He wrenched Donnie's hand and sent the knife flying before he backhanded him and kicked him down.

Aidan sneered at him. "I never once in my life thought I was better than you until now. I could never have hurt my family the way you have. Loyalty is everything to me. It always has been and always will be. But you . . . you don't know how to love. Your jealousy won't even let you recognize it when you have it. I can't hate you anymore, you wretched excuse for a human. All I can do is feel sorry for you."

Donnie shrieked before he ran at him. Aidan caught him and slung him back to the ground.

"You're pathetic."

Donnie pushed himself up. "You're the one who's pathetic. You got nothing now."

"Not true. I have my dignity and a million people in this world who love me. The only thing you have in your life is anger, bitterness, and a mistrust that you'll never overcome. All you know how to do is envy other people. You'll never have anything. Your hatred and greed won't let you."

Donnie launched himself at Aidan, but before he could reach him, Leta was there between them. She kicked Donnie back.

Aidan kissed her hand before he stepped around her. "Thank you, Donnie, for allowing me to recognize and appreciate real friendship. Had you not screwed me over, I would have married Heather and allowed her to make me miserable for the rest of my life, because unlike you, I don't walk away from important relationships. I don't turn my back on the people I love. Hell, I was even one step away from signing my entire estate over to her before we married. More than that, you flushed all the snakes out of my garden and set me free."

He looked at Leta and Deimos. "Now I know who I can depend on. I understand what real love is and what it means to put someone else above my own pettiness. I'm grateful to God that you're wretched and in trying to ruin me, all you did was make my life a hell of a lot better. Thank you."

He screamed and Aidan laughed.

The minute he did, Dolor looked up with a frown.

Donnie gestured toward the god. "Kill the bastard!"

Aidan braced himself for the fight, but didn't feel his anger rekindle. All he felt was pity for the brother who'd allowed his petty jealousy to ruin his entire life. More than that, Donnie's jealousy had caused him to kill the very people who loved him most.

His stomach wrenched at the thought of what Donnie had done to himself.

There was no more pain inside him now. No bitterness or hatred. Aidan felt nothing except gratitude that he wasn't Donnie. More than that, he was grateful that Leta had kept him from becoming his brother's shadow.

Dolor, who looked exactly like Donnie had when Aidan had left home to seek his fortune, stepped forward. Aidan wanted to weep over the fact that his nephew was dead. But there were no tears. Again, it was pity he felt for Donnie. For the first time since Donnie had turned on him, he didn't want revenge.

He was through with it.

"You're not fighting me," Dolor growled.

Aidan shook his head slowly. "I'll fight only for what matters." He looked over his shoulder at Leta. "Her safety."

Dolor's gaze followed his until it rested on Leta. Rage darkened his brow. He stepped forward, then froze.

Aidan frowned as he saw the god struggle, as if held in place by some invisible force. Dolor reached for him, then shattered into a shimmery dust that drifted down to the ground where it sparkled against the floor.

He looked around the room, expecting the god to rematerialize.

Dolor didn't.

Confused, Aidan turned to Leta. "What happened?"

"He's gone," Deimos said, brushing his hands against his pants. "You defeated him."

"How?"

Leta spoke in a quiet tone. "'*Pain is here,*

"'*sharp and clear.*

"'*Even so, it must fade,*

"*And a new way should be made.*'" She stepped forward. "That's what Lyssa was trying to tell us.

You released the pain and betrayal inside you . . . the fear . . . and it left him powerless to fight you."

"No!" Donnie shouted, rushing at Aidan.

Aidan turned to face him, but before he could he felt a sharp, stinging pain in his shoulder. He flipped his brother over his arm, and pinned him to the ground. It was only then he saw the knife in Donnie's hand. With a feral grimace, Aidan disarmed him.

Fury gripped him, but it didn't stay. Donnie wasn't worth it. He wasn't worth anything.

Deimos picked the knife up from the floor. "You want me to kill him for you?"

Aidan shook his head. "I want him to live with the knowledge that he destroyed everything and everyone in his life who loved him." He caught Donnie's hand as he tried to hit him and held it in his fist.

Donnie tried to spit, but Aidan dodged it.

Aidan swallowed against the lump in his throat that choked him. Even after everything that had gone on between them, there was still a part of him that wanted to love Donnie . . . to forgive him.

But in the end, he couldn't. Donnie would never allow that and he knew it.

"You were my brother, Donnie. I would have died for you. Done anything in this world you asked. But the problem is, you weren't satisfied with that. You had to take. May God have mercy on you."

"I don't need your pity, you prick."

Those words squelched any mercy that was left

inside him where his brother was concerned. There were people out there that no amount of compassion or love could save and it was time he faced the fact that Donnie was a lost cause. "And I don't need trash in my life." He glanced to Leta. "Any chance the cell phone will work?"

"Yes, why?"

"Because I want to call the cops to come get this sack of shit out of my house."

"This isn't over!" Donnie snarled.

Aidan shook his head. "Oh, yes it is. You're going to leave here in a few minutes and I will never again think about you and what you've done. I really don't care about you. You're not worth the salt in my tears or the brain power it would take me to even conjure your face."

"I won't let you rest."

Aidan snorted. "Believe me, I will sleep well at night. I have the resources and the drive to fight you to the bitter end for what matters most—my life and"—he looked at Leta—"my heart . . . I'm through with you."

"You—"

Deimos ended his words with a swift kick to his head that rendered Donnie unconscious. "Anyone else getting bored with his crap?"

Leta raised her hand.

Aidan stood up. "Did you kill him?"

"Nah. Against my better judgment, he's breathing.

Still say you should let me cut a few parts off his body."

"No. I want him intact so that the only thing he'll focus on is what he's done to himself. Sooner or later his lies will fade and he will see the truth. I'm not the one who hurt him. He is."

Deimos looked disappointed by the fact he couldn't kill Donnie. "Since this appears to be over, I'm going to head back and force Phobos to play another round with me. Later." He vanished.

Aidan let out an irritated breath at his abrupt departure. "I didn't have a chance to thank him."

"Don't worry about it. Demon hates thank-yous."

"Really?"

She nodded. "Like someone else I know, he gets uncomfortable whenever he's praised."

Aidan felt one corner of his mouth lift as he pulled her closer to him. "I think I'm getting over that."

"Are you?"

"Yeah, but only when it comes from you."

She returned his smile with one that left him weak in his knees. "I summoned the police a second ago. They'll be here in a few minutes."

"Cool." At least that was his thought until he realized something. "What happens to you now that Dolor's gone?"

"I have to leave."

His stomach shrank as a sick feeling went through him. "Leave?"

She glanced away as if unable to meet his gaze. "I'm a goddess, Aidan. I can't stay in the human realm. I don't belong here."

He wanted to beg her to stay with him, but he couldn't. She'd already told him why she couldn't stay. All begging would do was make her feel bad for something neither of them could help.

As she said, she was a goddess.

Maybe she could become mortal. But he didn't want that. She would grow old and die.

How could he ask that of someone who was forever young and beautiful? It would be selfish. "I'm going to miss you."

Leta swallowed at the pain she heard in his voice. He was trying so hard to be strong, but inside he was shattered. She could feel it.

Fear marked his brow. "Will Dolor be there, waiting for you?"

"No. When he failed to kill you and his human body disintegrated, he was rendered powerless. He's back in stasis now. It'll take another human sacrifice to reawaken him." At least that was what she believed had happened to him. The truth was, she didn't know and wouldn't know for sure until she returned home.

Aidan scowled. "Why does he have to have a human sacrifice to appear as a human when you don't?"

"With the help of Hades, I cursed him to it. My thought was that no one would be vicious enough to kill someone they loved in order to set him free. I thought I'd found a way to lock him out of the human world for all eternity."

Aidan looked to his brother, who was still unconscious on the floor. "I guess we both overestimated Donnie's humanity."

"Perhaps, but remember, not everyone else in the world is as sick as he is."

"But you're not really in this world, are you?"

"Aidan—"

He silenced her words by placing one finger over her lips. "Don't prolong the hurt, Leta. Just rip the Band-Aid off my skin and let the burn remind me that for one day, I had something more than misery. I told you earlier that I'd rather have one moment of incredible bliss than a lifetime of nothing." He placed a tender kiss to her forehead. "Now go. Just leave."

The problem was, she didn't want to leave him. She wanted to stay, but there was no way she could. Her temporary body wouldn't last in this plane of existence. "I'll visit you in your dreams."

"No," he said, his voice catching. "That would only make it worse. I couldn't stand seeing you there, knowing that I'm not really touching you. Let the wound heal. Let me be able to think back on this day and remember the woman who saved my life."

He was right, and it was killing her to admit it. "I won't forget you, Aidan."

Aidan didn't respond verbally, but the tormented light in those green eyes said more than words ever could.

He would remember her too.

The sound of police sirens pierced the air.

"Go, Leta."

She stepped back with her heart in her throat. All she wanted was to be with him. If only it could be. But the gods had decreed a different fate for them. There was no need to fight a battle they couldn't win.

"I love you, Aidan," she said before she flashed herself back to the Vanishing Isle.

Aidan stood there in the center of his cabin, staring at the space where Leta had been. It was only then that he let the tears he felt surface. The pain of them burned in his chest and choked him.

Eventually she would have betrayed you too. Everyone betrays you.

Perhaps, but he no longer believed that. Leta had taught him better.

He heard the thunder of the police running onto his porch. "Put your hands behind your head! Get down on your knees!"

Aidan didn't flinch as the cops flooded through his broken door with their weapons drawn. He obeyed their orders and knelt on the floor while one of the officers ran behind him and cuffed his hands together.

"For the record, I'm the victim."

But since they didn't know for sure, they followed

standard protocol of securing him before they called an ambulance for Donnie.

Once they realized Donnie was an escaped felon and Aidan did in fact live in the cabin and was the one who'd been attacked, they removed his handcuffs and let him get a cold towel to clean some of the blood off his face and shoulder.

"You sure you don't want to go to the hospital?" one of the male officers asked.

Aidan shook his head as he watched them haul a semiconscious Donnie out of his living room. There was no helping what really hurt him. Only Leta could do that. "I'll be all right."

"You sure?"

For the first time in years, he actually was. "Yeah. That which doesn't kill us—"

"Requires a lot of therapy to deal with."

Aidan gave a small laugh as the police officer shrugged.

"Hey, in my business, it's really true." The officer suddenly looked awkward as he glanced at the mantel where Aidan kept his Oscars. It was a bashful stance Aidan knew extremely well.

"You want an autograph?"

The officer's face brightened. "I didn't want to ask with you bleeding and all, but my wife's a really big fan of yours and this would score me some major points with her. If I could put that under the tree, I know it would make her Christmas."

Aidan smiled even though it hurt his split lip. "Hang on." He went into his office and pulled out a stack of publicity photos Mori had sent that he'd ignored and a Sharpie before he returned to the living room. "What's her name?"

"Tammy."

Another officer stepped forward. "Oh, man, can I have one too? I loved that movie *Alabaster.* You kicked major butt in it and the chick who was in it with you . . . Was she as hot in real life?"

"No, she was even better."

The officer laughed.

Aidan hesitated as the old joy he used to feel came flooding back. He could still remember the first time someone had asked for his autograph all those years ago. The first time someone had stopped him on the street to tell him how much they loved his work. There was nothing else like it. No matter when or where, he loved to be stopped by his fans. To share a few minutes chatting with them.

Donnie and Heather had tainted it with their poison. *"Those people don't care about you. They're just hanger-ons wanting to touch something they'll never be. God, I hate it whenever they come up to us. I can't even eat a meal in peace. Why don't you tell them to go away and leave us alone?"*

But Aidan had never minded. Even when it got to the point he couldn't drive on the street with his windows down or the times he had the press climbing into his backyard, he hadn't minded it. He was glad he did something that other people enjoyed, and if talking to him made them happy . . . There was no greater feeling than knowing he'd touched their lives and brought a smile to their faces, even if it was only for a few minutes.

This was what he'd wanted since he was a kid. What he'd fought his ass off to achieve. He'd suffered through enough slings and arrows to make Shakespeare proud.

And he loved every minute of it.

He handed the signed photo for Tammy to the officer before he looked at the other one. "What's your name?"

"Ricky . . . and can you make one out for my girlfriend, Tiffany? She'd just die if I came home with that. Oh, and my mom, Sara. She's been a fan of yours since that weird horror movie you did. I loved that too, but it was a major mind scrambler."

Aidan laughed at the man's enthusiasm. "It'd be my pleasure."

Before it was over, Aidan signed a total of twenty photos for the police and paramedics. Donnie was screaming in outrage from the ambulance, but no one cared.

"You have a Merry Christmas," Ricky said as he trailed the others out of Aidan's cabin. He hesitated at the splintered door. "You probably need to call someone to fix this. I don't think you should be up here without a good door, given what happened today."

"Thanks. I'll take care of it."

Ricky held his hand out. "You're a decent man, Mr. O'Conner. Thanks so much for the autographs."

"My pleasure, and call me Aidan."

Ricky grinned. "Aidan. It was a pleasure meeting you. I just wish the circumstances were better."

"Yeah, me too. You have a good Christmas and tell your mom and Tiffany I said hi."

"Will do. Thanks."

Aidan followed him out to the porch where he watched Ricky walk out to his car before all of them drove off. He could still hear Donnie's muffled voice cursing him as they pulled onto the road. Pity welled up inside him, but then again, maybe it was a good thing Donnie was still being eaten with hatred. One day Donnie would realize exactly what his jealousy had cost him—that in trying to ruin Aidan, he'd destroyed his entire life.

God help his brother then.

The pain of Donnie's betrayal rolled off his shoulders now. He really didn't care. "I am the last man standing."

The problem was, he was standing alone and for the first time in years that bothered him.

Closing his eyes, he felt the bite of the cold against him as he summoned an image of Leta in his mind.

"I miss you, baby." But there was nothing to be done about it.

Life was what it was.

Defeated, he turned to enter his house and saw that his door had been replaced. "Leta?" he asked with a hopeful note in his voice.

It wasn't her. Deimos was standing inside the living room, watching him.

Aidan couldn't understand his presence. "I thought you were playing chess."

"I was going to, but . . ." He hesitated as if there were something on his mind.

"But?" Aidan prompted.

Deimos indicated the door with a tilt of his head. "I remembered you had a broken door."

"Thanks for repairing it."

"No problem."

Aidan paused, waiting for Deimos to speak or do something. When he didn't, Aidan arched a brow. "Is there something I can help you with?"

"Not really. It's more along the lines of something I can help you with."

Now he had Aidan's full attention. "And that is?"

Deimos's gaze bored into him. "What would you give to have Leta with you?"

Aidan didn't hesitate. "Everything."

"You sure?"

"Yes." Suddenly, everything went black. Aidan

jerked around, trying to get his bearings, but he couldn't see, feel, or hear anything. It was just dark. "Leta?"

This time she didn't respond. There was no kind hand to ground him. No words of encouragement and he missed that even more.

When the light returned, he saw himself as a kid near a Christmas tree. He was eleven and at his uncle's house. Aidan frowned as he tried to remember the exact event, but he couldn't. He only remembered the setting.

"What did you get?" Donnie asked as he came over to where Aidan was playing.

Aidan held up his action figure. "G.I. Joe and some candy."

Donnie curled his lip. "That's not fair. I wanted a G.I. Joe."

Aidan was baffled by his anger. "No you didn't. You said you wanted Optimus Prime and Grimlock, which you got."

Donnie reached for the toy in Aidan's hand and snatched it away.

"Give that back!"

Donnie refused, and when Aidan tried even harder, he punched him with everything he had. Aidan shouted in fury which woke his uncle up from the nap he was taking on the plaid couch a few feet away from them.

Two seconds later, with insults ringing in their ears,

all the toys were in the garbage and both of them were grounded. Not to mention bruised from their uncle's anger.

"It's all your fault," Donnie snarled, shoving Aidan up the stairs as they headed to the room the two of them shared.

"I didn't take your toys, you took mine."

Donnie curled his lip. "That's because you need to learn to share. You're such a selfish scumbag. I hate you. I wish you'd died with Mom and Dad."

Aidan froze at the hostility on his brother's face as Donnie trudged past him. His heart heavy, he reversed course and returned to the living room. He sneaked around the corner, afraid of being caught. Luckily his uncle was back on the couch again, passed out from his Christmas drinking binge.

As quietly as he could, Aidan crept to the garbage can and pulled the toys out. Then just as silently, he made his way back upstairs where he handed the toys to Donnie.

"You can have them," he said, not wanting his brother to hate him anymore.

Donnie smiled.

But even though Aidan had won his brother back, there was no satisfaction in it. He merely felt relieved that Donnie didn't hate him . . .

The adult Aidan watched the scene as he finally remembered every buried emotion of that Christmas Day. He'd forgotten it all. Now every bit of it was clear to him. And he remembered other times when Donnie had acted that way. All the times he'd tried to placate him because Donnie didn't want him to have anything.

The entire world was supposed to be Donnie's.

Then the scene shifted and he saw his agent Mori at home with his latest wife. Tall, dark-haired, young, and beautiful, Shirley sat on the couch while Mori sat across from her in a brown leather chair.

"Why are you so unhappy?" she asked quietly.

Mori offered her an apologetic smile. "I'm sorry. I was just thinking about Aidan again."

She rolled her eyes. "I can't believe he'd walk away from that kind of money."

Mori's gaze turned introspective as he cupped his glass of brandy. His expression said that he found it more than plausible. "Money doesn't buy happiness."

She scoffed. "Anyone who says that isn't shopping in the right stores."

Mori didn't comment on that. "I hate what's become of him. He is without a doubt one of the finest actors of his generation. I just wish there was something I could do for him."

"You sent him a ham."

Mori cut her a bored look. "Not for a present. When I first met him, he was so full of life and laughter. When other actors got jaded by their fame, he didn't. He always enjoyed it. Even the parts of it that made lesser actors crumble and fall. Now . . .

now he's a soured recluse. If I had one single wish for Christmas, it would be to see him happy again."

Aidan was amazed by the fact that Mori wasn't as cold-blooded as he pretended. Wow. His agent had been keeping quite a secret from him. There really was a heart buried under all that swagger.

But that didn't change anything. He looked up at the darkness. "Is this supposed to mean something to me?"

His answer came as the scene blanked out again and reemerged, not in his future as he expected, but rather in a place he'd never seen before.

It appeared to be a dark cavern with walls that were bleeding . . .

Faint screams and moans echoed as he walked toward a large opening, and when he reached it, he froze. There was Leta in a long, flowing white gown, standing before two angry men who glared at her while a third man in white stood to her left.

"You would ask me for mercy for her?" the tall blond man sneered at the man in white. "Do you understand what she has done?"

"Yes, Zeus. I do. But what she did, she did to protect an innocent human."

Zeus sneered at the answer. "None of them are innocent. What's the death of one more human in this world?"

Leta started to answer, but the man beside her stopped her by putting his hand on her arm.

When he spoke, his voice was devoid of all emotion. "She was assigned the human by me and she carried out her assignment to the end. It was Dolor who—"

"Don't you dare defend her," Zeus snarled. "Because of his death, we have a rupture in the universe. Have you any idea what could have happened? The world could have ended."

"But it didn't."

Zeus blasted him.

"M'Adoc!" Leta said, rushing to where he lay on the ground.

Zeus cocked his head at that. "Are those emotions I hear from you?"

Aidan saw the panic in Leta's eyes but since her back was to Zeus, he was sure the god hadn't noticed it.

Instead a strange look passed between M'Adoc and the dark-haired god standing beside Zeus.

"They have no emotions, brother," the dark-haired man said. "She spent time with the humans and these are the residual effects."

Zeus's gaze narrowed dangerously as M'Adoc pushed himself back to his feet. "Are you defending them, Hades?"

Hades shrugged. "Not really. If you want me to punish her I will. It's what I live for."

Aidan frowned at the underlying sarcastic tone of the god's voice.

Zeus nodded. "Very well. Kill her."

"No!" Aidan lunged forward only to run into an invisible wall.

The gods turned as if they could hear him.

Aidan slammed his hand against the wall. "Don't you dare touch her!"

He realized that they could in fact hear him as Zeus came forward to stare at him as if he were an insect in a jar. "Have you any idea who I am?"

"I don't care. Leta did nothing wrong and I won't see her hurt for me."

"Nothing wrong?" Zeus asked, his nostrils flaring. "You stupid human. She could have destroyed the entire universe with her actions. The only thing that saved us was the fact that Dolor was in stasis and his powers restricted. Had he not been . . . We'll take a moment and be damn grateful for small favors."

Even though a small voice in Aidan's head told him not to argue with an ancient god, he couldn't stop himself. "She's not the one who killed Dolor. I did it."

Leta gasped at his words. "Aidan—"

"It's true," he said, cutting her off before she contradicted him. "I killed him. So if you're going to punish anyone, it should be me."

Zeus considered it.

"Ignore him, my lord," Leta said quickly. "He's noble but foolish. I was the one who ignored your mandate to leave Dolor alone. I killed him here while he slept in stasis—against your will. Because of that I'm the one who should be punished."

Zeus stiffened as if something offended him. "Are those emotions I hear in your voice? Have you feelings for this human?"

Leta shook her head. "No, my lord. It's only cold, hard logic."

Her words tore through Aidan, who couldn't bear the thought of her being false with him. "Leta?"

Her gaze was empty as she met his. "How could I ever have feelings for a human when I'm incapable of them?"

Zeus turned speculative. "So if I killed the human, you wouldn't care?"

Aidan wouldn't have thought her face could get colder, but he was wrong.

Even so, she didn't answer.

"She wouldn't care," M'Adoc answered for her. "She's not capable of it."

"Very well. Since the human was supposed to die anyway . . ." Zeus shot a lightning bolt out of his hand, straight at Aidan's heart.

9

Aidan staggered yet remained standing even as his entire body was shoved backward. He looked down, expecting to see blood from Zeus's attack. But there was no wound. In fact, there was no pain.

Confused, he glanced around until he saw Leta lying on the floor a few feet from him. "Oh, my God," he breathed, scrambling to reach her. She must have thrown herself in front of him to protect him.

He knelt on the floor and rolled her over, to see her struggling to breathe as blood coated her entire body.

"Leta?"

She coughed up blood before she spoke in a raspy tone. "I couldn't let you die, Aidan. I'm sorry."

Sorry? Why was she apologizing to him for saving his life? It didn't even make sense.

Zeus turned on M'Adoc. "I thought you said she was incapable of caring?"

M'Adoc maintained his stoicism. "She must have gone Skoti without our knowing."

Fury darkened Zeus's brow. He held his hand up and M'Adoc was instantly drawn forward into his grasp. "You don't make those kinds of mistakes."

Hades made a sound of extreme boredom. "You're wasting your time, Zeus. You stripped their emotions so if you're trying to make him afraid now—"

"Shut up," Zeus snapped at Hades before he shoved M'Adoc away from him. He stiffened before he gave M'Adoc a dire warning. "You better keep a wary eye on your brethren. I'm holding you personally responsible. You fail to corral them and it'll be your blood I bathe in."

Aidan saw the fury and fear flash in M'Adoc's eyes before he straightened and faced Zeus. Then his face was as blank as it'd been before Zeus attacked him. "I understand, my lord. Your will be done."

"You're damn right my will be done." Zeus glared at all of them. "Now get that human out of here and clean up this mess." With those words spoken, he dissolved into a light bronze dust and evaporated.

Still on the floor, Aidan held Leta close to him as she struggled to breathe. "You're going to heal again, right?"

"No," Hades said as he stepped forward. "She was hit with a god bolt from Zeus himself. There's no coming back from that."

Aidan frowned. "I don't understand."

"She's dying," Hades said in a tone that was devoid of all feeling.

It took several seconds for those words to permeate the fog in Aidan's head. "She can't die. She's an immortal goddess."

"Who was just assaulted by the king of the gods." Hades said in the tone of a teacher talking to a dense student. "Yes, she can die."

Aidan couldn't breathe as he looked down at her. "Why? Why would you have done this?"

"I love you, Aidan," she said as her eyes teared up. "I couldn't let Zeus kill you. I could never watch someone else I love die in front of me." She lifted her hand to lay it gently to his cheek. "It was why I had to kill Dolor. I knew Donnie would only summon him again and I didn't want him to hurt you anymore. I couldn't chance it."

His own tears swelled at her words. He crushed her against him before he looked up at Hades and M'Adoc. "We have to save her. Tell me what to do."

Hades let out a tired breath. "Thunder-Bluster wants her dead. There's nothing we can do. We heal her and he will rain down on her all kinds of pain. The kindest thing you can do is let her go."

"No! Save her!"

But the god wasn't listening. Hades stepped back and looked at M'Adoc. "Let's give them privacy to say goodbye."

Aidan saw the sympathy in M'Adoc's eyes before he faded away. Hades followed suit.

Alone now, he breathed in the scent of Leta's hair.

"I wish I'd been born human," she breathed against his neck.

"I would have changed nothing about you."

He felt her smiling as she tightened her grip in his hair. An instant later, she expelled her last breath and fell limp in his arms.

For three full heartbeats, Aidan didn't move. He couldn't. It took that long for reality to set in.

Leta was dead. She'd given her life to save his.

He refused to believe it. Pulling back, he looked at her. Her eyes were partially open, her face grayish. There was no life in her eyes. Blood coated both of them.

"Wake up," he breathed, knowing it was an impossible request. "Don't leave me, Leta. Please."

But all the begging in the world changed nothing. She was gone and he was alone.

His heart shattering, he pulled her against him and did the one thing he hadn't done since the night his parents had died. He sobbed.

Rocking her in his arms, he held her for what seemed to be forever as he cried. All he wanted was to go back in time and change all of this. To start fresh and new.

To tell her he loved her too.

"I love you, Leta," he whispered into her ear, knowing she couldn't hear him.

Why hadn't he said it earlier?

But then he knew. He'd been afraid to voice it.

Afraid she would somehow use that to hurt him. Now she would never know just how much she'd meant to him. It was so unfair.

"She knows."

He looked up to find a tall, beautiful blond woman standing over him. "Who are you?"

"Persephone." She knelt by his side with sympathy in her eyes. "I'm sorry for your loss. Leta was a wonderful woman." Pulling out a small black handkerchief, she wiped his eyes. "You need to return home now. I'll take care of her for you."

"No!"

"Aidan," she said quietly. "You can't stay here. Believe me, you don't really want to. I will make sure Leta is taken care of, but you have to go."

Aching deep inside his soul, Aidan knew she was right. He pressed his lips to Leta's cold temple before he allowed Persephone to take her body from his arms. "Will you bury her with her family? She doesn't like to be alone."

Tears welled in her eyes as she nodded. "You do love her, don't you?"

"More than my life. I wish to God she'd let me die in her place."

Persephone sniffed as she took Leta from his arms. "Deimos," she said, summoning the god to appear in front of them. "Can you take him back to his world?"

Deimos nodded before he and Aidan vanished.

As soon as he was home again, Aidan turned on him. "Why did you take me there?"

"I wanted you to know how much she cared for you."

"Why? So that it would haunt me for the rest of eternity? No offense, Deimos, but as the ghost of Christmas Present, you suck. At least Scrooge was given a chance to fix his life. I can't fix this. Why the hell did you show it to me?"

Deimos shrugged. "Zeus was going to kill her anyway. As you told Persephone, she didn't like to be alone. I thought it would be nice for her if you were at least there when she died. She needed you."

He was right, but it did nothing to stop the pain inside Aidan. "Thank you, Demon. For everything."

He saw the sympathy on the god's face before he left.

Alone, Aidan stood in the center of his living room, feeling bereft. Closing his eyes, he could feel Leta here. Hear her laughter. Her jacket was still on his tree where she'd left it.

Needing to be closer to her, he walked over to it so that he could touch its softness. "I wish I had you back, Leta. If I did, I'd take better care of you than anyone you've ever known."

And if wishes were horses, even beggars would ride.

Aidan pulled the small hat out of her pocket and

lifted it to his nose. It contained her scent and that brought another set of tears to his eyes. His chest tight, he went to the mantel where he had pictures of Donnie, Heather, and Ronald. One by one, he plucked them off and tossed them into the fire where the glass heated and shattered and the pictures burned.

The only photo he left was the one of his parents. He set Leta's knit hat beside it and stepped back.

Yeah. That was his family, and only they deserved a place of honor on his shelf.

Aidan woke up to the sound of someone knocking on his front door. He looked at the clock . . . it was just after noon on Christmas Eve.

"Leta?" he breathed, tossing back his covers to run to the front door. Wearing nothing more than a loose pair of green boxer shorts, he threw the door open to find Mori and his wife with a medium-sized suitcase.

Shirley raked a hungry and amused look over his body. "I know it does nothing for you, Mor, but that just made getting on an airplane and coming to this godforsaken place worthwhile. Thanks!"

Mori rolled his eyes as he pushed past his wife and came into the house. "Merry Christmas, Aidan."

Aidan stepped back and allowed Shirley to sashay in behind her husband before he closed the door. "What are you doing here?"

He'd barely closed the door before another knock sounded. Frowning, Aidan saw Theresa and Robert on the porch, holding a small tree between them.

He'd hired Robert to be his manager two weeks before Donnie had started blackmailing him. Short and tiny with brown hair and bright blue eyes, Theresa was his publicist. "And again I say, no offense, but what are you doing here?"

"We couldn't stand the thought of you spending one more Christmas alone," Robert said. "Mori called and asked if we could come out to make you a decent meal on Christmas Eve and we agreed. It's time you realized that there are people in this world who do love you, Aidan."

Before Leta had come into his life, he would have tossed them out of his house and locked the door behind them.

Today, they were more than welcome.

"Come on in. Let me go get some clothes on."

"I don't know," Theresa said with a laugh. "I kind of like your Christmas suit."

Shirley laughed. "You mean 'birthday suit,' don't you?"

Theresa set the tree in the corner by his fireplace. "I'd like that even better, but he *is* dressed in holiday green. Christmas suit."

Aidan smiled before he went to his bedroom and pulled on jeans and a sweater. By he time he returned, Shirley had poured eggnog for everyone while Robert and Mori decorated the tree with tinsel and Theresa unwrapped a HoneyBaked ham in the kitchen.

He was amazed by their actions. "You know you guys don't have to do this. I know all of you have family you'd rather be with."

Robert scoffed. "Your surly butt or my klepto aunt Coco who always steals the silver by putting it in her purse when no one's looking . . . hard choice, buddy."

Theresa chided him. "You're our family too, Aidan. And this year, I think you need us the most."

She had no idea just how right she was. "Thank you, guys."

Robert grinned. "You say thank you until we burn your house down with these Christmas lights."

Aidan laughed at him as Shirley handed him a glass of eggnog.

"To Aidan," she said cheerfully. "Which reminds me of an old toast my grandfather used to give."

"And that is?" Aidan asked.

"To those who know and love me, I wish you well. All the rest may go to hell."

"Here, here," Mori said as he paused to lift his own cup.

Robert agreed. "Very fitting."

Aidan nodded. "Yeah. I'll have to remember that."

"I'm sure you will."

Aidan took a sip before he realized something. "I don't have presents for any of you."

Mori scoffed. "Don't worry. You're here with us and that's all the gift any of us need. We really are here for you, Aidan. Not because you pay us, but because we really do care about you."

And for the first time in years, he believed that. "Thank you. *All* of you." Then Aidan looked up at the ceiling and whispered "thank you" to it as well, hoping that somehow his words would get back to Leta. He was sure she'd had a hand in this.

The afternoon went by fast as Theresa warmed up the food she'd brought and they had a good lunch of ham, potatoes, gravy, and green beans, with pecan pie for dessert. Aidan could count the traditional Christmases like this that he'd had in his life on one hand.

And none of those had been nearly as special as this one. But all too soon, it was over and his guests were leaving.

He stood on the porch, watching them drive off with a lightness in his heart that had never been there before. Smiling, he picked up his phone and called Mori, who answered on the first ring.

"Did we forget something?"

"You can call the studio on Monday. I'll take the job."

"Are you screwing with me?"

"No, Mori. I'm serious. I'll do it."

The rented Town Car stopped in the driveway and Mori got out to look up at him. He pulled the phone from his ear. "I love you, man!" he shouted. "In a purely platonic kind of way."

Aidan laughed as several birds took flight in fright. "Love you too, Mor. Definitely in a platonic way."

Mori saluted him before he got back into the car and drove off.

Aidan hung up the phone and returned inside where the smell of pecan pie warmed him all the way to his toes. The day would have been perfect if only . . .

He couldn't finish that thought. It was too painful.

Yeah. There was also something to blight the happiest times of his life. But even so, he'd needed this and he was grateful to his friends for making this day special.

Sighing, he started for his den when he heard a light tapping on his door. He glanced into the kitchen to see if Theresa had forgotten something. She was always misplacing and leaving things behind. But he didn't see anything.

He opened the door, then froze.

It couldn't be.

Eyes so blue they didn't seem to be real stared up at him.

"Leta?"

Her smile dazzled him. "Can I come in?"

"Abso-fucking-lutely."

She launched herself into his arms.

Breathless, Aidan held her close, trying to make sense of this. "How can you be here?"

"Hades released me from the Underworld."

"I don't understand. Wouldn't you need a sacrifice?"

"Not if he does it. Once I died, Zeus no longer had power over me. Only Hades." She squeezed him so hard, his back popped. "Persephone was so touched by what you said that she told Hades I had to be with my loved one . . . You."

"For how long?"

She shrugged. "I'm human now. Just like you."

He couldn't believe it. More relieved than he'd ever been before, he scooped her up and closed the door with his foot.

She frowned at his actions. "Where are you taking me?"

"To my bedroom where I plan on nibbling on you from the top of your head to the tips of your toes. I love you, Leta, and I intend to make sure you never doubt me."

She brushed his hair back from his eyes. "I would never doubt you, Aidan. And you will never, *ever* have a reason to doubt me."

EPILOGUE

One Year Later

Aidan smiled as he watched Leta finish decorating the tree. Her three-carat wedding ring sparkled in the candlelight—they'd gotten married on Valentine's Day. "You know it kills me that you celebrate my holidays with me when you used to be a Greek god."

Leta shrugged. "All gods and traditions deserve respect."

She was amazing and his life had been nothing short of a miracle since the moment she'd walked into it.

Her presence was breathtaking as she crossed the distance to him and handed him a small box. "For you."

He was confused by her present. "I thought we weren't exchanging gifts until midnight?"

"I know, but this has been killing me for weeks now, and if you don't open it, I might die from it."

He sucked his breath in sharply. "Don't joke about that. I've already lost you once. I'm not about to lose you again." Ripping through the paper, he found a gold foil box that he opened.

It contained a single sheet of paper that had her handwriting on it. "July twenty-third. What's July twenty-third?"

"Look under it."

He did and what he found there stole his breath. It was the sonogram of an infant. "Is this . . . ?"

She beamed. "July twenty-third."

"Oh, my God," he breathed, staring at her as it sank in. He was going to be a father. Laughing, he scooped her up and twirled around with her. "I love you, Leta. Thank you so much for my life."

"No, Aidan, thank you for reminding me of what it's like to feel again. To wake up every morning in the arms of someone who loves me."

Aidan laughed as joy raced through his entire body. He was finally the last man standing. But for the first time in his life, he wasn't standing alone. He was standing stronger than ever before because he knew he had a person at his back who would never betray him. Someone who would and had died to keep him safe.

Life truly never got any better than this.

"Merry Christmas, Aidan."

"Merry Christmas, Leta . . . and baby."

HOLIDAY
GATHERINGS

New Orleans
Sanctuary Bar
Christmas 2007

Aimee Peltier paused as she watched the gathering around her. This was the one day a year when Sanctuary officially closed. Even though very few members of their extended family and staff were Christian, they still took time to honor the holiday. To remember their own beliefs and to think back on those they'd loved and lost.

As the bar's name implied, this was the haven for were-animals, shapeshifters who were hunted by each other and by the humans. Her parents had set up the bar over a hundred years ago after Aimee's older brothers had been killed in the senseless war that divided her people from each other.

It had been her mother's solemn vow that no other mother would ever weep over the loss of a child if she could help it. But since then, her mother's view of what was right and what was wrong had shifted a bit. And in order to keep the peace here at the bar, her mother had made decisions that Aimee didn't always agree with.

But then mother–daughter disagreements were even older than the were-animals themselves.

The bar was dim, lit only by candles. Her brother Dev was at the counter, pouring drinks. He'd pulled his long, curly blond hair back into a ponytail while he joked with Colt and Angel, who were in human form, sitting on the stools in front of the bar, drinking beers.

Aimee's mother, Nicolette, was off to the side in human form as she played with Zar's bear cubs. There were several tigers, a jaguar, and bears lounging about or playfully fighting while others were in their human forms as they played cards, pool, or just hung out for the night.

"You feeling okay?"

She turned at the deep voice behind her to find Maxis standing there. Tall and gorgeous, he had dark blond hair and silvery-green eyes that shimmered in the dim light. Stunned, she had to blink twice just to make sure she wasn't imagining his presence. Maxis had come to Sanctuary severely wounded. One of the rare dragon Katagaria, he didn't mix with other groups easily. He preferred to stay isolated in the attic where he could sleep in dragon form and not be disturbed.

"What are you doing downstairs?"

Max folded his arms over his chest. "I felt your pain and was wondering what caused it."

His concern touched her deeply. It was true, watching the family around her made her ache for the one thing she wanted most.

Fang Kattalakis. A wolf who'd been half dead, he'd been brought here by his brother, and Aimee had nursed him back to health the same way she had Max. But unlike with Max, she'd fallen in love with Fang even though she knew there was no chance of there ever being anything between them.

If only she could convince her heart of that.

She offered Max a smile she knew was fake. "I'm okay."

"You're not okay, Aimee. You haven't been okay since the night Fang left."

She glanced about nervously. "Please keep your voice down . . ."

"Is this better?"

She could only hear his voice in her head. Nodding, she patted his arm. *"I'll be fine, Max. Thank you for your concern, but you know me."*

"I do know you, Aimee. And I know that solitude is a dungeon of spikes that pierces every layer of armor you try to build for it." He held his hand up so that she could see the tattoo he'd placed there in remembrance of his family. *"I lost what meant most to me. Don't make the same mistake."*

"But Fang and I aren't mates. There are no marks . . ."

"Neither were there marks for us. And still my

heart is broken. Don't let the Fates rule your life. Sometimes we have to take responsibility for it ourselves."

He stepped back and swept his gaze around the others. "I don't like being here with these people and animals. I'm going to retire, but remember, courage is doing what we know is dangerous. It's risking our safety for a chance at something better. Don't let your fears shape your reality because no matter how cautious you are, someone or something always sneaks in the back door to manifest that fear. Better to face it and defeat it than to let it attack you unawares."

Before she could comment, he vanished.

Aimee stood there as she considered his words. He was right, but knowing something and acting on it were two entirely different things.

"What did he want?"

She hesitated at her father's question. Over seven feet in height, her father intimidated almost everyone who saw him. But not her. As his only daughter, Aimee knew he'd never harm her. "He was wishing me a Happy Holiday."

Her father smiled before he pulled her against him and kissed the top of her head. "You attract the strangest creatures."

"Is that such a bad thing?" She looked meaningfully at her brothers.

Her father laughed.

But his laughter didn't ease her. "Papa? Can I ask you something?"

He narrowed his gaze on her. "I'm not sure I like that tone of voice, but you can try."

Before she spoke, she glanced to where her mother played with the cubs. "Had you not been fated for Maman, would you have still stayed with her?"

His gaze turned dark. "Why do you ask?"

"Curiosity."

His expression hardened and she could see that her response didn't appease him. "Don't lie to me, Aimee. I can smell it on your skin. You're thinking of that wolf, aren't you?"

She looked away, unable to answer him. Not that he didn't already know.

Her father's eyes snapped fire at her. "He is not our kind."

And in her mind that changed nothing. "I know that, Papa. I tell it to myself every day."

"If you leave us for him, I don't know if Nicolette could handle it. Your mother can be harsh, but she does love you and she only wants what's best for all of us."

"I know."

He leaned down to whisper in her ear. "But this is your life, *ma petite coeur*. I will always be here for you."

Aimee closed her eyes as those words eased her heart. "Thank you, Papa. I love you."

"I love you, too. Now smile and join the party." He left her to speak to her brother Serre while Aimee felt suddenly out of place and she didn't know why. This was her home. These were her people and family, and yet . . .

She'd never experienced anything like this before and it made her ache.

"You okay, sis?"

She nodded at her brother Kyle as he paused by her side. "I have a headache starting."

"You want me to get something for you?"

She smiled at his youthful face. He was the most precious of all her siblings. "It's okay, baby. I think I'm going to lie down for a few minutes. Tell Maman that I'll be back down shortly."

"Okay."

She squeezed his arm before she made her way from the bar through the door that connected this building to the house where they all lived. It was eerily silent with everyone in the bar. This was the only time when the house was truly quiet.

Aimee made her way up to her room.

Pushing open the door, she paused as she caught a familiar scent.

Fang.

Her heart pounded as she slammed the door shut to look for him. But he wasn't here. She wanted to cry . . . at least until she realized his scent was still strong by her dresser.

She looked underneath a pile of papers to find a small box. Lifting it up, she inhaled the scent that was uniquely Fang's. How she missed him. Her eyes tearing, she unwrapped the gift and opened the box to find a small locket. It had a bear claw engraved around a diamond on the front. On the back was the paw of a wolf. But it was what was inside it that made her tears fall.

It was a piece of his fur. Aimee sobbed at the sight of it. Animals didn't give out things like this. With this fur, an enemy could track him through time.

But he trusted her enough to let her have it. Nothing had ever touched her more.

Her hand trembling, she closed the locket and hung it around her neck. The long chain fell down between her breasts, and she tucked it into her bra so that she could keep it as close as possible to her heart and keep it out of the sight of others.

As she reached for the box, she realized there was a note in the bottom. Unfolding it, she smiled at a typical Fang comment.

Miss you.

No "I love you." Nothing sappy or romantic. Just a short, clear truth.

"I miss you, too," she breathed, trying to stop the tears that fell. And it was then she looked up to see the remnant of a hand print on her mirror.

Fang's.

Aimee held her hand up to it, placing her palm

against the imprint of his. "One day, Fang. One day . . ."

Fang blinked as he watched Aimee through the window. In wolf form, he was able to hide himself against the darkening sky. He wanted to hold her so badly, but he knew better than to try. His mere presence jeopardized her.

"One day, Aimee . . ."

His heart breaking, he backed away and padded across the roof until there was enough distance between them that he could change over to human form, flash into the clothes he'd been wearing, and climb down. He made his way to where he'd left his Suzuki GSX-R. He pulled his helmet on before he started the Jixer and headed home for the night.

It was so hard to be with his family when what he really wanted was Aimee. His brother Vane was a lucky wolf. His human mate, Bride, had accepted him, and the Fates had decreed them as partners for life.

If only a wolf could mate with a bear.

Sighing, Fang parked his bike and entered the house through the back door.

Bride had decked out the entire house for the Christmas holiday. There were bells, holly, and poinsettias everywhere. He heard laughter coming from the living room as he dropped his keys on the counter.

His brother Fury paused in the doorway. He cocked his head before he made a wolf sound in the back of his throat. "You better wash the bear off you before you get near Vane. You go in there smelling like that and he'll skin your ass raw."

Fang started to tell him what he could do with his warning. The last thing he wanted was to remove Aimee's scent from him, but it was Christmas.

Time for peace and family.

"I'll be down in a few minutes."

Fury nodded as he watched Fang head for the back staircase. He felt so bad for his brother. If he could, he'd hand Aimee over to him, but it wasn't meant to be. The bears would never tolerate their only daughter mating with a wolf. It just wasn't done. And if the Fates didn't decree it . . .

Man, it must suck.

"Fury?"

He turned to see Maggie coming down the hallway to join him in the kitchen. "You need a hand?" she asked.

"Nah," he said, heading for the fridge. "I was just getting some water. I don't like to drink that human stuff. It screws with me and I don't think you want your dad to see me flash into wolf form while he's here." Her father had no idea that he was surrounded by animals that were taking human form to placate Maggie and Bride's families. "My luck, I'd be so drunk I'd piss on his leg."

Maggie's mate, Wren, laughed as he joined them. "For that, I might pay you."

Maggie elbowed her mate in the stomach. "You promised me you'd behave."

"I'm behaving. But if Fury happens to piss on your dad . . ."

"Wren!"

He held his hands up in surrender before he gave her a wink.

"You are all so evil."

Wren only smiled as he grabbed water from the fridge before they returned to the living room where Bride's family was singing Christmas carols. Bride sat on the couch with her son in her lap while Vane sat on the floor, holding her hand as he cringed a bit from the disharmony of the a capella song.

Fury felt a deep need to howl, but the sharp look from Vane kept his jaw locked shut. He caught Fang's gaze as his brother rejoined them. His dark hair was still wet from his quick shower.

Sniffing, Fang made a very wolf-like cringe as his nose was assailed by the human scents around them. It was hard whenever there were this many around. But they'd become masters at blending in.

Sometimes.

Fury walked over and handed him a bottle of water. "Merry Christmas, brother."

Fang nodded before he unscrewed the top and took a drink. But even so, Fury saw the longing on his brother's face and wondered what was worse. Knowing what he wanted and not being able to claim it or to be like him and have no idea if he'd ever find someone who could tolerate him . . .

New Orleans
Hunter Household

Kyrian Hunter looked around at his friends and family who were gathered for Christmas dinner. His son, Nicky, and daughter, Marissa, were playing under the tree with his mother-in-law while his best friend, Julian, and his wife Grace were helping their kids open the last of their presents.

His wife's family, the Devereaux clan, were all here, laughing and celebrating.

He had to be the luckiest bastard on the planet. It seemed like only yesterday he'd been alone in the world with no one to love. No one who cared about him.

And one night a lethal enemy had almost taken the very people who were now crowded into his home.

His sister-in-law, Tabitha, stood up and clanked her glass to get everyone's attention. "Sorry to interrupt, but I wanted to take a second and say Merry Christmas to all of you."

A shout went up, but Tabitha motioned them to

silence. "You know, my Romanian grandmother always said that enemies and lovers make strange bedfellows."

Kyrian met Valerius's gaze over Tabitha's head. The two of them had spent centuries hating one another. But for the sake of their wives who were twin sisters, they'd buried the ax—just not in Valerius's head as Kyrian had wanted. He raised his glass in a silent toast to Valerius who returned the gesture before his gaze went to his brother, Zarek, who was holding hands with his wife, Astrid. Like Kyrian, Zarek had spent eternity hating Valerius, too.

Now the brothers were reunited.

Miracles did happen. The people in this room were living proof.

"To family," Tabitha said, holding up her glass. "And to those we've lost, but who we still hold in our hearts, I'd like to propose a moment of silence for them . . ."

Everyone bowed their heads in respect.

But it wasn't sadness Kyrian felt, it was gratitude that all of them were here tonight, alive and well.

He lifted his head at the same time Talon and Sunshine did. Kyrian smiled at them, remembering a time when he and Talon had been the only two Dark-Hunters to patrol New Orleans. Boy, how things had changed from that fateful day when he'd awakened handcuffed to his wife, Amanda.

And thank the gods for it.

* * *

Nick stepped back from the window as he watched the group inside lifting their heads from prayer. He placed his hand against the window and remembered Christmases past when he and his mother had been in Kyrian's house, celebrating.

Every year his mother had demanded he attend midnight mass with her. Every year until she'd been brutally murdered.

Now Nick had no one.

You could tell them. Kyrian and Amanda would welcome him back. But he couldn't allow them to. He'd sold his soul to the devil for vengeance and whatever he saw, Stryker saw.

And Stryker wanted Kyrian's daughter.

No matter how much Nick might hate Acheron for allowing his mother to die, he couldn't let Kyrian suffer. He owed Kyrian too much for that.

Closing his eyes, Nick turned away from them and pulled his collar up higher on his neck to block the chill. There really should be some kind of do-over for mistakes. But there wasn't. Life was cold, and it was brutal.

For him, there could never be forgiveness. There was no way back to the life he'd once had.

No way back to the mother he'd once loved more than his own life. He'd screwed everything up royally.

His heart broken, Nick left Kyrian's home and crossed the street to where he'd parked his Jag. After getting inside, Nick paused to stare at Kyrian's house. The red and white lights sparkled in the night and he could hear the laughter that came from the party inside.

"Merry Christmas," he breathed before he started his car and drove it over to the St. Louis Cemetery on Basin Street. He parked at the gas station across from it and crossed the empty street until he was at the locked gates. Nick looked to his right and then his left before he leapt to the top of the ten-foot wall and then jumped to the ground inside.

It was pitch black, but as a Dark-Hunter, he could see better at night than in full daylight. He ignored the hungry souls that reached out for him as he made his way to his mother's tomb. Because of his ties to Stryker, he was immune from possession by their souls.

Nick parted his coat and pulled out the roses he'd brought for her. Shattered by the tragedy of his life, he knelt down before her tomb and placed his forehead against the cold stone. "I miss you, Mom. And I'm sorry."

And there in the darkness for the merest sliver of a moment, he thought he could feel her presence. But he knew better. She was as lost as he was.

Falling to his knees, Nick curled up against the

tomb and squeezed his eyes shut as overwhelming grief racked him.

Stryker rolled his eyes as he saw the image of Nick at his mother's grave in his mind. "Why did I make him my servant again?"

His sister, Satara, looked up from her corner. "What?"

Stryker sighed as he shifted himself on his throne. "Your pet. He's whining again. Go get him."

Satara let out a loud sound of disgust. "Why don't you kill him already?"

Stryker considered it. "Because he will be my tool to kill Acheron. Trust me."

"Trust you . . ." She blew him a raspberry. She lifted her hand to form a ball so that she could see Nick. "Oh, just leave him. Let him wallow in his grief. The more he feels her loss, the better for us."

Perhaps his sister was right.

Even so, watching Nick with his mother reminded Stryker of the loss he'd once suffered, and it pained him to see Nick grieve like that. But more than his loss, he thought of his own son.

Urian.

The pain of his son's death still burned deep inside him, and it made him hate the goddess he served who had demanded he kill his own child.

"One day, Apollymi, I will serve to you what you have served to me." And he would laugh while she cried over the death of her precious Acheron.

Katoteros

Ash smiled as he watched his daughter, Simi, and her sister, Xirena, opening presents. Dressed in a Goth Santa's Helper dress, Simi had red and black hair. Her demon's wings were a matching red, and they fluttered while she unwrapped a large box.

Xirena's hair was blond, and she was dressed in dark green and gold.

Suddenly, Simi squealed in delight. "BEGoth dolls!" She beamed at Acheron as she ripped open the box for her Slayer Storm doll and set it next to her Pandora doll. "Akri, you spoil your Simi and she loves her akri. Thank you!"

Xirena let out a similar noise as she opened her gifts to find a collection of Voodoo Babies. She turned to Ash's servant, Alexion. "Oh akri, you know what your demon likes. Thank you."

Danger leaned against Ash's back to whisper up in his ear. "What do you think they'll do when they open their Tokidoki bags?"

A shrill, piercing scream answered her question. Ash actually cringed. "I think I've lost all hearing."

Alexion snorted. "I think we just lost some glass in the windows."

Danger rolled her eyes at her husband before she left Ash's side to put her arm around Alexion's waist. "Shouldn't you see about replacing it then?"

"I don't—" Alexion paused as if he suddenly caught her meaning. "Um, yeah, I think I should." He looked at Ash. "If you'll excuse me . . ."

Ash didn't have time to answer before the two of them vanished.

Simi frowned. "Where are they going?"

"Sweaty human sex," Xirena answered before she ate one of the plastic qees for her handbag.

Ash cringed at Xirena's comment which was most likely true. "Xirena, do you mind?"

She looked up innocently. "What? It's what they're going to do. It's what they always do. All that huffing and—"

"Xirena, please!"

Simi let out a long-suffering sigh as she caught her sister's attention. "It's not you, Xirena. Akri afraid his Simi is going to find another human to have sex with."

Xirena made a strange demon noise. "I keep telling you, you need to let me introduce you to some of my demon friends. They have a lot more stamina than them humans do. They can go for days without pausing. And they're so much better-looking. No man turns blue when—"

Ash stood up. "Lady-demons? Do you mind? I'd really like to change this subject."

Simi huffed. "Listen to him. You'd think akri had never had sex before the way he carries on, which the Simi knows is definitely not true. Akri has more sex than any ten sweaty humans you can name."

"Simi! Mercy, please." The last thing he wanted was to have open sex talks with his daughter.

Ash paused as a sudden idea hit him. He snapped his fingers. QVC came onto the TV, and the demons immediately flashed themselves to the monitors.

Thank the gods he knew at least one thing that could distract them. He let out a relieved breath as they stretched out on the floor and manifested cell phones so they could begin ordering.

"Having demon troubles?"

Ash froze as he heard his brother's voice behind him. Alexion had warned him that he'd allowed Styxx to cross over to their side of Katoteros for the holiday.

Even so, it irked him.

Ash turned around to face the one person who was an almost-identical copy to him. The only difference was their eyes. Styxx's were a vibrant blue while Ash's were a swirling silver. "I thought you'd pass on this. It's not exactly your holiday."

Styxx looked at the Christmas tree in the corner

of Ash's throne room—half the ornaments were missing since the demons had decided to snack on them earlier in the evening. "Never thought I'd see something like that in the hall of the Atlantean gods. You think a lot of your family, don't you?"

Ash hesitated. As a human, he'd once begged his brother to love him. At the very least, acknowledge him as family. And every time he'd reached out for Styxx, Styxx had brutally slapped him away.

Now the tables were turned, and Styxx was the one reaching for him. His instinct was to return the favor.

But Ash refused to be like that . . . at least today.

"It took me a long time to have a family that would claim me."

Styxx sighed. "I'm never going to be able to prove myself to you, am I?"

"How many times have you tried to kill me now?"

Styxx placed his hand on Ash's shoulder and gave him a sincere stare. "I've apologized for that."

"And I've accepted your apology."

"But you don't trust me."

"Would you?"

Styxx looked away as he removed his hand from Ash's shoulder, and Ash felt sorry for the hurt in his brother's gaze. He wanted to trust his brother, but it wasn't that simple. Centuries of betrayal separated them.

"Look, we're taking this slowly, Styxx. Give me time."

Styxx nodded. "At least you're not throwing me out on the street naked, huh?"

Ash went ramrod-stiff at the callous words and the memory that tore through him of the day Styxx and their father had done that to him.

Styxx looked horrified as he realized what he'd inadvertently said. "Oh gods, Acheron. I forgot. I'm so sorry."

That was why there was still a wedge between them. Styxx had forgotten an event that had left an indelible scar on Ash's soul. It was one of abject humiliation and bitterness.

And it made Ash want to put his brother through the wall behind him. He had the powers to do it without making a move.

So easy . . .

But he refrained for the time being. "What are you doing here, Styxx?"

"I don't like being alone all the time."

When Ash spoke, he made sure there was no emotion whatsoever in his voice. "Yeah, it really sucks to be alone, especially on days of celebration."

Styxx flinched. "I was stupid, Acheron. Please, give me another chance."

"You want me to throw him out?"

Ash looked past Styxx's shoulder to see Urian approaching them. Tall and lithe, Urian had white blond hair that he normally wore tied back in a queue. Since the day Urian's father, Stryker, had cut his throat and left him for dead, Urian had lived here with Ash, Simi, and Alexion.

"It's all right, Urian. I have it."

"You sure? It's been a whole day since I last killed someone, and I'm getting antsy."

Styxx turned a menacing glare on him. "You can't kill me. If you do, Acheron dies."

Urian tsked. "Nice try, but I know better. The tie only works in reverse. I kill Ash, you die. I kill you, it's just another day to rejoice."

Ash shook his head. "I thought you were spending the holiday with Wulf and Cassandra."

"I was, but then Cassandra got all weepy-eyed over the holiday and I couldn't take it."

In spite of his harsh words, Ash felt the grief Urian still carried over his dead wife, Phoebe. She'd been Cassandra's sister, and no doubt that was what had made Cassandra so sad on this day.

"It's still your day off."

Urian shrugged. "I hate days off. They're such a waste. Hell, there aren't even any Daimons out and about. They're all holed up as if there's some kind of truce or something."

"Don't worry. They'll be out in force for New Year's."

Urian looked hopeful. "Flash me forward in time, Ash. I want to start cleaning house."

"You know I can't do that."

Urian scoffed. "You mean you won't. We both know you can."

"Just because you can—"

"Doesn't mean you should." Urian shook his head. "I really wish you'd get another saying. That one is lame." Urian swaggered over to the demons and plopped down on the floor between them. "Any chance we can watch a horror movie?"

Simi lifted her head to look at him. "Is there any where the demons win?"

"Not really."

"Then pooh on them. I'd rather shop."

Urian grimaced. "I'd rather have my eyes gouged out."

Simi arched a brow. "If I do that, can the Simi eat them?"

Xirena pulled a bottle of barbecue sauce out of her purse. "You have to share if you do."

Urian whimpered in feigned pain.

Ash paid them no attention as he started away from Styxx.

Styxx took his arm and pulled him to a stop. "You can't ignore me forever, brother."

"True," Ash agreed. "But I can ignore you for now." And with that, he snapped his fingers and left Katoteros to visit Olympus.

Normally, he'd be like Urian and would rather

have his eyes gouged out than be here. Today, however, it was different.

He opened the doors from the balcony of Artemis's temple to find his daughter, Kat, visiting her mother in the main room. Kat sat on the cushioned throne with her long, blond hair gleaming. Her husband, Sin, stood behind her with one hand possessively on her shoulder while Artemis glared at him. Her long, wavy red hair fell around her body, and Ash could tell she was one step away from blasting Sin out of her temple.

"Did I miss something?" Ash asked as he joined them.

Artemis turned on him with a hiss. "Kill Sin already."

"I would, but I think Kat would miss him."

"Like I care?"

"Matisera!" Kat said, placing her hand on her distended belly. "Be nice. He is the father of your grandchild."

Artemis let out a squeal of pain before she flashed out of the room.

"Grandma, grandma, grandma," Sin said in a very infantile manner.

Ash gave him a droll stare. "Is that really necessary?"

Sin laughed. "Absolutely, and don't pretend for even an instant that you're not loving every minute of it."

Ash couldn't resist smiling. "Not every *single* minute."

Kat rolled her eyes at them. "You two are rotten."

Joining the laughter, Ash moved forward to take Kat's hand, and as he did so, he caught a bright flash of something in his mind.

He gasped.

"Solren?" Kat asked, using the Atlantean term for father. "Is something wrong?"

Ash couldn't speak as a strange feeling overcame him. There was something . . . something . . .

No, it was someone, he realized, and it was casting a dire pall over everything. He looked at Kat as he tried his best to home in on it.

It was no use. Whatever it was, it was gone now. But even so, it left behind a rift.

Something was coming for him.

And it was going to change him forever . . .

SANTA WEARS SPURS

PROLOGUE

Danger. O'Connell felt it on the back of his neck and deep in his bones as he raced his pinto across the dead winter Texas plains toward a town he'd never known existed.

After all this time, he ought to be used to danger. He had lived his life under its constant stalking shadow, and kept it as his faithful companion. Danger was his ally and his enemy.

It defined everything about him. There had only been one time in his life when he had felt safe. But that was a long time ago.

It was biting cold out, not that he felt it much. His thrumming blood kept him warm as he rode through the night.

"You should have been there, Kid. It was like taking candy from a baby." Pete had laughed. "Hah, now that I think about it, I *did* take candy from a baby. I just wish I could see their faces when they wake up and find their money gone."

Then as now, O'Connell hadn't found the words amusing. He knew Pete could be as cold-blooded as they came—the bullet wound in his arm was testimony to that. But not even *he* had thought Pete would steal from an orphanage just two days before Christmas.

The man had no soul.

There was a time when O'Connell had been just the same. When hatred had strangled his heart and left him unable to feel for anyone save himself.

And then he'd met *her*.

His heart lurched, just as it always did when he thought of her. She had shown him another way, another life, and had changed everything about him in the process. She'd given him hope, a future. A reason to live. And life without her had been nothing more than a bitter hell.

In all honesty, he didn't know how he managed to make it through the endless, miserable days that had turned into years.

Somehow, he just survived. Cold. Empty.

Alone.

God, how he missed her. How he ached for some way to go back and relive just one second of the time he'd shared with her. Just to see her face one more time, feel her breath on his skin.

For a moment, O'Connell let his thoughts drift to the past. And like they always did when he was unguarded, they went to a remembered dream of long dark brown hair and eyes as clear and warm as a summer's day. Of a woman who had told him she loved him without making a single sound.

Closing his eyes, he saw her bright smile and heard the music of her laughter as she lay naked beneath him while he claimed her for his own. He clenched his teeth at the white-hot desire that coiled through his belly. And for a moment he swore he could still feel her hands against his back as she held him tight and cried out in ecstasy.

Not even five years could dull the memories. Or his craving for her touch. He could taste the salty sweetness of her body, feel her hot and tight around him, and smell the sunshine that had always seemed to be in her hair.

Catherine had touched him in ways no one had before or since.

"I remember you," he breathed. But most of all he remembered the promise he had made to her. The promise he had broken. And in that moment, he wished Pete's bullet had gone straight through his useless heart.

Lord above, if there was one last wish he could have, it would be to set things right. He'd sell whatever was left of his blackened soul for a way to go back and change what he'd done to her.

But it wasn't to be.

He knew that.

There was nothing left for him to do except see

the money back to the orphans Pete had stolen it from.

After that, he didn't know where he'd go. He'd have to find another place where the law and Pete couldn't find him. *If* such a place existed.

Briefly, he considered trying to find *her*. After all, she had been his safe harbor. His greatest strength.

But then, she had also been his greatest weakness.

No, it wouldn't do to seek her out. Too much depended on him staying away from her. Because one thing his brother, Pete, had taught him years ago—there was no such thing as a second chance.

1

"All I want for Christmas is a man as handsome as the Devil himself. One with a charming smile, at least some semblance of intelligence, and a great, *big,* bulging—"

"Rebecca Baker!" Catherine O'Callahan gasped, shocked at her friend's words.

"Bank account," Rebecca said as she dropped her hands down from the graphic illustration she had been providing. She picked up the frying pan near Catherine, then placed it on top of the black iron stove. "I was only going to say *bank account.*"

Trying not to smile lest she encourage her friend's libidinous conversation, Catherine looked askance at Rebecca as she continued washing dishes.

Rebecca's olive cheeks colored ever so slightly as she walked back to the sink. "Well, maybe I wasn't. *But* as a married woman yourself, you know what I mean. How long am I supposed to go around mourning Clancy anyway? Good grief, it's been almost four years since he died. And I barely knew him before we married."

As was her habit, Rebecca gestured dramatically with her hands to illustrate her next words. "My father practically dragged me to the altar to marry a man almost twice my age. I tell you, snuggling up to a man whose hands and feet are colder than icicles in January isn't my idea of wedded bliss."

Catherine could well agree with that point.

Rebecca sighed dreamily as she idly put the plates on the shelf above her head. "What I'd like to have is a gorgeous, *warm* man I could be cow-tied to forever. A man who could enter the room and make me all hot, and cold, and all jittery." She looked at Catherine and smiled. "Know what I mean?"

Blushing, Catherine grew quiet as she rinsed a large black pot. She knew *exactly* what Rebecca meant. She'd lain awake many a night as memories washed over her of a pewter-eyed demon who had promised her everything, including the moon above.

A man who had made her body so hot there had been times when she was certain she'd perish in flames.

But unlike her friend, she wasn't a widow. For all she knew, her husband could come waltzing up to the front door at any time and knock on it.

As if *that* would ever happen, Catherine chided herself.

When would she give up her useless, unwavering

hope of seeing him again? Why couldn't she just put him out her mind?

What was it about him that made her yearn for him after all this time?

Of course, she knew the answer to that question—everything about him. He'd been so wonderful and kind, considerate and giving. Up until the day he left her without so much as a by-your-leave.

She must be insane to still yearn for him.

And after five years, he *might* be dead. Heaven knew, a lot had happened to her since he'd run off. She'd moved to a new town, started her own restaurant and boardinghouse, and created a respectable life for her and her four-year-old daughter, Diana.

Last summer, after the yellow fever epidemic, she and Rebecca had taken in five of the town of Redwood's orphans.

A *lot* had happened.

Rebecca sidled up to her and took the pot from her hands to dry it. "So, tell me, if not a gorgeous St. Nick to come knocking on the door, what *do* you want for Christmas?"

"Oh, I don't know," Catherine said as she reached to wash a pan. "I guess if I had my druthers, I'd like for our money to be returned. It bothers me that someone would steal from the children right before Christmas."

Rebecca agreed. "I know how much you wanted to spend it on them. It's such a shame. I can't imagine what kind of monster could so something so terrible."

Neither did she.

They didn't speak for a few minutes. Only the sound of sloshing water and clanging dishes broke the silence as they worked.

All of a sudden, the hair on the back of Catherine's neck stood up. Turning her head, she saw Rebecca staring at her.

"What?" she asked.

"Is that really all you want for Christmas?"

Catherine handed her another pan to dry. "Why, yes. I'm quite happy with everything else."

Rebecca arched a questioning brow.

"I am," Catherine insisted.

"Methinks the lady doth protest too much," Rebecca said, putting the pan away. "Can you truly tell me that you haven't once given thought to having a handsome man come sweep you off your feet?"

Catherine laughed halfheartedly. "I already had that happen, and I must say I found the experience less than desirable."

Rebecca shook her head. "You know, I came to work here almost four years ago and never in that time have I heard you speak of your husband. That is who you're talking about, isn't it?"

Catherine nodded, refusing to meet Rebecca's inquisitive brown-eyed stare as she moved to pump more water into the sink. "There isn't much to tell."

Rebecca nudged her away from the pump and took up the motion. "Come on, Catherine. All the children are in bed for the night. Why not open up a little?"

Catherine buried her hands back in the suds and sighed. "What do you want me to tell you? Plain preacher's daughter fell in love with the gorgeous stranger who came to work for her father's ranch? He married her a month after they first met, took her off to Nevada, and left her the first chance he got."

"That's it?"

"That's it."

Rebecca paused. Her brown eyes darkened in anger. "I'll never understand a man who could do something so cold-blooded or mean."

"Me either," she whispered under her breath.

"I don't see how you stand it."

Catherine shrugged. "I got used to it. Five years gave me time to lay aside my hatred. Besides, I have Diana to think about. I'm the only parent she has and I decided on the day she was born that I would never mention his name or dwell on what he did to us."

"Well, I respect you for that. Me, I wouldn't have rested until I found the polecat and skinned him alive."

Catherine relished the image of her husband's tawny skin being flayed from him as he screamed for mercy. Now that Rebecca mentioned it, she did rather enjoy the thought of him being skinned. It would certainly serve him right. "You know, I do want something after all."

"And that is?"

Catherine scrubbed her pot with renewed vigor, wishing it were her husband's head she held beneath the water. "I wish I could lay eyes on him one last time to tell him what a no-good, lousy, rabid dog he was for leaving me."

"That's my girl." Rebecca laughed as she patted Catherine on the back. Then, she leaned forward and said in a low tone, "But the real question is, was he any good where and when it counted?"

"Rebecca!" Catherine gasped, trying her best not to think about just how good he had been *there*.

Though why Rebecca's words continued to shock her after all these years of knowing her, she couldn't imagine. Rebecca had never had an ounce of shame in her.

But then, it was her outspokenness Catherine liked most of all. She always knew where she stood with Rebecca. Her friend never held *anything* back. And after having lived with her husband and his secrets, she found Rebecca's candor a true blessing.

Suddenly a knock sounded on the door.

Catherine wrung the suds off her hands, then wiped her hands dry on her apron. "Why don't you go on to bed?" she said, rolling her sleeves back down her forearms and buttoning them against her wrists. "I'll get the door. I'm sure it's just someone needing a room."

"Poor soul to be out on Christmas Eve without a bed," Rebecca said. She inclined her head to the sink. "You sure you don't want me to finish up the dishes?"

Catherine shook her head. "There are only a handful left, and we already have all the gifts under the tree. Why don't you just go and enjoy what's left of Christmas Eve?"

"All right, then. I'll look in on the kids and then retire. Let me know if you need me."

"I will."

Rebecca headed to the back stairs while Catherine took the lantern off the kitchen table and walked down the narrow hallway to the front door.

Through the lace curtains, she could see the outline of a tall man with broad shoulders.

A smile twitched at the corners of her mouth. Perhaps Rebecca would get her wish after all.

Rolling her eyes at the very indecent thought that flicked across her mind, Catherine opened the door.

She took one glance at the handsome stranger, who had his head turned to look at his horse, and dropped the lantern straight to the floor.

O'Connell cursed as the lantern's fire exploded on the pine boards of the porch. Reacting without thought, he dropped his black Stetson and saddlebags, and stamped at the flames, his spurs jingling loudly as he stomped. Then, to his chagrin, the flames spread to his boots and set fire to the toes of his left foot.

He hissed in pain as he whipped his black duster off and put out the fire on his smoking boot. Then he quickly used the duster to extinguish the rest of the fire.

Luckily, the fire didn't do much in the way of permanent damage, but the porch and door would need a good washing come morning.

"Good Lord, woman," he snapped as he surveyed the damage. "You ought to be more . . ." his words trailed off as he looked up and met wide, startled brown eyes.

His jaw went slack. Those were the same eyes he'd been dreaming of not more than a few minutes before.

"Catherine?" he whispered in disbelief.

Catherine couldn't move as she stared into the handsome, devilish face that had coaxed her away from everything she had ever known.

Ask and ye shall receive, her father's favorite phrase, echoed in her head.

Stunned by his sudden appearance, she took his form in all at once. He was still as handsome as sin. His dark brown hair was short in back with long bangs that draped becomingly into eyes so silvery gray they appeared almost colorless.

Captivating and searing, his eyes could haunt a woman night and day. And she ought to know, since they'd done nothing but torment her since the moment she had first seen them.

That same air of danger still clung to him, seducing her, wooing her. Oh, but he was a man to make any woman's heart pound.

His face had grown thinner over the years, adding sharp, angular planes to it. But they in no way detracted from the perfection of his patrician features. Dark brows contrasted sharply with his silver-gray eyes, and his broad nose still had the tiny bump in the center where she'd broken it.

Glory, but he was scrumptious. Completely and utterly scrumptious, like a rare treat of succulent chocolate after a long abstinence.

He'd always possessed a powerful, compelling, masculine aura that was downright salacious in nature. An aura that reached out and captured the attention of anything female within its mighty grasp.

And heaven only knew, she was far from immune to it.

But the Devil would move his home to Antarctica before she *ever* let him know that.

"What on earth are you doing here?" Catherine asked as she finally found her voice.

"Needing a doctor," he said sardonically, shaking his left foot.

Catherine looked down to see the charred black leather in the bright winter moonlight. A rush of embarrassment filled her.

"Why is it," he asked, "every time we meet, I end up needing a doctor?"

She lifted her chin at his playful tone. Her days of finding him amusing were long past. "Are you trying to charm me?"

Not even the dark could mask the wickedly warm look in his eyes. "And if I were?"

I'd probably end up surrendering to it.

But she had no intention of letting him know that, either. *Fool me once, shame on you. Fool me twice, shame on me.* She couldn't afford to let him break her heart again. The first time had been painful enough. And in truth, she wasn't sure if she could survive losing him again.

Instead, she sought to protect herself by putting an end to whatever thoughts might be playing through his mind.

"I'm not a girl anymore, Mr. O'Callahan. I no longer dance to your tune."

O'Connell took a deep breath as he sized her up. He'd almost forgotten his old alias. But the cold tone of her voice chilled him more than the winter wind at his back.

Still, it did nothing to daunt the fire in his gut that her presence stirred. She looked even better than he remembered. Gone was the willow-thin frame of her youth and in its place were the luscious curves of a woman full grown.

She wore her hair in that tight bun he'd always despised. Catherine had such beautiful hair—long, thick, and wavy. He, the man who was wanted in six states, had spent hours brushing her hair at night. Running his hands through it.

And he wondered if it still smelled like springtime.

In that instant, he remembered the way he had left her. Without a word, without a note. He had simply gone off to work and had never returned.

Shame filled him. He should have at least sent a letter. Although, honestly, he had tried to write one a thousand times. But he'd never completed it. What did a man say to a woman he'd been forced to give up against his will?

Especially when he didn't want her to know the real reason he'd left?

Picking his hat up from the porch, he cast a sweeping, hungry look over her body, and wished for the millionth time, that things had been different between them. That he could have had a long life spent by her side, being the husband she deserved to have. "It's good to see you again."

Her look froze him as she untied her apron, then stooped to pick up the broken glass and place it in the cloth. "I wish I could say it's good to be seen by you, but in this case I think you'll understand if I'm a bit cool toward you?"

"Cool" was a mild term for her demeanor. In truth, he suspected icebergs at the North Pole might be a shade or two warmer.

He'd expected more anger from her. The Catherine he remembered would have been cursing him like a slow-walking dog for leaving her.

This Catherine was different. She was composed and serious, not laughing and playful.

Passionate, he realized with a start. That was what was missing. She'd lost the verve that used to have her laughing one minute, sobbing the next, and then kissing him blind two seconds after that.

And without a doubt he knew he was to blame for it. Being abandoned had a way of affecting a person adversely. His gut drew tight. He had a lot to answer for in his life. He just wished she wasn't one of those things he'd messed up.

"Where's your anger?" he asked as he leaned over to help her pick up the mess.

Catherine considered her answer. She should be enraged at him, but oddly enough, once the initial shock of the encounter wore off she found herself completely numb to him.

Well, not completely numb.

In fact, "numb" described his effect on her like "handsome" described Abe Lincoln.

A woman would have to be dead not to feel a vigorous stirring for a man so incredibly handsome as her wandering polecat. Especially a man possessed of such raw, primal appeal.

Everything about him promised sheer, sexual delights. And all too well she remembered the way he had felt in her arms, the strength of his long, lean body caressing hers in playful abandon as he sent her spiraling off into blissful ecstasy.

And right then, with his head just inches from her own, she could smell the raw, earthy scent of him. That leather and musk that had always titillated her. That warm, wonderful smell was a part of him like the innate power and authority that bled from every pore of his body.

And those lips . . .

Full and sensuous, those lips of his had kissed her until she lost all reason, until her entire body buzzed with lust and desire. And those wonderful, sensual lips had teased and tormented her body to the ultimate pinnacle of human pleasure.

Good heavens, how she ached for him. Even after the way he had hurt her.

What are you thinking?

Catherine mentally shook herself. No, she didn't hate him for leaving her the way he had—five years had given her time to lay her hatred aside.

She wouldn't get mad at this point.

She would get even.

He deserved to feel the sting of rejection. Then he

would understand exactly what he had done to her. How it felt to be denied and forgotten.

"I got over my anger for you, Mr. O'Callahan," she said tartly, rising to her feet carefully lest she cut herself on the glass in her apron.

She raked a look from the top of his head down to his still-smoking boot, took a step back into the house and spoke, "And then I got over you."

With one last stoic look at him, Catherine closed the door in his stunned face.

2

Catherine's words rang in O'Connell's ears as he stared in disbelief at the closed door.

Well, what did you expect? he asked himself as he retrieved his charred duster from the porch.

Her hatred, in all honesty. That he had been prepared for. But her apathy toward him . . .

Well . . .

It was . . . insufferable.

Anger over her rejection blistered his gut. How dare she dismiss him so? What did she think he was, some lost little puppy come to lick scraps off the floor?

Well, he wasn't a lost puppy. He was a man. A man sought by every woman who had ever laid her eyes upon him. Not that he was vain about it. Not overly so, anyway. It was merely a fact he'd long grown accustomed to. A fact everyone who knew him just plainly accepted.

Women had always been partial to him.

In Hollow Gulch where O'Connell had been

working the last few months, the women had singled him out the moment he rode into town—baked him fresh pies, batted their lashes at him. Hell, one gutsy blonde had even snuck into his room and hidden herself naked in his bed while he'd been out drinking.

Not that he had been interested in the blonde or any of the others. Unlike any normal, *sane* man, he'd sent her home as soon as he tossed some clothes on her body. And all the while she'd whispered to him the torrid, lusty things she'd do to give him pleasure.

Her salacious comments had set fire to his loins, but even so, she hadn't appealed to him in the slightest. His heart belonged to Catherine. It always had.

And he refused to sully Catherine's memory by bedding down with any other woman. That was the one vow he'd never break.

Hell, he'd given up everything he valued to see Catherine safe.

And she had banished him from her thoughts?

He saw red.

In the last five years there hadn't been an instant when he hadn't been consumed by thoughts of her. Not a minute he hadn't wondered what she was doing. *How* she was doing.

And she felt nothing toward him.

Nothing.

He didn't even warrant her hatred.

"Fine," O'Connell muttered at the closed door as he shrugged his duster on, then settled his Stetson on his head. He grimaced at the front of the brim that had been partially burned away by the fire. "I don't need you to feel anything for me, woman. I don't need you at all. In fact, I can put you right out of my mind, too."

Spinning on his heel, he took a step for his horse. Pain exploded across his foot and he cursed out loud as he limped away.

The woman had damned near maimed him. And all the while she felt nothing toward him.

Nothing. . . .

"What do you mean, you got over me?"

Catherine turned around to see *him* standing in the doorway. His face awash with shadows, she could feel his angry glare more than see it.

Go ahead and seethe, Mr. O'Callahan. Stew in your rage until your entire body becomes pruney from it.

It was terrible to take such delight in a man's misery, but delight in it she did. Catherine kept her face from betraying her glee. She'd known he couldn't resist her words. That was why she'd left the door unlocked. The last thing she wanted was for him to break it down. And knowing him, he most certainly would have done it had she tried to bar him from her house.

Come into my parlor, said the spider to the fly. He wouldn't escape her clutches until she had exacted five years of rejection from his rotten hide.

"Did you need something?" she asked coolly.

O'Connell forced the emotions from his face as he swept his hat from his head. How could she stand there so all-fired calm and dismiss him like an old shoe?

Well, he wasn't some old shoe, to be cast aside and forgotten. They had been more than merely intimate. The woman had actually touched his unrepentant soul. And after all the years he had tortured himself with guilt over his actions, she had forgotten him?

Oh, he wasn't about to leave here until he made her remember what they'd shared. Stepping into her house, he closed the door behind him.

"What do you mean, you got over me?" he asked again as he closed the short distance between them.

She shrugged casually. "It's been five years, Mr. O'Callahan."

As if *he* needed her reminder. It had been five long, gut-wrenching years of missing everything about her. Of feeling her presence, smelling her scent. Of longing to hear her voice, feel her tender caresses on his flesh.

Like an arrogant fool, he had assumed she'd missed him as well. Obviously, he'd been wrong.

Well, he wasn't going to let her know how much it bothered him. If she wanted to play this with a cool hand, he was certainly one to give it right back to her. He could hide his emotions better than anyone else alive. Indeed, how many times had that trait made her loco?

"You're right, Mrs. O'Callahan," O'Connell said in a deceptively calm voice. "It has been five long years. For the sake of old times, could you at least tell me where I might find a doctor for my foot?"

A becoming pink stained her cheeks as she glanced down to his injured member. "I'm afraid Dr. Watson died a few months back and as yet we have no replacement. But since I'm the one who burned you, I'll tend it."

"Well *it* would definitely appreciate that since it is throbbing."

And now that he mentioned it, the other *it* was throbbing, too. Especially as his gaze dipped of its own volition to her succulent breasts. His body grew even hotter and stiffer as his palm itched to caress the firm round mounds, and his mouth watered to suckle the soft pink tips until they hardened into rippled buds under his tongue.

And she felt nothing for him.

Nothing.

Stifling his growl, he vowed that that would soon change. If it was the last thing he did, he would make her remember how good they were together.

How much pleasure he could give her.

And if any other man had dared enter her bed in the last five years, the law could add the crime of murder to his wanted poster.

"If you're through ogling me," she said, "I keep my medicinal basket in the back."

"I wasn't ogling you," O'Connell muttered, unwilling to admit to her what he'd been doing.

She headed down a narrow hallway toward the back of the house. "Then please forgive me," Catherine said over her shoulder. "I guess after five years, I've forgotten what an ogle looks like."

Biting back his response, O'Connell limped his way down the narrow hallway, past the stairs. He looked around at the burgundy walls and the paintings lining the hallway. She had a beautiful home. He just wished he'd been the one to give it to her.

Even worse, a homey feel enveloped her boarding-house.

There had been a time once, long ago, when he had dreamed of having such a place to call home. And the thought of sharing such a place with Catherine had been his idea of paradise.

But fate had turned her back on him and he had long given up that delusion. He could never have a life with her. He knew that.

"Nice place you have here," he said.

"Thank you. I made the down payment on it with the money you left behind."

"See?" he said defensively as he limped. "I wasn't all bad."

"Which is why I don't hate you."

O'Connell cursed under his breath. Back to square one. That hadn't helped his case the least little bit.

He wanted her anger, her hatred. He wanted . . . no, he corrected, he *needed* her to feel something for him. Something other than apathy.

There had to be some way to stir her up.

He paused in the doorway of the kitchen as she crossed the floor to put the apron and glass in a wooden trash receptacle. "If you'll sit at the table and remove your boot, I'll be right back with the burn salve."

She disappeared into a room off the kitchen.

O'Connell crossed the floor to the table. He set his hat down on the table, shrugged off his duster, then straddled the wooden bench seat and did as she ordered.

Grimacing in pain, he removed his scorched sock. He had to admit his foot had looked better. And it had most definitely felt better.

He blew air at his throbbing toes, noting the reddish skin that was already showing signs of blistering.

Damn, but it hurt. Even more so than his nose had when she'd accidentally smacked him in the face with a broom handle because of some spider web she couldn't stand being in the corner of the room. Personally, he'd have much rather suffered the spider than the broken nose.

Being around Catherine could be quite dangerous

to one's health. Though, to be fair to her, he'd never seen her clumsy around anyone but him.

Then again, he'd never really minded her clumsiness, since she had such wonderful ways of making amends for it.

His breath caught in his throat at the memory of how she had made amends for his nose. Closing his eyes, he could still see her lowering herself down on him, feel her mouth teasing his flesh. Her teeth nibbling him all over.

And his body grew harder, hotter, until he could barely stand it.

Lord above, but she had such a sweet little mouth that tasted like honey and felt like hot silk as it slid over his flesh.

It really was true a body couldn't feel pain and pleasure simultaneously. Because when she teased his flesh with her tongue and teeth, all his pain evaporated like dew on a hot July morning.

Catherine returned to the kitchen, carrying a small wicker basket in her hand. She placed it on the table beside his hat, then leaned over to examine his foot. A stern frown drew her brows together. "Did I do all that?"

"Yes, you did," he said petulantly.

"I'm sorry," she said. "I'd best get some butter for it." As she reached for the porcelain butter jar on the table, she accidentally brushed the wicker basket off the side.

It landed straight on his injured foot.

O'Connell sucked his breath in between his teeth as pain exploded up his leg.

"I'm sorry," she repeated as she bent over to retrieve the basket.

His gaze feasted hungrily on the site of her round bottom as she fished for the basket under the table. Oh, but she had such a nice, round bottom. One that felt incredible under his hands, or against his loins.

He forgot all about his foot until she straightened, teetered ever so slightly, then grabbed his injured foot to steady herself.

This time he cursed out loud.

Color exploded across her face. "I'm—"

"Don't," he snapped, cutting her off. "I know you didn't mean to, just please give my foot time enough to recuperate before you do anything else to it."

Her cheeks darkened even more as she set the basket back on the table. "It's your own fault, you know."

"How is that?"

"You make me nervous," she confessed.

"I make *you* nervous?" he asked in disbelief. If anyone had a right to be nervous, it should be him, since he never knew what injury she might inflict on him next.

"Yes, you do. The way you sit there and stare at me like I'm some prime roast and you haven't eaten anything in a week. It's quite disconcerting, Mr. O'Callahan. If you must know."

He stopped fanning his foot and looked up at her. "Why did you never tell me that before?"

"I used to not mind the way you looked at me."

"And now?"

"I mind it and I wish you'd stop."

O'Connell locked his jaw at her words. There had to be some way to chisel away the ice around her.

Of course, he'd never in his life had to practice chiseling ice away from a woman. Women had always melted in his presence. They had only shown a token resistance before lifting their skirts to him.

Catherine had been the only one he'd ever courted. But then, she'd always been different in his book. Her shy innocence had been what captivated him. The way her smile carried all the warmth of the sun in it.

Pete had mocked him for his love of her. "The woman's as plain as yesterday's bread."

But to him, she'd always been beautiful.

Catherine leaned over him and gently spread the butter on his foot. Her light touch shook him to his core, and a thousand needles of pleasure tore through him.

In spite of himself, he smiled. Her ministrations on his foot reminded him of how they first met.

He'd just turned nineteen and had only been working for her father a few weeks. The main gate to her house had been damaged by a storm and he'd been trying to patch it when all of a sudden she had come riding up over the hill like the Devil himself was chasing her. He had barely ducked out of the way before her horse leapt over him.

The post he'd been hammering into the ground slipped sideways and as he tried to grab it, the hammer had fallen from his hand and crashed down on his toes, breaking the little one. If that hadn't been painful enough, the entire post had also fallen on him.

She had instantly turned around and come back to check on him. Even now he could see her in the dark green riding habit that had no doubt cost more than a year's worth of his pay as she helped him push the post off his legs. Without any thought to her dress, she had knelt down on the muddy ground, carefully removed his boot, and checked on his toe even while he told her not to.

She had insisted that since she broke it, she should tend it.

That had been the first time in his life anyone had ever truly been kind to him without expecting something back in return.

Later that night when she brought out a tray of steak, potatoes, and biscuits to the bunkhouse he shared with the rest of the ranch hands, he'd known he was in love.

She had looked like an angel coming through the door with that large silver tray in her hands.

And that stupid daisy she'd put on it . . . The other men had mocked him for weeks after that. But he hadn't cared.

Nothing had mattered to him, except her smile.

"You're doing it again," Catherine snapped, drawing his attention back to the present as she reached for her burn ointment. Her touch even more gentle, she spread it over his burned toes.

"Doing what?" he asked.

"Ogling me."

O'Connell smiled at her. "Do you know why I'm ogling you?"

"I can't imagine."

"Because you're still the most beautiful woman on earth."

Disbelief was etched onto her face as she straightened and looked at him. "Is that why you left me?"

"No."

"Then tell me why."

3

O'Connell barely caught himself before he spilled the truth out. Now as then, he couldn't stand the thought of her knowing what he'd been.

What he'd become.

He'd never been proud of what desperation and family obligation had led him to. He knew he should have walked away from Pete and his crazy schemes years ago. But every time he thought about hurting Pete, he remembered his childhood, when Pete had been the only thing that stood between him and starvation.

The world was a harsh, cold place for two orphans alone, and filled with unscrupulous people who would quickly take advantage of them. But Pete, who was seven years older than him, had always kept him safe.

If only Pete could let him go. Unfortunately, his big brother saw them as inseparable twins joined at the hip.

And no matter what he did to escape, his brother managed to track him down like some possessed bloodhound.

No, there was no way he could ever have her while Pete trailed him. Sooner or later, his brother would show up and use her as leverage against him—just as he'd done five years ago in Nevada.

O'Connell could only stand strong against Pete when just the two of them were involved.

Catherine made him weak. Vulnerable.

Besides, she was a good woman, with a good heart, and he would rather she think him a sorry good-for-nothing lowlife than ever learn she'd married an outlaw. No good could come of her knowing the truth.

So he answered her question with the first stupid answer that occurred to him. "I don't know."

She arched one dark brown brow at him as she lifted her gaze from his foot to his face. "You don't know?"

"It just seemed like the right thing to do," he offered as a consolation.

By the irate look on her face, he realized too late he should have just kept his mouth shut.

Catherine narrowed her eyes on him. "Why don't you just go and . . ." her voice trailed off.

He waited for her to finish.

She didn't. Instead, she stared strangely at his right arm.

"And?" he prompted.

She stepped around the bench until she rested by his side. She grabbed at the sleeve of his black shirt, and bent down to look closer at it. The contact brought her head right up under his nose. His gut wrenched. She still smelled like springtime. Her hair held that same delectable scent of fresh flowers and warmth.

And right then, all he wanted to do was lay her down on the kitchen table, lift her skirt up, and bury himself deep inside her warm body.

It took all of his willpower not to yield to that desire as the scent of her circled him, making him dizzy. Hungry. Inciting him beyond thought or reason.

A full minute passed before he realized she was staring at his blood on her hand.

"You're bleeding?" she asked.

Unwilling to explain to her that Pete had shot him as he ran off with the stolen money, he rose to his feet. "I probably should be going now."

"Sit!" The sharp tone coming from her was so unexpected and out of character that he actually obeyed.

"Take your shirt off and let me see what you've done now."

"Yes, ma'am," he murmured sarcastically as he unbuttoned his shirt and obliged her.

Catherine opened her basket, then made the mistake of glancing back to him.

His slow, languid movements captured her gaze

as those long, strong fingers of his worked the buttons through the black cambric. She had always loved those hands. The way they felt laced in hers, the pleasure and comfort they had always managed to give her.

Her throat dried at the memory.

He opened his shirt, then set to work on the buttons of his white union suit. And with every white button that opened, she saw more and more of his perfect, tawny flesh.

She had forgotten just how nerve-wracking the sight of his bare skin could be. The years had done nothing but make his muscles leaner, more defined. And all too well she remembered what it felt like to slide her hand over those taut ripples. The way his hard stomach felt sliding against her own as he held himself above her and drove her into paradise with long, luscious strokes.

Her body growing hot, it took all her concentration to force herself to reach for the makeshift bandage on his right biceps. His arm flexed seductively as her fingers brushed his skin, and a jolt of molten lust tore through her. There were few things on earth that felt better than those hard, strong biceps flexing beneath her hands.

Catherine clenched her teeth in frustration. How could he make her so breathless after what he had put her through?

Why was her body so determined to betray her?

And right then, she wished desperately for an off switch to stop the overwhelming desire coursing through her veins.

Tend his wound, tend his wound—she mentally repeated the words over and over, hoping to gain some control over herself.

I will not succumb to him!

By all that was holy, she wouldn't.

Untying his bandage, Catherine immediately saw the bullet wound. "You've been shot?"

"And can you believe it wasn't by you?"

She stiffened at his playful tone. "You're not funny."

"Not even a little?"

"I told you, Mr. O'Callahan, I'm immune to your charms."

Don't you wish! If only she could live up to those brave words.

"I wish you'd stop calling me that," he snapped at her. "I have a name and you used to use it."

She didn't dare use it right then, because if she did, she had no doubt she would be his to do with as he pleased. Just the sound of those syllables on her tongue would be enough to finish her off.

She struggled to bring herself under control. "I used to do a lot of things with you that I don't do anymore."

"Such as?"

"Use your imagination."

That silver-gray gaze dipped to her breasts, which

drew tight and heavy at his heated perusal. "Oh, I'm using it, all right. And I can *well* imagine the sound of your sighs of pleasure in my ear as I nibble the flesh of your neck. Do you remember?"

"No," she lied, her voice amazingly calm.

But in spite of her denials, she felt her body melt against the heat of that silver-gray stare. Even worse, she could smell the warm, uniquely masculine scent of him. It was all she could do not to bury her face in the crook of his neck and inhale the intoxicating scent.

Tend his wound, tend his wound! She forced herself to concentrate on the task at hand.

"Is the bullet still in there?" she asked as she examined the hole in his arm.

"Woman," he said huskily, his gaze never leaving her breasts, "right now I have a loaded gun just waiting to . . ." his voice trailed off.

He finally looked up and met her gaze, but she couldn't read anything in the smoldering depths of his eyes except the raw hunger that scorched her through and through. "Did I just say that out loud?"

She nodded.

He cleared his throat and looked across the room. "No," he said quickly. "The bullet passed clean through."

Disregarding his answer, she gingerly examined the wound to see for herself. As he predicted, it looked to be clean. "It needs to be stitched."

He met her gaze again. Only three inches separated their faces and she could feel his breath on her face as he spoke. "Then by all means, have at it. I'm sure nothing would give you greater pleasure than to take a needle to my hide."

She should take pleasure in it, but she knew she wouldn't. How could she ever delight in hurting the man who had stolen her heart?

But she would never let him know that. Not after he'd hurt her. No, she'd never let him know just how much power he still held over her.

Never.

"Actually, I won't feel anything," she said, reaching for her basket.

O'Connell clenched his teeth in repressed frustration.

I won't feel anything, he mocked silently as she reached for a needle and thread.

You stitch the wound, and when you're finished, I promise you you'll feel something, all right. She was going to remember his touch if it was the last thing he did.

O'Connell felt himself harden even more as she placed the thread between her lips and licked it. The tip of her tongue poked out as she threaded the needle.

I can't stand this. His mind screamed from the needless torment. If he didn't know better, he would swear she did it on purpose.

When she set to work on his wound, he felt no pain, only the pleasure of her soft hands against his bare flesh. Her breath fell against his shoulder as she leaned so close to him he could smell the fresh sunshine of her.

Over and over he could envision letting her hair down and burying his hands in the thick waves. Feeling it fall across his chest as he placed her above him and feasted on those plump, luscious breasts.

Catherine could barely steady her hand as she closed the wound. Her memory of touching his hard, hot muscles couldn't compete with the reality of her hand against him now.

Her head swam at the contact. Worse, she could feel his heat surrounding her, feel his breath against her neck. His shoulder pressing against her right breast.

A thousand chills shot through her. It was all she could do not to moan and demand he take her right then and there. Oh, it was torturous. Especially after all the years she had yearned to see him again, all the years she had lain awake remembering the feel of him lying against her. The feel of him sliding inside her.

After what seemed an eternity, she finished the four tiny stitches that closed the wound. She had barely tied the knot off when he reached up, cupped her face in his hand, and took possession of her lips.

Catherine sighed at the contact.

He'd been the only man who had ever kissed her and the taste of him had been branded into her memory long, long ago.

He pulled her to him possessively and sat her down on the bench before him as he plundered her mouth.

Catherine buried her hands in his silken hair and pressed her breasts against his hot, naked chest. She should stop him, she knew it. But for her life she didn't want to. All she wanted was to savor him like she'd done all those years ago.

Volcanic heat poured through her body, pooling itself between her legs as she ached for him in the most primitive of ways. She wanted him desperately. And only he could pacify the aching heat that demanded his body inside hers.

He was her husband and the part of her that still loved him came rushing to the forefront. Under the assault of his scorching kiss, that part of her took possession of her common sense and forced it to flee her mind.

Before she knew what was happening, she felt her hair fall down around her shoulders and it was only then that he pulled back from her lips to kiss her cheek, her eyelid, the tip of her nose. His lips were hot and moist as they branded a fiery trail over her face.

"My precious Catherine," he whispered in her ear. "Let me love you the way you deserve to be loved."

She felt his hands unbuttoning her shirtwaist. She

wanted to tell him no, but in truth she couldn't. The words lodged in her throat because deep down she wanted him. She had always wanted him, and no matter how badly he had hurt her, there was still a part of her that needed him.

And she gave herself over to that part.

He opened her shirtwaist, then buried those hot lips against the tops of her breasts as his hands reached around back to unlace her corset. She sighed in pleasure as she buried her face in his hair and inhaled the wicked, warm scent that was her husband.

O'Connell's head swam from the scent of her as he buried his face between the soft mounds of her breasts and licked her salty skin. It had been so long since he tasted her, felt her, and he knew that he would spend the rest of this night making up for the five years they had been apart.

The five long years he had been without a woman.

In her arms, he had always felt that anything was possible. That he could do anything, be anything. No other person had ever lifted him to the heights of goodness and pleasure that she did.

She was the one truth in his life that he could depend on. The one person he truly needed.

He ran his tongue over the tops of her breasts, delighting in the way she shivered in his arms as he struggled with the corset laces.

And at that moment he despised whoever had invented the cursed thing. It had to be some old, doddering matron seeking to preserve her daughter's virtue, for no man would ever design so inconvenient a contraption.

At last he loosened it to where he could free her breasts to his hungry mouth.

Catherine cupped his head to her as she stifled a moan of pure pleasure. His hand caressed her swollen breasts, drawing the taut nipples so tight she could barely stand it. Heat tore through her body as an ache started deep in the center of her. It was a familiar longing that she only felt in his presence.

No other man had ever aroused her the way he did. No one. And she doubted if anyone ever could.

And then his hands were under her skirt, stroking and teasing as they skimmed over her calves and thighs. One hand cupped her buttocks as he wrapped his other arm around her and drew her up tight against him.

He reclaimed her lips for one hungry, pulsating kiss, then pulled back.

He cupped her face in his hands and tilted her head to look at him. His lips were swollen from her kisses and he stared at her as if he were dreaming.

The need and hunger in that silver-gray gaze mesmerized her. Her breathing ragged, she could do nothing but stare up at him in wonderment.

"Say my name," he demanded, stroking her swollen lips gently with his knuckles.

She hesitated.

But what was the point? She had already surrendered herself to him. And for some reason she couldn't fathom, she wanted to please him.

"Michael," she breathed.

He smiled, then returned to torture her mouth with sweet bliss.

He rose with her in his arms. "Where's your room?"

"In there," she said, pointing to the back hallway and the room on the left.

Limping all the way, he carried her to it then shut the door with the heel of his burned foot. "Where's the lamp?"

Catherine squirmed out of his arms and moved to find her chest of drawers to the left of the door. Too dark to see, she groped along the smooth top as he came up behind her and cupped her breasts in his hands.

She moaned as he toyed with her and heat swept through her body.

"You're making this difficult," she said, then sighed at the feel of his lips on the back of her neck as he pressed his swollen shaft against her hip.

He gave one last possessive squeeze to her breasts, then released her. "Light the lamp," he said, his voice ragged. "I want to see you. All of you."

Quickly, she found the glass lamp. Lifting the globe, she took one of the matches beside it and lit it. She turned the wick down to a low, warm glow that made their shadows dance on the far wall.

Michael came up behind her again and placed a kiss on her shoulder as his arms wrapped around her waist to pull her close to his chest. She leaned her head back, savoring the feel of him. The strength and warmth in his powerful arms. His deep groan echoed in her ears and she sighed contentedly.

Slowly, he began undoing her clothes.

"Michael, what—"

"Shh," he said, placing a finger to her lips. "I want to savor you like a wrapped gift. Slowly. Carefully and with relish."

And so he did. She didn't move as he took her shirtwaist off, then her skirt and petticoats. Her corset went next, exposing her upper body to him. She shivered from the cool air against their skin, but his hot gaze warmed her as he untied her pantaloons, then dropped them to the floor.

She swallowed as she stood naked before him.

O'Connell thought he'd go mad as he stared at her bare body. Not even his memory had been able to hold on to the true beauty that was his Catherine.

And for this one night she was his.

All his.

He reached out and ran one hand over her right breast, delighting in the way her nipple hardened to his touch. Then, he trailed his hand over her abdomen to the curls at the juncture of her thighs. She moaned as he slid his fingers against her.

His mind reeled at the hotness of her body, at the

sleek wetness in his hand. She was as ready for him as he was for her, but he didn't want to rush this.

He wanted this night to last a lifetime.

"I am going to savor you," he told her. "Every single inch of you."

Catherine couldn't respond verbally. Her mind numb, she could do nothing more than watch him watch her.

He picked her up again and carried her to the bed, where he removed her shoes, then carefully rolled down her stockings, nibbling her legs as he went.

As she started to sit up, he held her in place with one hand and shook his head. "Let me look at you lying there. I want to see you naked in your bed."

And look he did. His gaze traveled from the top of her head down to her breasts, to her stomach, her hips and legs, and then it returned to the center of her body, which thrummed with a hot, demanding need.

He lifted his hands to her thighs and spread her legs wider.

"Michael—"

"Let me look at you."

So she did, and his look burned even more than his touch. He leaned his head down and placed a tender kiss just below her belly button. His hot breath scorched her as his teeth tormented her flesh. He trailed his kisses lower, down to the inside of her thighs. Catherine closed her eyes and moaned as his lips brushed up against the center of her body.

Then he pulled back.

As if sensing how she ached for him, he quickly shed his own clothes, then climbed up between her legs. His entire body caressed hers in a long, luscious stroke.

She moaned at the erotic pleasure it delivered as her body arched to meet his. She felt him from the tips of her toes to the tips of her aching breasts, all the way to her forehead, where he placed a tender kiss.

His hot, stiff shaft rested on her belly.

Wanting him too badly to wait, she reached down between their bodies and stroked the velvety hardness of him. He hissed in her ear as she cupped him gently, then sought to guide him into her.

But he would have none of it.

Without entering her, Michael rolled to her side before his mouth returned to hers. He skimmed his hand over her body, then buried it between her legs.

Catherine hissed in pleasure as her hips lifted instinctively toward his hand.

He pulled back to stare down at her. "So," he whispered as his fingers toyed with the sensitive flesh between her thighs. He plunged one finger deep inside her, swirling it around and teasing her with pure, unadulterated pleasure. "Do you remember me now?"

"Yes," she gasped as his fingers did the most wicked things to her body.

He teased and toyed, his fingers circling and delving, faster and faster, until she was breathless from her aching need.

"And do you remember this?" he asked as he circled the core of her body with his thumb.

"Yes," she gasped again as her entire body throbbed.

He smiled a tender smile. "Now tell me what you want."

"I want to feel you deep inside me. Now."

He released her.

Catherine whimpered until he picked her up and moved her yet again. "What are you doing now?"

He led her to where her mirror stood in the corner. "You'll see," he whispered in her ear, raising chills on her arms.

He stood her before the mirror, where she could watch his hands as they caressed her body, kneaded her breasts, and masterfully stroked the flesh of her stomach.

He brushed her hair over her right shoulder to where it covered most of her and buried his lips in the curve of her neck.

Reaching up over her head, she buried her hand in his hair and groaned in pleasure.

"You still smell like sunshine," he whispered in her ear before swirling his tongue over the sensitive flesh. And when he plunged his tongue inside her ear, she melted and moaned as her entire body erupted into flames.

Catherine trembled all over as she watched his hands cup her breasts possessively. He pressed them, kneaded them, caressed them until she could barely stand it.

"I want to touch you," she said hoarsely, trying to turn around in his arms.

He stopped her. "You will," he said. "But not yet. Not until I *devour* you."

"Then devour me."

His rich laugh echoed in her ear. "Yes, ma'am," he whispered. "I'm more than happy to oblige you."

And then he trailed kisses down her spine. Slowly, methodically, covering every tiny inch of her flesh. She didn't know how her legs managed to keep her standing, for they trembled until she was sure she would fall.

His warm breath caressed her flesh as his hot, wet mouth teased her skin. He paused at the small of her back, his tongue gently stroking her buttocks. His hands circled around in front of her as he knelt on the floor at her feet.

Then his lips kissed the backs of her thighs, her knees, her calves, and when he got to her ankles, she jumped in erotic pleasure.

He laughed, then nudged her legs farther apart.

Fevered and hot, she did as he wanted and watched in the mirror as he positioned his body between her legs and kissed the front of her knees, her thighs.

He paused at the juncture of her thighs.

Her gaze transfixed by the sight of him in the looking glass, Catherine's entire body pulsed as his hot breath scorched her skin. He ran his left hand through her dark, short curls, kneading her erotically. Then, using both hands, he gently separated the tender folds and buried his mouth at the center of her body.

Tremors of ecstasy shook her.

O'Connell wanted to shout in victory as he tasted the most private part of her. She was his and this part of her was for him alone.

He would never share her! Never.

He ran his tongue over her, delighting in her moans and sighs. In the taste of her body, hot and moist against his starving tongue.

"Please," she begged. "I can't stand any more."

He nipped her tender flesh. "Oh, yes, you can, my love. I've only started with you."

Deciding he had tortured the two of them enough for the moment, he moved to nibble the sensitive flesh of her hip. She buried her hand in his hair. He delighted in the feel of her hands on his scalp.

More hurriedly than before, he kissed his way up her body until he could bury his lips in the hollow of her throat.

He held her tightly against him, reveling in the feel of her naked flesh against his, the feel of her tight nipples burning into his chest.

Catherine lifted one leg up to cup him to her as she arched her body against him, needing desperately to be closer to his heat. His lips burned her throat. She rubbed her hips against his in a silent plea for him to have mercy on her and to squelch the fire scorching her from the inside out.

To her chagrin, he pulled back. Then he took her hands in his and braced them on the frame of the mirror as he moved to stand behind her.

She met his lustful, hot gaze in the mirror. Never had she seen such a look of love and lust intermingled. His breathing ragged, he whispered to her, "I want to see you see me take you."

And then with one powerful stroke he drove himself up inside her. She sucked her breath in sharply at the feel of his fullness stroking her.

"Oh, yes, Michael, yes!" she cried out.

O'Connell thought he would perish at the sound of his name on her lips while she surrendered herself to him.

At that moment, he knew what paradise meant. Nothing could ever be more pleasurable than being with the woman he loved, hearing her sighs, and feeling her body from the inside out.

"Show me," he said in her ear. "Show me that you remember me."

She hesitated only an instant before she lifted herself on her tiptoes, drawing her body up to the tip of his shaft. Just as he was sure she'd drive him out, she dropped herself back against him, wringing a deep-seated moan of pleasure from him. He ground his teeth in the bittersweet torture of her milking his body with hers.

To hell with dreams! he thought rabidly. They were nothing compared to this reality. To the true feeling of her body sliding against his.

Catherine smiled at the look of ecstasy on his face as she watched him in the mirror. Unabashed, she gave him what he wanted and took what she needed. Perspiration broke out on his forehead as he met her gaze in the glass.

She could feel her body starting to teeter, to spiral to the pinnacle only he had ever shown her.

But before she would go there, she wanted something else from him. She delivered one last, long stroke to him, then paused.

He arched a questioning brow.

"Did you ever remember me?" she asked.

"Every minute of every hour. I've never stopped wanting you."

The sincerity in his gaze told her he spoke the truth. Joy spread through her as she again rocked herself against him, then pulled away.

He looked at her questioningly.

"I want to hold you when it happens."

Unwilling to make the short distance to the bed, he laid her down on the floor and again entered her.

Catherine moaned at the sensation of him thrusting between her legs as she encircled his body with hers. Wrapping her legs around his waist, she ran her hands down his spine and cupped his buttocks to her, urging him on. Her pleasure mounted higher and higher until she felt herself slipping again.

This time she let herself teeter over the edge.

Crying out, she shook as tremors of pure pleasure tore through her.

Still he thrusted, deepening her ecstasy until he threw his head back and cried out as well.

With a contented sigh, he collapsed on top of her and she reveled in the weight of him.

It had been too long. Far too long.

O'Connell couldn't breathe or move. Not until the throbbing returned to his arm and foot. "Ow," he breathed.

"Ow?" she repeated.

"My foot," he said as he rolled off her. "It's hurting again."

A blush stained her cheeks. She rose slowly from the floor and reached her hand out to him. "I think I know a way to make you forget about that."

He smiled and rose to her invitation. She took him to the bed and laid him back against the soft, feather mattress.

Surrendering himself to her whims, he watched as she crawled up his body like a naked wildcat. She wriggled her hips and then straddled his body.

O'Connell moaned at the feel of the hairs at the juncture of her thighs caressing his bare flesh as she sat down upon his stomach. She leaned forward, spilling her breasts across his chest as she wiggled that delectable bottom against him.

"Now let's see how much I remember," she whispered before burying her lips just below his ear. "Does this help the pain?"

"A little," he moaned.

She trailed kisses over his skin until she got to his chest. She stroked his nipple with her tongue and he hissed in pleasure. She nibbled him ever so gently.

"And that?" she asked.

"A little better than before," he said.

"Still not gone entirely?"

He shook his head.

"Well, then, let's see what it takes."

She moved to his side and as she bent over him her hair fell against his flesh, raising chills all over him. She lashed his chest with her hair, over and over, and he arched his back against the pleasurable beating.

"Better?" she asked.

"Somewhat."

She arched a brow. "Somewhat?"

He shrugged.

Her smile was wicked and warm. "In that case . . ."

She lowered her head and took him into her mouth. O'Connell pressed his head back into the pillows as his entire body jerked in pleasure.

"Catherine," he said hoarsely. "Next time, you can set fire to my entire body if that's the cure for it."

She laughed against him. "Don't tempt me," she

said, looking up an instant before she returned to the part of him that was steadily growing larger. Harder.

Before he could move, she straddled him again and lowered herself onto his shaft. "How's that?"

"Hot and wet, just like I like it," he said.

And this time when they came, it was in unison.

O'Connell didn't know what time they finally fell asleep. All he knew was that for the first time in five years, his body had been fully sated. He couldn't remember the last time he had felt this good. This free.

He cradled Catherine's slumbering form against his chest and buried his face in her hair. If he could, he would die right then and there.

Because with the dawn that would invariably come, he knew he would have to leave her. And he would rather be dead than walk out on her again.

But he had no choice.

4

Catherine awoke to the sound and feel of Michael's breathing in her ear, to the warmth of his body pressed against her own. It had been so long since she last had the pleasure of him sleeping by her side.

How could she have told him she didn't remember, when all she did was remember the feel of him? The smell of him? The *essence* of him?

And how could she ever reject a man she loved so dearly?

Catherine opened her eyes and saw him lying on his side, facing her. His left leg snuggled between hers, he had his left arm draped possessively across her body.

Impulsively, she brushed the brown wisps of hair off his forehead and placed a tender kiss to his brow.

"I still love you," she whispered, knowing he couldn't hear her. That was one thing about Michael—once he slept, it would take the end of the world to wake him.

She heard footsteps outside in the kitchen. Afraid it was one of the children or Rebecca, someone who might enter her room to wake her, she quickly got up and dressed.

With one last look to savor the sight of him sleeping naked in her bed, she drew her quilt up over his sleeping form and tiptoed from the room.

Entering the kitchen, she didn't see anyone.

How strange.

She had definitely heard someone a moment ago.

With a frown, she walked into the parlor where they had placed the Christmas tree and toys. To the right of the tree, hidden in the shadows, she found her daughter, Diana, cradling the doll St. Nick had brought her.

Catherine paused, staring at the product of her love for Michael. Diana was a bit small for her four years. She had Catherine's long, wavy dark hair and Michael's silver-gray eyes. It never failed to amaze Catherine that something so pretty and smart had come from her.

Smiling, she approached her daughter who looked up, her eyes brimming with tears.

"Diana, what is it?" she asked, instantly concerned as she knelt by her side. She brushed the dark bangs back from her daughter's face.

"He didn't come," Diana whimpered as a solitary tear fell down her face.

"Of course St. Nick came, sweetling. You have the doll and everything."

"No, Mama, *he* didn't come," she repeated, hugging her doll even closer as more tears fell. "It was all I wanted for Christmas and he didn't come."

"Who, baby?"

"Daddy," she sobbed.

Catherine's breath caught in her throat at the unexpected word. Diana had only started asking about her father a few short months ago, and the fact that he *had* shown up in the night . . .

It was enough to give one the shivers.

"What are you talking about?" Catherine asked her daughter.

"You told me St. Nick could make miracles, remember, Mama?"

"Yes."

"And I told you I wanted a *special* miracle."

"I thought you meant the doll."

Diana shook her head. "I wanted St. Nick to bring me my daddy. I wanted to see his eyes like mine."

Catherine wrapped her arms around her small daughter and held her close. She wasn't sure what she should do. Part of her wanted to take Diana into the bedroom to meet her father, and the other part of her was too terrified of how Michael might react.

She should have told him last night, but she had turned coward.

It was one thing for him to abandon her. She could deal with it. But hurting Diana was another matter.

No, it would be best to wait and tell him about

their daughter when Diana wasn't around. That way only she would be hurt if he ran for the door. Again.

With the edge of her shawl, Catherine wiped Diana's eyes. "No tears on Christmas, please?"

Diana sniffed them back.

She kissed the top of Diana's little dark head and squeezed her tight. "I'll talk to St. Nick after breakfast and see what I can do."

"But he's already gone back to the North Pole."

"I know, sweetling, but didn't anyone ever tell you that mommies have a special way of letting St. Nick know what their babies want?"

Diana wiped her tears with the back of her hand. "After breakfast?"

Catherine nodded. "Keep your fingers crossed and maybe he can manage something."

"I will. I promise."

She smiled at those silver-gray eyes that shone with innocence. "Good girl. Now go check your stockings and see what else St. Nick might have left while I go start breakfast."

Diana scooted out of her arms and Catherine rose slowly to her feet.

In truth, she felt ill. Her stomach knotted. How would she break the news to Michael?

Would he even care?

Taking a deep breath for courage, she knew one way or the other she had to tell him. Even an irresponsible scoundrel deserved to know he had fathered a beautiful little girl who wanted nothing more than to meet him.

"Just don't hurt her," she whispered. "Because if you do, I'll kill you for it."

O'Connell came awake slowly to the smell of bacon and coffee, and the sound of children laughing outside his door. At first he thought it was a dream.

How many times had he yearned to experience just such a morning?

Many more times than he could count.

"Catherine, do I need to set extra plates for whoever was at the door last night? I didn't know if he, she, or them stayed, or what."

He heard Catherine's mumbled reply through the walls, but couldn't make out any of her words.

All of a sudden the memory of the night before came crashing back through him.

It had been real. All of it. This was no dream. He was, in fact, sleeping in Catherine's bed on Christmas morning.

O'Connell leaned his head back into the pillow as an overwhelming joy ripped through him. He felt like shouting or singing or doing something. Anything to celebrate such a glorious event.

Impulsively, he pulled Catherine's pillow to him and inhaled the fresh sunshine smell of her. Intoxicated, he listened to the children sing "God Rest Ye Merry Gentlemen" as someone jingled china and silverware.

"It's not a dream," he whispered.

He laughed softly as raw euphoria invaded every piece of him. He had his Christmas miracle.

Smiling, he rose from the bed and dressed, then made the bed up. Catherine had always complained he twisted the sheets into knots and she hated a messy bed.

This would be his gift to her.

He left the room warily and made sure no one spied him lest Catherine have some serious explaining to do. The last thing she needed was a tarnished reputation, and the last thing he needed was nosy questions he couldn't answer.

He saw the stairs behind him and made like he was coming from one of the rooms upstairs.

As he drew flush with the kitchen door, he saw Catherine standing in front of the stove, frying eggs.

He delighted at her trim form. She'd left her hair long in the back with a braid wound about the top of her head to keep it out of her eyes. Her dark green dress hugged every one of the curves he had feasted on the night before. And a white shawl draped becomingly over her shoulders.

Never had he seen a more glorious image, and he wished he could stay here forever.

"Rebecca?" Catherine called, stepping back from

the stove and looking out the doorway on the oppo-site side of the room. "Are the children still outside?"

"Making snow angels, last I saw," a woman called as she came into the room. The petite brunette stopped dead in her tracks as her gaze fell to him.

Catherine caught the woman's gaze and turned to face him.

"Morning," he greeted them.

Catherine blushed, and he didn't miss the light that came into the short brunette's eyes.

"Morning," the brunette said warmly, suggestively.

Catherine cleared her throat. "Rebecca, this is our visitor from last night."

"Pleased to meet you," Rebecca said. "Mister . . . ?"

"Burdette," he said, falling into his most recent alias. "Tyler Burdette."

He glanced to Catherine, who took his name in with a frown.

"I'll just go set another place at the table for you, Mr. Burdette," Rebecca said.

As soon as they were alone again, Catherine approached him, waving a spatula dripping with hot grease dangerously near his nose. "Tyler Burdette?" she asked in a miffed tone. "Is there something you need to tell me?"

That was a loaded question and he wasn't sure how to answer it. Luckily another visitor, a man, spared him a few moments to think.

But to be honest, all he thought about was the

fact that the distinguished-looking, gray-haired man spent a little too long staring at *his* Catherine.

"Miss Catherine?"

"Marshal McCall," she said, stressing the title, no doubt for his benefit.

And it worked. O'Connell was immediately on guard.

By the look on the man's face, it was obvious he wanted to ask Catherine something of a personal nature. Worse, the man stuttered and shifted nervously before he came out with, "I just came for my morning cup of coffee."

O'Connell's gaze narrowed. The damn man was infatuated with *his* wife.

He flinched as an image of her in the marshal's arms tore through his mind.

Would the insults never cease?

As Catherine moved to fetch a cup of coffee, the marshal glanced to O'Connell. "How do?" he asked, amiably enough.

"Just fine, Marshal," O'Connell returned, trying to remain pleasant in spite of the urge he had to choke the man. "And you?"

The marshal frowned as he looked him up and down. "Don't I know you from someplace?"

Probably from about a dozen or so wanted posters, but he didn't dare say that. Instead, O'Connell shook his head. "I don't know any marshals." He made it his habit to avoid them at all costs.

"No?" the marshal asked. "You sure look familiar to me. You got any family in Reno?"

O'Connell shook his head. "Not that I'm aware of."

He seemed to accept that. But still he took a step forward and extended his hand. "Dooley McCall."

"Tyler Burdette," he said, shaking his proffered hand.

"Burdette," the marshal repeated. "Nah, I don't reckon I do know you after all."

Catherine handed the marshal his coffee.

"Thank you, Miss Catherine. I keep telling my deputies no one on earth makes a better pot of coffee than you do."

"Thank you, Marshal."

O'Connell didn't miss the blush staining her cheeks. For a moment, he had to struggle to breathe. How dare she blush at another man? So what if he had been gone five years, it still didn't give her the right to do *that* for someone else.

She was *his* wife, not the marshal's.

The marshal nodded, then took his coffee and left.

O'Connell wasted no time sneaking to the doorway to see the marshal sitting in the parlor with a paper, sipping his coffee as if everything were right in the world.

"What the hell is a marshal doing here?" he asked Catherine in a low voice.

She gave him a haughty glare. "He *lives* here."

"Lives here?" he repeated.

"I run a boardinghouse, remember? He's one of my regular tenants."

"Why would you let him live *here*?"

"I don't know," she said sarcastically. "Maybe I like having him here because it keeps out the riff-raff," she said with a pointed stare, "and he pays two months' rent in advance."

Catherine didn't miss the heated glare Michael gave her. Licking her lips, she felt a wave of misgiving run up her spine. Michael was entirely too interested in the marshal.

Something was wrong.

"Are you wanted?" she asked all of a sudden.

He stared at her with those clear silver-gray eyes. "It depends," he said in a serious voice. "I was hoping you'd want me."

Her breath caught. Did she dare hope that he might actually be able to settle down with her and Diana?

"And if I did?" she asked.

He looked back at the marshal. "This is a bad time. I really need to leave."

"Leave?" she gasped. "You can't."

"Why not?"

"Because you just got here. You can't just show up on my doorstep, roll around in my bed, and then take flight as soon as the sun comes up. I thought we had shared something special last night. Or were they all lies again?"

He winced as if she'd struck him. "I've never lied to you, Catherine."

"No. But you lied to my boarder and housekeeper. Is that not true, Mr. *Tyler Burdette*?"

"I—"

"Miss Catherine, Miss Catherine?" An excited boy came bursting through the kitchen with Pete's saddlebags in his hands. The blond head bobbed as the kid jumped up and down. "I just found these outside by the front door, and look," he said, flipping one open. "They're filled with money! Can I keep it?"

O'Connell went cold as everything came together in his mind.

"*I found this little orphanage in a town called Redwood*," Pete had said. "You'd probably like it a lot, Kid. It had a real *homey* feel to it."

O'Connell cursed as his stomach drew tight. Pete knew. He had sent him purposefully to find Catherine.

Panic swept through him. That meant Pete wouldn't be far behind. He had to get her to safety before his brother showed up and used her to drag him back into robbery.

But how? She'd never leave her business or her orphans.

"This is bad," he whispered. "Real bad."

Catherine looked into the saddlebags. "Where did this come from?" she asked the boy.

"I was told it was stolen from you," O'Connell said as he double-checked where the marshal sat.

Looking up at him, Catherine frowned. "By whom?"

"Is it yours?" O'Connell asked, seeking to delay the inevitable explanation of how he'd come by her money. "Were you robbed?"

"Yes, we were. But how did you get it?"

So much for delaying the inevitable.

She looked at him sternly. "Did *you* take it?"

"No!" he barked. "How could you even ask that?"

"Well, what am I to think?" she asked as she set the saddlebags on the table and excused the boy.

She moved to stand just before him, hands on hips. "I thought I knew you, and yet every time I blink I learn something about you that scares me. Now tell me how it is you have my money."

O'Connell didn't have a chance. Before he could say a word, the back door opened to show Pete holding one of Catherine's little girls in his arms.

"Knock, knock," Pete drawled. He flashed an evil grin to O'Connell, then lifted the little girl's face to where O'Connell could see her tear-streaked eyes. "Look what old Uncle Pete found out in the yard."

5

O'Connell felt the air leave his lungs as he gazed into a pair of eyes indistinguishable from his own. They were set in a face that looked identical to Catherine's, right down to the dark brown curls spilling over Pete's arm.

In an instant, he recognized his daughter.

Sobbing uncontrollably, the girl looked to Catherine. "Help me, Mama! Make the mean man let me go."

Catherine took a step toward the girl, but O'Connell grabbed her arm and pulled her to a stop.

No one approached his brother. If Catherine tried to take the girl, there was no telling what Pete might do to her.

"Let her go, Pete," O'Connell said, his calm voice belying the volatile state of his mind and body.

Pete gave an evil smile. "I told you in Oak River, you can't escape me, Kid. Now I ask you again, are you coming with me or what?"

"Oak River?" he heard Catherine repeat under her breath.

That was the town where he'd left her. Only then, Pete had used Catherine as his leverage. It was either go with Pete to rob another bank or see his wife hurt.

After the robbery, O'Connell had lacked the heart to go back to her. He couldn't face her after what he'd done for Pete. Worse, he knew that sooner or later Pete would show up again with the same threat.

And the last thing he wanted was to kill his brother for hurting his wife.

So long as there was life in his body, he would protect his Catherine.

You're my second chance. That's what O'Connell had told her on their wedding night. Catherine hadn't known what he'd meant by it. But he had.

For a time, he had been stupid enough to believe it. But second chances were for fools.

And Catherine could never again be his.

"I'll come with you, Pete. Just put her down."

Pete nodded. "Good boy. I knew you'd see things my way once you saw them again." Pete squeezed the girl's cheeks and tilted her head up to where he could look into her face. "She is kind of cute, isn't she?"

Rage infused every cell of O'Connell's body. "Take your hands off her, Pete, or I'll kill you for it."

His brother met his gaze and for several seconds they stared at each other in mutual understanding. "You know. Kid, I believe you would."

"You can count on it."

O'Connell didn't breathe again until Pete set the girl on her feet, and she ran to Catherine's outstretched arms.

Pete glanced to Catherine and the little girl. "Since it's Christmas and all, I'll give you five minutes with them. I'll be waiting outside by the horses."

O'Connell waited for him to leave before he turned to face Catherine, who cradled the little girl to her chest.

His daughter.

He felt so much pride and delight, he thought his heart might burst. But the joy died as he remembered his brother waiting for him outside.

O'Connell reached a hand out to touch the dark brown curls. The softness of his daughter's hair reached deep inside him, carving a place in his heart.

"She's beautiful," he breathed.

Catherine saw the pain deep inside him and she noted the tenseness of his hand on Diana's hair. "Her name is Diana."

He gave a bittersweet smile. "Named for your mother?"

She nodded.

"Why didn't you tell me about her in Nevada?" he asked, his eyes misting.

"I didn't know I was pregnant until after you left." She narrowed her gaze on him as she finally understood everything that had happened. "You left because of him, didn't you?"

"He's my brother," he said simply. "I had no choice."

"We always have choices."

He shook his head. "No, we don't. You don't know what kind of man my brother is, but I do. I know he's cruel, but I owe him. If not for Pete, I'd have never survived after the death of our parents. He's harsh because that's the way the world made him."

"He's harsh because he's—"

O'Connell stopped her words by placing his fingers on her lips. His heart tearing apart, he leaned over, kissed her gently on the mouth, and whispered, "Until the day I die, I'll always remember you."

He touched Diana's hair one last time, then he turned and walked away.

O'Connell met Pete by his pinto, which Pete must have saddled. His brother was as fair-haired and fair-skinned as O'Connell was dark. The two of them had always been opposites in most everything. Even Pete's eyes were a brownish green.

And never before had O'Connell felt so much resentment and hatred for the brother who had once protected him.

"Why can't you just let me go?" he asked Pete. "I've paid my debt to you a thousand times over."

Pete gave him a hard glare. "You're my family, Kid. Like it or hate it, it's just you and me." Pete smiled wickedly. "Besides, you're the only man I know who can blow a safe and not destroy half the money with it."

"You're not funny."

Pete shucked him on the shoulder. "Now, don't get sore on me, Kid. You can do better than her. I told you that years ago. She ain't nearly pretty enough for you."

He grabbed Pete by his shirtfront. "I'm not a kid anymore, Pete, and I'm no longer scared of you. Catherine is my wife and she deserves your respect. If you ever say anything else against her, as God is my witness, I'll tear your hide apart for it."

For the first time in his life, he saw a glimmer of fear pass through Pete's eyes. "All right, Kid. Whatever you say."

O'Connell let him go. He had barely taken a step when he heard the front door of the boardinghouse open.

The marshal strode out across the porch with two men in tow. And all three of them carried shotguns in their arms. By the grim, determined looks on their faces, he knew what they wanted.

Him and Pete.

His blood went cold.

The marshal stared at Pete as he leveled the shotgun on them. "Pete O'Connell," he said slowly.

"Never did I expect to receive such a great Christmas present. Imagine the bounty of *both* O'Connell brothers."

Pete swore, then went for his gun.

O'Connell didn't think. He merely reacted. He was tired of his brother's schemes, and tired of the lives Pete had taken for no reason.

It was time for it to end.

He grabbed his brother's gun, and the two of them struggled for it.

Catherine watched the men tussle from the parlor window. She had sent Diana upstairs with Rebecca, then immediately sought out the marshal to let him know there was a possible outlaw outside.

She pressed her hand to her lips as terror sliced through her as she watched the two men fighting for possession of the gun. What had she done?

A gunshot rang out.

Catherine stopped breathing. Michael and Pete froze and locked gazes. Time seemed suspended as she waited.

Who had been shot?

Then Michael staggered back, and she saw the red stain on his shirtfront right before he collapsed on the ground.

"No!" she shouted as tears stung the backs of her eyes. It couldn't be Michael! It couldn't be.

Pete just looked down at him, his face indecipherable.

Dropping her shawl, Catherine ran for the door, down the steps, and across the yard to Michael's side.

His brother stood coldly to the side as the marshal and his men put irons on his wrists.

Sobbing, she knelt by Michael's side. Terrified and shaking, she touched his cold brow.

"Michael?" she breathed.

He opened his eyes and looked up at her. In that look she saw the love he had for her. He opened his mouth to speak, but she pressed her fingertips to his lips.

"Save your strength," she whispered. She looked up to Marshal McCall, who stared angrily at Pete.

"I always heard you were mean, but damn, to shoot your own brother on Christmas? You're a sick man, O'Connell," the marshal said to Pete.

His face blank, Pete glanced down to her and Michael, then back at the marshal.

"What are you, stupid? Do we *look* like brothers?" Pete drawled slowly. "My brother got killed in Shiloh last month during our last holdup. That there's just some stupid cow-poke thinks he's a bounty hunter. Bastard's been trailing me for weeks. I don't even know his name." Pete locked gazes with Catherine, then shocked her with his words, "But I think the lady over there knows him. Ask her who he is."

The marshal gave her a probing stare. "That true, Miss Catherine? You know this man?"

A tremor of panic shook her as she realized Michael's entire fate was in her hands.

What should she answer?

She looked down at Michael's calm, deliberate stare. He expected her to betray him. She could read it plainly in his eyes as he waited for her to denounce him.

But she couldn't. She didn't know everything yet, but before she handed him over to the marshal, she wanted some long-overdue answers. Answers he couldn't very well give her locked up in jail.

"He's my husband," she answered honestly. "Michael O'Callahan."

The marshal gave her a hard stare. "I thought you said your husband ran off."

"He did," she said, looking back at Michael. "But he came home to me last night."

"Farley," the marshal shouted to his deputy. "Help me carry Miss Catherine's husband inside while Ted locks up O'Connell."

The marshal helped her to her feet.

"Where you want us to take him?" the marshal asked.

"To my room," she said, leading the way back into the boardinghouse.

* * *

Michael O'Connell didn't say anything for the rest of the day. His head swam with what had happened.

Why had Pete lied?

Why had Catherine protected him, when she could have easily seen him in prison for the next ten to twenty years?

None of it made any sense to him, and worse, Catherine had avoided coming into the room for him to question her. If he'd been able to, he would have gone after her himself, but he was too weak to do much more than just breathe.

The door to his room creaked open. He glanced over to see a tiny dark head peeking in.

He smiled at the sight of his daughter in the doorway.

When Diana saw him look her way, the little girl smiled from ear to ear.

She fanned the door back and forth as she twisted in the door frame. "Are you really my daddy?" she asked.

"What did your mama say?"

"She said St. Nick brought you to me last night."

O'Connell gave a half laugh at her words, but he couldn't manage any more than that, since pain cut his breath off. Pete had been called a lot of things over the years, but this was the first time anyone had ever referred to his brother as St. Nick.

"Yeah," he said with a grimace. "I guess maybe he did."

Releasing the doorknob, she ran across the room and scrambled to sit next to him on the bed. He winced at the pain she caused by dipping the mattress, but in truth he didn't mind it at all. To have his daughter near him, he would suffer a lot worse than that.

"You sure are pretty for a man."

O'Connell smiled at her words. No one had ever said *that* to him before.

She reached out one little hand to touch his eyelid. "You do have eyes like mine. Mama told me you did."

He cupped her soft cheek, amazed at what he saw in her face. It was so strange to see parts of him mixed in with parts of Catherine.

Never in his life had he seen a more beautiful little girl. "We get them from my mother."

"Was she pretty, too?"

"Like you, she was as pretty as an angel."

"Diana!"

He started at Catherine's chiding tone.

"I told you not to disturb him."

"I'm sorry, Mama."

"She's not disturbing me," he said, dropping his hand from her face.

Catherine shooed her out anyway. At first he thought she'd leave as well, but she hesitated in the doorway.

"Why didn't you tell me who you really were?" she asked.

He stared at her. "I liked the man you saw me as. To you, I was a decent man, not some no-account outlaw drifter. The last thing I wanted was for you to change your mind about me and hate me."

"So you lied to me?"

"Not really. I just didn't tell you everything."

She shook her head. "I always knew you were hiding *something* from me. I was just never sure what. Funny, I used to think it was another woman you loved, not a lunatic brother."

He gave her a hard, meaningful look. "I could never love anyone but you."

"Do you mean that?"

"On my life."

And then she gifted him with one of those loving smiles that had kept him warm on the coldest days. "So tell me, Michael, where do we go from here?"

EPILOGUE

Christmas Eve. Two years later

"Hey, Pa, where do we go from here?"

Michael looked up at nine-year-old Frank's question. After Catherine had given him his second chance, the two of them had decided to adopt the orphans she'd been keeping. And every day of the last two years, he had spent every minute making up to her for the time they had been apart.

She would never again have cause to doubt him, and he reveled in the blessing of his family and home.

"I think you'd best be asking your mother that question," he said to Frank. "Catherine?"

"It's the big white house at the end of the street," she said as she waddled up to them beside the train station.

Michael grinned at the sight of her pregnant body. He'd missed seeing her carry Diana, but he was definitely enjoying her now.

The way Catherine figured, they had two more months before the baby would join them. Just enough time to visit her parents with their passel of children in tow, and then make it back home in time for the little one's birth.

Four of the orphans still lived with them. Five children total with Diana. Michael smiled as he watched all of them climb aboard the wagon he had rented.

He'd always wanted a big family.

"You nervous?" he asked Catherine as he draped a comforting arm over her shoulders. She hadn't seen her parents since the day they had eloped almost seven years before.

"A little. And you?"

"A little."

Even so, he was too grateful for his life to mind even a lengthy visit at his in-laws'. He still found it hard to believe Pete had lied to save him.

"I've ruined your life enough, Kid. This is one place I think I'd best go to alone," Pete had told him.

Pete would be in prison for a long time to come. Maybe it would make his brother a better man.

All he could do was hope that one day his brother would find the peace that had always eluded him.

Michael placed a tender kiss on Catherine's brow as he took Diana's hand in his and helped her up into the wagon.

Every day for the last two years, he had been grateful that his wife had stood by him, even though it was the last thing he'd deserved.

"Thank you, Cathy," he breathed as he helped her climb into the wagon seat.

"For what?" she asked.

"For making my life worth living."

Her smile warmed him to his toes. "It's been my pleasure, Mr. O'Callahan. Merry Christmas."

And a Merry Christmas it would be, too. For in this life, there were second chances, and this time, Michael wouldn't waste the one he'd been given.